Praise for
THE ANNIVERSARY DAY SAGA

… the Anniversary Day Saga could become a milestone in the field.

—*Amazing Stories*

Anniversary Day is an edge-of-the-seat thriller that will keep you turning pages late into the night and it's also really good science fiction. What's not to like?

—*Analog* on *Anniversary Day*

The suspenseful storyline is fast-paced and filled with twists as the hero comes out of retirement to confront his worst nightmare.

—*Midwest Book Reviews* on *Blowback*

Fans of Rusch's Retrieval Artist universe will enjoy the expansion of the Anniversary Day story, with new characters providing more perspectives on its signature events, while newcomers will get a good introduction to the series.

—*Publishers Weekly* on *A Murder of Clones*

This new Retrieval Artist Universe novel is action-packed and continues where *A Murder of Clones* leaves off. These must be read in order to fully appreciate the suspense and mystery that is taking place.

—*RT Book Reviews* on *Search & Recovery*

The Anniversary Day Saga just keeps getting more interesting and more complicated. Each addition is eagerly anticipated and leaves the reader anxious to discover what will happen next, who the bad guys are and what it is they are hoping to achieve.

—*RT Book Reviews* on *The Peyti Crisis*

Praise for
THE RETRIEVAL ARTIST SERIES

One of the top ten greatest science fiction detectives of all time.

—*io9*

[Miles Flint is] one of 14 great sci-fi and fantasy detectives who out-Sherlock'd Holmes. [Flint] is a candidate for the title of greatest fictional detective of all time.

—*Blastr*

Part *CSI*, part *Blade Runner,* and part hard-boiled gumshoe, the retrieval artist of the series title, one Miles Flint, would be as at home on a foggy San Francisco street in the 1940s as he is in the domed lunar colony of Armstrong City.

—*The Edge Boston*

What links [Miles Flint] to his most memorable literary ancestors is his hard-won ability to perceive the complex nature of morality and live with the burden of his own inevitable failure.

—*Locus*

Instant addiction. You hear about it—maybe you even laugh it off—but you never think it could happen to you. Well, you just haven't run into Miles Flint and the other Retrieval Artists looking for The Disappeared. ...I am hopelessly hooked....

—Lisa DuMond
MEviews.com on *The Disappeared*

An inventive plot and complex, conflicted characters increases the appeal of Kristine Kathryn Rusch's *Extremes*. This futuristic tale breaks new ground as a space police procedural and should appeal to science fiction and mystery fans.

—*RT Book Reveiws* on *Extremes*

Part science fiction, part mystery, and pure enjoyment are the words to describe Kristine Kathryn Rusch's latest Retrieval Artist novel.... This is a strong murder mystery in an outer space storyline.

—*The Best Reviews* on *Consequences*

An exciting, intricately plotted, fast-paced novel. You'll find it difficult to put down.

—*SFRevu* on *Buried Deep*

A science fiction murder mystery by one of the genre's best.... A book with complex characters, an interesting and unpredictable plot, and timeless and universal things to say about the human condition.

—*The Panama News* on *Paloma*

Rusch continues her provocative interplanetary detective series with healthy doses of planet-hopping intrigue, heady legal dilemmas and well-drawn characters.

—*Publishers Weekly* on *Recovery Man*

...the mystery is unpredictable and absorbing and the characters are interesting and sympathetic.

—*Blastr* on *Duplicate Effort*

THE RETRIEVAL ARTIST SERIES:

The Anniversary Day Saga:

Other Stories:

VIGILANTES

A RETRIEVAL ARTIST NOVEL

KRISTINE KATHRYN RUSCH

*wmg*PUBLISHING

Vigilantes

Book Six of the Anniversary Day Saga

Published 2015 by WMG Publishing
www.wmgpublishing.com
Cover and Layout copyright © 2015 by WMG Publishing
Cover design by Allyson Longueira/WMG Publishing
Cover art copyright © Eugenesergeev/Dreamstime
ISBN-13: 978-1-56146-621-4
ISBN-10: 1-56146-621-2

For Dean

Acknowledgements

So many people have made this long project possible. Paul B. Higginbotham helped me design the legal system. I greatly relied on his expertise in this series. Annie Reed makes sure I remain consistent from book to book. Dean Wesley Smith lets me know if the plot falters. Colleen Kuehne monitors the details. Allyson Longueira designs the lovely covers, shepherds the books into production, and keeps track of all the publishing details. I couldn't do this without any of them. Any mistakes you find, however, are all my responsibility. (And probably result from the fact that I didn't listen to someone I listed above.)

I greatly appreciate the support from all of you readers. From the beginning of the Retrieval Artist series to the Anniversary Day Saga, you've stayed with me and kept me on track. Thank you so much!

Author's Note

Dear Readers,

I got horribly stuck when I reached the middle of the first draft of Vigilantes. Every single character showed up on the Moon with a story. It was rather like the first day of grade school after summer vacation, only the speeches could have been called, "Guess what I did on the way to the Moon?"

I didn't want you to guess. I wanted you to know. Because everything these characters did was important.

Here's where I need to put in the disclaimer:

If you bought this book without buying any of the others marked Anniversary Day Saga, then you're entering book six of one long story. The story starts with the novel called Anniversary Day. You can start there, or if you want to read the first seven standalone books in the Retrieval Artist series, start with The Disappeared.

If you've read some of the standalone Retrieval Artist books and picked this one up thinking it will stand alone, I'm afraid it doesn't. The Anniversary Day saga is one long story, and it runs for eight novels. I'll return to standalone novels in the series after 2015.

What's happening here is that in consultation with WMG Publishing, I've decided to release the remaining six books in the Anniversary Day Saga in the first six months of 2015. Vigilantes is the April release.

If you had asked me what came next after I finished Blowback, I would have pointed to some of the events in The Peyti Crisis, and some that you'll find here. You'll find others in the next two books.

As I wrote the remaining six books, I started with The Peyti Crisis, and tried to cram six books of material into one novel. So I split it off into Vigilantes, *and as I wrote that book, I stalled.*

I got tired of characters reporting on their adventures. I finally threw in the towel when a character walked into Flint's office and reminded Flint of their shared history, then told a story of explosions and near death. You won't find that scene in any of the books. At that point, I realized that I, as a reader, wouldn't tolerate that scene, and I, as a writer, couldn't finish it.

Instead, I wrote the sequence which, unsurprisingly, isn't in this book. You'll find part of it in Starbase Human *(the next book) and even more of it in the final book,* Masterminds.

Once I realized what the problem was, I could solve it. I almost wrote that I could solve it easily, but that's not true. I had to write entire novels to explain what some characters were doing, and expand some existing character arcs to show what others were doing.

And, I have to admit, writing the story the way it wanted to be written was so much fun.

Once I got Vigilantes *on track, it proved to be the easiest book to write—and the most enjoyable. I hope you enjoy it as well.*

—Kristine Kathryn Rusch
Lincoln City, Oregon
June 30, 2014

VIGILANTES

A RETRIEVAL ARTIST NOVEL

ANNIVERSARY DAY

RA

BOOK SIX

SAGA

FORTY YEARS AGO

1

THE GRAY DOOR BEFORE CLAUDIO STOTT HAD FIFTEEN LEVELS OF PROTECTION on it. Stott knew because he had actually studied the manual for this part of the Forensic Wing of the Alliance's Security Division. Most of the other candidates had downloaded the manual and used AutoLearn to figure out the massive information contained within.

The problem with that, of course, was that the other candidates gave similar answers to the verbal quiz Terri Muñoz gave them before making her final selection for this job.

Now that Stott stood in the corridor outside the most secure part of the Forensic Wing, he wasn't certain he wanted this job after all. The door stood at the end of several long corridors, buried in the center of the starbase, and the first rooms beyond the door were clean rooms. He would have to use both a sonic shower and a shower with specialized liquid before entering and leaving the section, something not mentioned in the manual, because, apparently, it irritated everyone involved.

Muñoz told him that several employees of the section actually had gotten enhancements to keep their skin moist and to prevent rashes from the four-to-eight-times-per-day showers. The showers themselves sounded like wasted effort. Stott wanted to know why a decontamination chamber wouldn't work better, one calibrated for foreign DNA.

Then, even as he had the thought, he realized the problem with his question. The Forensic Wing didn't care about foreign DNA. They cared about the DNA that every single human being sloughed off through the course of every second of every day.

The showers, in theory, would prevent the sloughing long enough for the staff to don specially made environmental suits without contaminating the exteriors of those suits.

He should have known all of that; after all, he *had* studied the manual.

He looked at Muñoz. She was slight, her skin tending toward a greenish-olive that made her seem just a little ill. He had seen a holo of her from the days when she was first hired. Then her skin had been a creamy brown.

So many people looked different as they aged that he hadn't attributed the change to anything. But now that he was contemplating half a dozen showers just to get to work, take his outside breaks, and eat his lunch, he wondered if that greenish-olive color reflected the beating her skin had taken after decades inside this facility.

This facility sounded so impressive. Special DNA Collections sounded like something positive instead of something scary.

He'd gotten past the scariness of it all by reminding himself that this was where the most interesting work in the Forensic Wing occurred. Where real science got done.

He'd initially signed on to the DNA testing unit right out of university, with a newly minted degree in biological sciences. Because he'd been granted admission under the Alliance Poverty Program, he had to spend at least five years working off the cost of his degrees within the Alliance government.

He'd almost decided to move into the private sector when this opportunity had come along. The salary was double what he made in the regular DNA testing section of the Forensic Wing, and he got to do actual work, rather than monitor the machines that did the testing almost automatically.

He once told one of his colleagues that he hadn't gotten a degree to babysit computer programs and make sure they ran right. Nor had he gotten one so that he could testify in court, verifying the computer's results.

He had gotten the degree so that he could learn the secrets of DNA, secrets that—after thousands of years of study—human beings still didn't entirely know.

Stott worried about working for corporations. He believed they often acted in amoral ways, particularly when it came to their employees. He knew too many people who had become actual sacrifices for the corporations: sent into newly aligned alien territories, forced to work in uncharted conditions, and then punished for violating alien laws that no human had known about.

Some corporations had Disappearance services, which helped employees and their families escape the long arm of alien (and Alliance) justice. But Stott knew from personal experience that the Disappearance services often came on the scene too late and did too little to save lives.

He shuddered and made himself focus on Muñoz. She was holding a tablet close to her chest. Apparently, the tablet was part of the security system.

Her dark eyes met his. "Are you changing your mind, Mr. Stott?"

He straightened. Double the salary. He didn't have to work with aliens. And he got to do real science. Surely several daily showers and lots of security procedures was worth all of that.

"No," he said, then decided his voice sounded wobbly. So he made himself speak more firmly. "No. I want to work here."

"Good," she said. "Because once you go through those doors, you're not going to be able to change your mind about this assignment."

He nodded. He had heard that warning before. It had been part of the application process at every single step. This was an irrevocable assignment, particularly because he would learn things that would be dangerous in the wrong hands.

"I'm ready," he said. "Let's go."

2

THE INTERIOR OF THE SPECIAL DNA COLLECTIONS UNIT WAS EVEN LESS impressive than the corridors leading to it. Getting through the fifteen layers of security at the main door had taken ten minutes. Then the showers, which were even more hideous than Stott had expected, followed by the debacle of the environmental suit.

He was actually timed on how long it took him to put on the suit. Anything over thirty seconds meant that he had to go through the damn showers again. He had missed the first time by nearly a minute, the second time by five seconds. He made it the third time, but by then, his skin was red—and it stung.

He was definitely going to look for information on the enhancements.

The environmental suit was a thin version of the one used in the most hostile environments known to humans. The staff had to have freedom of movement—hence the thinness—but they also could not contaminate their environment in any way. So the suit clung to every part of him, and it ran a continual diagnostic. If there was even the slightest breach—something that wouldn't even kill him in one of those hostile environments—he would have to go back to the clean rooms, scrub down again, and switch suits.

No one had warned him about any of this, and now it was too late to change his mind.

Fortunately, today's suit had no breaches. Yet.

After he'd put the suit on, he'd followed Muñoz into next part of the wing. Again, he was confronted with doors. And they had another layer of security. The manual had told him why: once he got assigned to one section, he couldn't move into another section without a promotion or being accompanied by a supervisor.

These doors were labeled only on the internal links provided to the Collections staff. The labels spread across his vision in red, except for the one he was allowed to enter, which was green.

He had been assigned to the Dangerous Criminal Division. He would be one step above glorified prison guard here. The Dangerous Criminal DNA needed protection against cloning services. This division stored all of the collected material from mass murderers, serial rapists, and other very famous criminals. Nothing could leave this section because of the rampant identity theft that had started up two decades ago.

Some cloning companies, both legal and illegal, had started selling designer criminal clones—and not just as fast-grow clones, which couldn't think for themselves. There was a disturbing trend in creating regular criminal clones and attempting to raise them in an environment that would make them into the same kind of criminal that their original had been.

Stott didn't mind starting here. In fact, he was intrigued. Because in addition to his guard duties, he would be studying the DNA to answer a question that science had gone back and forth on since DNA was discovered: was criminality in the genes or was it just a product of environment and upbringing?

After hundreds of years of study, the answer still eluded everyone.

Stott took a deep breath, then coughed at the flood of pure oxygen into his lungs. He never used pure oxygen when he wore an environmental suit. He quickly changed the mix to something closer to Earth standard (even though he had never lived on Earth).

Muñoz watched him. Maybe she could see his hesitation. Or maybe his coughing unnerved her.

"Are you ready?" she asked.

Stott was glad she hadn't asked if he had changed his mind, because he wasn't sure how he would answer her honestly, not with his skin still stinging from those showers.

He glanced at the red-labeled doors. *Biohazard, Mixed Species, Experimental,* and *Unknown.* Those were only the doors he could see. He knew that another section had even more doors.

Most of the work on this side was done with 100 percent human DNA except in the Mixed Species area, where experimenters tried to see if different DNA were compatible. Corporations were doing the same thing, and much of the study in Mixed Species was of creatures that were nonviable or had been confiscated from some of the larger companies.

That division intrigued him, as well.

"Mr. Stott?" Muñoz asked him. "Are you all right?"

He nodded.

She ran through the five layers of security on the *Dangerous Criminals* door, and then it slid open. She walked in first. He followed slowly, half expecting a temperature change like he felt when he walked into the lab he'd been promoted out of.

But of course he couldn't feel one; he worked in an environmental suit now.

And that was the only visible difference in setup. Work stations spread across the center of the room. Lab equipment was through a windowed door toward the back.

And the DNA was stored in various compartments built into the walls. The labels were funneled through his links, and all were in red. He was on probationary status: he wouldn't have access to any of the criminal DNA for another year—unless given to him by a supervisor for analysis.

The only difference in this entire area from the lab he'd previously worked in was a small, round case built into the center of a pillar to the left of the door. That case had a double helix imprisoned within. He could see at a glance that this wasn't an artistic rendering of a double helix: It actually belonged to someone.

"What's that?" Stott asked Muñoz.

"A reminder for the humans in the room," she said. Her answer startled him.

"There are aliens working here?" he asked.

"In this division, yes," she said. "Criminals aren't just human."

"I thought the designer criminal clone phenomenon was human only," Stott said.

She shook her head, her lips turned downward. "I wish," she said.

Then her eyes narrowed, and met his. She seemed suddenly cool toward him.

"I know you haven't worked with other species in your years here," she said. "Was that by choice or circumstance?"

This was his chance to get out of the assignment. He had a split second to answer. If he answered honestly, he could avoid the eight daily showers. But he would either be stuck in that lower-level position forever, overseeing and testifying, or he would have to leave and work for a corporation, which was a hell of a lot riskier.

If he wanted to use his degree—and his brains—he would be better off here.

"Circumstance," Stott lied. "I've had very little contact with other species since I left school, so I was surprised."

Muñoz nodded. He wasn't sure if she believed him, so he moved the conversation forward.

"You said this image was a reminder for the humans in the room?" he asked.

She crossed her arms and moved closer to the pillar. She studied the double helix for a moment, as if it spoke to her. Then she turned to him.

"You're inside now, so you get a new level of security clearance. Before you leave, you'll get a chip that'll go in your elbow."

"Not my hand?" he asked. That's where most people wore their chips. The chips were so tiny as to be almost impossible to see (unless someone enhanced theirs as a fashion statement), but people seemed comforted by the chip's proximity.

"No one puts chips in elbows," she said. "So, if someone wanted to steal your security clearance, they wouldn't find the chip easily—unless they made you talk."

He shuddered. That would happen? Someone would try to steal his clearance?

She clearly saw the question on his face. "No one has tried for nearly fifty years," she said. "But we remain vigilant."

"I asked about the image," he said, nodding toward that clear case, "and that prompted you to mention a chip."

"Because, when you receive the chip, you'll be able to read all the labels in this room, not just the level-one labels. And this one is of particular significance to humans." Muñoz touched the edge of the case, as if she could reach inside it. "This double helix shows us everything we need to know about the physical make-up of Pier-Luigi Frémont."

Stott frowned for a moment. The name was familiar, but he couldn't place it.

And then he did. He'd heard about Frémont as a cautionary tale. Poor boys, like Stott had been, were considered prime targets for deluded messianic leaders like Frémont. Frémont had committed genocide, eliminating his followers in not one but three different attempts at starting his own colony.

Stott couldn't remember if Frémont had been a religious fanatic or not, and doubted it mattered. Frémont was used as an example of the bad things that human beings could do if left to their own devices.

He wanted to ask if Frémont was truly an evil genius but wasn't sure how Muñoz would take the question. Instead, Stott asked, "Is there anything in the DNA that later predicted Frémont's behavior?"

"Good question," Muñoz said. "In the twenty-five years since his death, the answer has changed more than once."

She nodded toward the labs.

"Every now and then, someone in this division suggests slow-growing a batch of baby Frémonts, raising them differently from each other, and seeing which one of them ends up like the original. I'm sure you can understand the folly in the suggestion?"

Was this another test? If so, it caught him by surprise.

"If they phrase the purpose of the experiment the way you just did," he said, "then they'll skew the experiment to get the results they want."

She smiled at him, as if he had just become her very best student ever.

"And that's why this division doesn't ever do that kind of experimentation," she said.

But something in her tone caught him. If this division didn't do that kind of experimentation, did that mean another division did?

Stott wasn't going to ask. Not on his first day at this new job. But he stored the question for later.

If those teams existed, he wondered how hard it would be to join one. How many years of experience would he need in this division to get there? Or would he need to move his way through the other divisions, from *Biohazard* to *Mixed Species* and beyond?

He felt giddy. He had made the right decision after all.

His future was here.

He could use his abilities, grow, and become the person he had always wanted to be.

For the first time since he had been a child, he would be doing something useful. He might even make a discovery that would save lives.

Which was something he needed to do.

TWELVE DAYS AFTER
THE PEYTI CRISIS

3

Torkild Zhu stopped half a block away from Sevryn's, and waited as two cops walked through the door. His stomach twisted. The day before, cops had assaulted him in that deli, deliberately pouring hot soup and some lemony drink all over him.

No one had defended him. The owner had actually thrown Zhu out as if it had all been his fault.

He wanted to go back in now and say something. He'd been turning it over and over in his mind ever since it happened. And what he wanted to say was this: He was as entitled to eat somewhere as those cops were. Hadn't they ever done something difficult for their jobs?

But he wasn't that tough, except in a courtroom. Defending someone else. Using his brain.

The moment he got to the point where he had to defend himself, particularly physically, he was the quiet kid in school all over again. The one who thought of the good lines *after* the fighting was over. The one who curled up into a fetal position whenever the bullies went after him.

He ran a hand through his dark hair. He kept it neatly trimmed now, just like he wore actual silk suits, paid for by his employers, the exclusive law firm of Schnable, Shishani & Salehi. S³, as everyone called it, made more money than Zhu could even imagine.

Other people dressed well on this street. The problem was that the ones who went to work early weren't the well-dressed ones, but the ones heading to jobs that required uniforms.

Like cops.

Zhu sighed and adjusted the suit. It fit perfectly. Some employee of the clothing company that S³ used had arrived at the office to confirm the measurements the holo system had sent. Probably because Zhu had lost so much weight in the last year. He suspected the company was making certain that the person who ordered the clothes was entitled to the clothes.

He was entitled to a lot through S³—or, at least, he had been.

He'd been a junior partner with the firm for nearly a decade, and six months ago he had nearly been fired. He'd left the S³ offices to come home to the Moon, and had drunk himself silly. He'd expected to be out of a job.

Instead, it turned out that he was the only S³ lawyer on the Moon when the Peyti Crisis occurred.

He went from being a sloppy about-to-be-fired drunk to running a branch of S³ in the space of a few hours.

Of course, the price had been his soul.

The price in the law was always someone's soul. Same old story, told since the law became a profession. Zhu had a moment of clarity right after his boss, Rafael Salehi, contacted him. Zhu could either stand by his principles and starve to death (or take some humiliating job for someone of his education and intelligence) or he could get filthy rich by representing thugs, killers, and mass murderers.

Zhu had said no initially. But his spine was wobbly. He'd changed his mind within an hour.

He was now representing *all* of the Peyti clones, the ones who had caused the Peyti Crisis. At least until Salehi got here, which would be Any Day Now.

Then Zhu could become a glorified office manager if that was what he wanted. Or at least, he could go back to being a junior partner instead of the guy who answered all the stupid questions that the staff was asking.

The thick yellow light of Dome Daylight covered the center of the street, missing the corner by a few meters. This part of Armstrong had a brand new dome (brand new, as of a few years ago), and its Dome Daylight program was more sophisticated than in other areas of the city. The daylight moved across the dome, mimicking the way that sunlight moved on Earth.

Right now, they were in the early morning phase of Dome Daylight. The sun was strong, but its reach was limited.

Zhu actually liked the design of the program. It was different than it had been when he was growing up here, when the transition between Dome Dawn, Dome Daylight, and Dome Twilight happened in a moment, destroying the illusion of an Earth day.

He swallowed hard. No matter what he did to distract himself, he couldn't quite make himself walk the rest of the way to the office. He could call one of the new company cars, or he could take a different route.

But he had told himself he wouldn't let the fear overtake him. He knew that the harassment would only get worse, as long as S^3 represented those clones.

The level of hatred in Armstrong was palpable. Which he could understand, given what had happened to the folks on the Moon.

Even when he tried to think about it, he couldn't entirely comprehend what it meant to have lost millions of lives Moonwide in less than a year.

He scanned the street, looking for more cops. They seemed to hate him more than anyone else. They had made that clear the day before. Maybe because they were constricted by the injunctions S^3 filed. Or maybe because they couldn't get to the Peyti clones any more.

He shuddered to think what those clones would have been subjected to if S^3 hadn't stepped in.

Then he shook his head a little. He didn't shudder to think, because he tried not to think about the clones at all. They had attempted something awful. And they had perverted his profession to do it.

If he were honest with himself, he hated those clones too.

But it was pretty normal for a defense attorney to hate his clients. That was the first thing he had learned when he worked off his student loans in the most notorious part of the court system, which was nick-named the Impossibles. Most potential defense attorneys first worked in the public defender's office, where every case was a loser, everyone was guilty of something, and every lawyer was so overworked they couldn't remember their clients' names from one hour to the next.

But he didn't do the job for the clients. Nor, he learned in the last year, did he do it for the money. (Although he had to admit that the money was nice.)

He did it because he actually believed his job had value to the entire society. And the value in these cases (this case, since they were tied to-gether by the same client) wasn't in the clients.

It was in the cause.

What he was doing, in defending the clones, was, as Salehi said, try-ing to guarantee rights for all clones.

Because right now, the Peyti clones weren't considered individuals under the law. They were property, and in Armstrong, at least, property could be destroyed or damaged without sanction, even if it were part of an upcoming criminal trial.

Zhu heard footsteps and instinctively stepped closer to the faux brick wall, protecting his back. But the footsteps retreated, heading down a side street.

He shook his head at himself, then took a deep breath. If he hadn't believed in the cause, the cops might have scared him off.

Hell, everyone might have scared him off.

Even his ex-fiancée, Berhane Magalhães, who had come to see him at the beginning of the week. She wanted him to stop doing this work, and had even offered him one of those humiliating jobs, which her ex-ceptionally wealthy father would probably pay him to do, if Zhu would only give up his job with S^3.

Berhane's opinion mattered to Zhu. Perversely, it mattered now more than it ever had when they were engaged. The Anniversary Day bombings had brought out a side to Berhane that he had only caught glimpses of, and he admired her deeply now. Loved her even, where before—if he were honest with himself—the love had slowly disappeared (if it had ever existed at all).

The argument he had with her crystalized what he believed for him. Because of her. Because he respected her. Because part of him wanted to be the guy who left S³ and helped her with her charities and her good works.

Instead, he felt like he was doing good works of his own.

Sure, the Peyti clones had tried to do something horrible, but that didn't mean all clones had to pay for it. And they would, particularly after the Anniversary Day bombings, which had been caused by yet another group of human clones.

Most of those clones had died on Anniversary Day (many by their own hands), so S³ didn't concern itself with them. Yet.

But Zhu had a hunch S³ would. Eventually.

Not that it was his problem. He needed to get the law firm up and running in less than a week, plus he had to make certain that the police, courts, and prison system honored the injunctions he had slapped on them. No organization, from the Earth Alliance to the United Domes of the Moon to the domed cities themselves, could do anything to the Peyti clones until their status was litigated.

Or so the injunctions said.

Zhu had a hunch he'd issued them just in time.

And, if yesterday's incident were any indication, he had done the right thing.

Because if cops were willing to go after a defense attorney working with one of the most high-powered firms in the Alliance, then they would have no qualms about hurting—or even killing—the clones.

Better that the cops hated him than hated the clones.

He was shaking just a little. He slowly looked over his shoulder, trying not to appear as paranoid as he felt.

He didn't see anyone behind him. But that didn't mean he was alone. Someone could be watching him, spying on him, wanting to hurt him.

Zhu had gone into Sevryn's several times before anyone attacked him, but not enough to establish a pattern. And yet the cops had found him there.

The smart thing would be to turn around and find a different route to the office. But he didn't want to do the smart thing. He needed to become stronger. He needed to accept the hatred and live with it.

He needed his own bodyguards. He would recommend that to Salehi as well when Salehi arrived Any Day Now.

Zhu took a deep breath. He had to make a decision, instead of cowering on the street corner. He had a lot of meetings today. He was still hiring support staff and lawyers, most of whom were newly minted or had come from places as far away as Earth.

The cops hadn't come out of Sevryn's. Zhu wasn't sure if he was waiting for them to do so. If they walked down the street, would they come toward him? Would they try to harm him again?

This time, no one would witness what they did—except maybe whoever was behind that feeling he had.

That thought was enough to make him look around one more time.

Jeez, he was being a coward. (*So what else is new?* that naggy little voice inside him asked.) He had as much right to be on this street as everyone else did.

He straightened his shoulders and took a step forward. Right now, he didn't have a personal bodyguard, so he would have to let his attitude protect him.

He had to show those bullying cops that he wasn't afraid of them.

He walked down the street, and this time, his footsteps echoed. The expensive shoes that he'd bought with S^3's money had an even stronger ring to them than the footsteps he had heard earlier.

The hair rose on the back of his neck, like it did every time he walked with his body exposed. He ignored the feeling. He had to.

He walked past Sevryn's and didn't look inside—at least, not directly. He turned on one of the few enhancement chips he owned, the ones he'd bought when he first left the Impossibles. The chips expanded his peripheral vision, and let him see everything except what was directly behind him.

He could walk with his gaze straight ahead and still see what was happening behind his ears.

He used that additional vision to get a glimpse of the interior of Sevryn's. The cops, sitting at one of the only tables the place had, quite close to the windows.

Watching him go by.

In fact, everyone in line (and there was always a line at Sevryn's) turned to watch him pass.

He didn't move his head or do anything to betray that he had seen them. If they wanted to intimidate him, fine, they had. But they didn't need to know that.

He ducked into the deli next door. He had ordered dinner from that place yesterday for the entire office, and had it delivered. The sandwiches were better than Sevryn's, but some of the baked goods weren't.

Still, the place smelled fantastic. Fresh coffee, cinnamon, and a touch of baking bread. His stomach rumbled.

The woman behind the counter smiled at him. She was older and a little heavyset, her curly hair tired, probably because of the steam rising around her.

He ordered coffee and a bagel.

And then he smiled at her.

Because he could. Because this was his life now.

Because this was the life he wanted.

Finally.

4

For the second time in two days, Bartholomew Nyquist found himself inside the area between the Peyti and human sections of Armstrong's Reception Center. That was the euphemistic name of the maximum security prison just outside Armstrong's dome, where the accused were kept while awaiting trial. The Reception Center had its own dome, with varying environments so it could house various members of the Alliance.

Once again, Nyquist had been given an environmental suit and mask. He hadn't needed them the last time, and he hoped he wouldn't need them this time, either. The things were ancient or filthy or both.

Because he was in a prison, he couldn't bring his own suit. Apparently, prison officials believed he (or other visitors) would smuggle something in with their suits. Even though he would never share the same area as the prisoner, never be able to touch him, never be able to slip him anything. Rules sometimes made no sense.

The area between the two sections was called the Tunnels for obvious reasons. Accompanied by two mouthless android guards, Nyquist had gone through what looked like Disty warrens between the two sections. Eventually, he ended up in a clear, round room that looked like it floated.

It was a one-person protective bubble that provided its own environment. The guards used these things to peer into the sections that lacked an environment they could function in. But Nyquist couldn't control his own little bubble. He had no idea where the control panel was, and he didn't have the access codes.

He had to wait wherever the guards wanted him to. And he couldn't talk to the android guards, because they were designed to protect and defend, not communicate.

All of his links were down, including his emergency links, which irritated him. He could contact the prison through a link it had set up, and no one else. He truly felt trapped in a sterile environment.

At least there was a table and a chair. He could rest his head on the table and snooze if he wanted to. He wasn't getting much sleep, between worrying, talking to DeRicci, and trying to figure out what was happening to his beloved city.

But he wasn't going to sleep. It would show weakness. Although he might rest his head if they left him in here as long as they had the day before.

At least the wait had given Nyquist a chance to study everything around him, including the blue water-like substance outside the protective bubble. He prepared himself for the interview, reviewing the questions over and over again in his head.

He had a long list, and he doubted he would get to all of it. He hadn't had enough time with Uzvaan, the Peyti clone, the day before. Nyquist doubted he would have enough time today, either.

Uzvaan had been the lawyer for Nyquist's old partner, Ursula Palmette. Her experiences during the first explosion in Armstrong had turned her somehow, and she had been trying to bomb Armstrong herself on Anniversary Day. Nyquist still wasn't certain of the connection, and Palmette wouldn't talk.

But he had used Palmette as an excuse to bring Uzvaan into the station on the day of the Peyti Crisis, to hold him in place and prevent him from bombing the city.

It had worked.

And now, Nyquist was using the same excuse to convince prison officials to let him see Uzvaan. The officials believed that Nyquist was here on the Palmette case. So far, no one from S³ had figured out what Nyquist was doing, but he had a hunch they'd figure it out soon enough.

Hence all the questions he had to ask today, which he had mentally ordered from most important to least important. Even so, he doubted he would ask them in that order, because interviews were organic things. But he would do his best.

Only a few minutes after Nyquist arrived, another bubble made its way through the blueness. Inside sat Uzvaan, limbs at his sides, legs pulled back, his maskless face still looking unbelievably alien to Nyquist.

He was so used to seeing the Peyti with their masks that Uzvaan looked like an entirely different creature without it.

The bubble stopped not too far from Nyquist's. Uzvaan's eyes still dominated his face, even without the mask. So Nyquist decided to focus on them.

Nyquist made sure he had started recording.

"Detective," Uzvaan said, in that sarcastic tone of his.

Nyquist had figured out the day before that Uzvaan used the sarcasm to mask his desperation. If Uzvaan didn't get Nyquist's help, he would probably die horribly. If Uzvaan cooperated, he might be able to live—although Nyquist had no idea why someone like Uzvaan would want to live.

"I have a list of questions for you," Nyquist said, his voice cold. He was supposed to tell Uzvaan before they even started that they had a deal. DeRicci would sign some kind of order declaring Uzvaan an individual under Alliance law, *not* a clone. But Nyquist couldn't quite bring himself to tell Uzvaan about the deal.

This bastard had tried to kill him, and that still angered Nyquist more than he could say.

"I told you my conditions," Uzvaan said, sounding like the lawyer he still was.

"You're not in a position to deal," Nyquist said.

"Detective, you believe I have information or you wouldn't be here. So I *am* in a position to deal. And I won't talk to you until you talk to your friend Noelle DeRicci."

Nyquist wanted to hit the release button, sending his little bubbly ship out of the Tunnels. He would have too, if this damn meeting weren't so important.

"Well, lucky you," Nyquist said. "Security Chief DeRicci believes you actually have some value to the investigation. She's willing to sign an order granting you individual status *after* we've heard what you have to say."

"Before," Uzvaan said.

"Look," Nyquist said, leaning forward, elbows resting on the table. "If it were my choice, you wouldn't get a fancy deal. You might get protective custody or you might be able to have your case severed from everyone else's, but to be considered an individual, a *person*? I think you lost that chance when you tried to kill thousands."

Uzvaan raised his head slightly. The bluish tinge near his eyes betrayed how deeply that comment had disturbed him, but his expression hadn't changed.

"You would not believe an apology," he said softly.

"No," Nyquist said. "I wouldn't. And I think, if you were truly sorry, or if you were truly forced to do this against your will, you would talk to me because it's the right thing to do, not because you'll get something out of it."

Uzvaan's entire face turned blue. He looked down, and said softly, "I am a lawyer, Detective. I have not been trained to think of anything from that angle."

"Yeah," Nyquist said. "We know how susceptible you are to training."

Uzvaan flinched. Nyquist felt a sense of satisfaction. He wasn't sure he liked that about himself.

Then Uzvaan nodded, as if part of the conversation had gone on without Nyquist. "I—am—you are right. I—um—it is logical to repent for one's actions by going above and beyond."

Nyquist half expected Uzvaan to add, *I often told my clients that*, but Nyquist couldn't quite imagine Uzvaan ever giving that advice.

"Ask your questions," Uzvaan said. "I will not withhold my answers."

Nyquist wanted to believe that Uzvaan was trying, but Nyquist had already made DeRicci's offer. Uzvaan knew that if his information was valuable, he would get a deal.

Of course, Nyquist didn't have to tell DeRicci that Uzvaan took the deal. Twice since he started negotiating with Uzvaan, Nyquist had felt the urge to lie about any kind of deal with Uzvaan.

For once, Nyquist had to fight himself to tell the truth about what was happening in these little rooms.

"All right," Nyquist said, hoping that his ambivalence hadn't shown on his face. "Someone created all of you clones of Uzvekmt. Who? And why? And how many of you are there?"

"That is more than one question," Uzvaan said, then caught himself and looked away. "But I shall endeavor to answer all of them."

He pulled a little from side to side, his arms remaining in place. His hands were strapped to the sides of the chair. That had to hurt, considering he had been in the same position the day before.

"Who created us?" Uzvaan said. "This I do not know, at least, not exactly. I do know that a corporation titled—"

And then he spoke Peytin, which irritated Nyquist. He was trying to record this conversation like he had recorded the one yesterday, but he wasn't certain if the prison officials would let him leave with it. Yesterday, the officials hadn't noticed the recording chip that Nyquist used. He couldn't guarantee that they would miss it today.

"The name has many translations," Uzvaan was saying, "but I believe that the one the corporation's founders intended was a little known meaning for the phrase. It is *legal fiction*."

"You were part of a corporation called 'Legal Fiction'?" Not even Nyquist could believe that.

"I was not part of any corporation with that name. That corporation—named in Peytin—" and again, he said the unintelligible words—"is the one that housed, fed, and educated me and about one hundred of my fellows."

He did not say the word "clones." Nor did he look at Nyquist as he said this last part.

Nyquist paused for a moment. He could either follow his list or he could go with the conversation. At the moment, he wanted to go with the conversation.

Jin Rastigan, the head of Earth Alliance Security Office Human Division on Peyla, had observed clones of Uzvekmt killing each other in rather horrible ways, not long ago. She had contacted DeRicci about it. Nyquist wondered if Uzvaan had lived through a similar experience.

Nyquist would approach this issue slowly.

"Did all of your fellows, as you put it, go to law school?"

"No," Uzvaan said, still looking down.

"Did all of them survive their upbringing?"

Uzvaan looked at him quickly, as if startled. Uzvaan opened his mouth, then turned his head a little, his face grayer than Nyquist had ever seen it.

"Why do you ask?" Uzvaan asked.

"Answer the question," Nyquist said.

"No, not all survived." Uzvaan spoke softly.

"Because some of the clones were not viable?" Nyquist asked.

"Because some of them failed," Uzvaan said.

In spite of himself, Nyquist felt chilled. "The cloning techniques failed? That means the embryos weren't viable."

"No," Uzvaan said, speaking even softer than he had before. "They—the individuals—they failed."

"At what?"

Uzvaan's eyes narrowed. "Whatever they were assigned."

The chill Nyquist felt settled around his heart.

"What happened to the ones that failed?" he asked, even though he knew. Or he thought he knew.

Uzvaan closed his eyes. He twitched. Then he opened his eyes. They seemed bigger than before, glassy.

"I would like to move on to more recent events," he said.

"I would like an answer," Nyquist said.

"It is not relevant," Uzvaan said in his lawyer's voice.

"I decide what is relevant," Nyquist said.

"They died," Uzvaan said so softly that Nyquist almost missed it.

"They died because they failed?" Nyquist repeated.

Uzvaan nodded, his face so tense that his eyes had narrowed.

"Isn't it more accurate to say that you and the other survivors killed them?" Nyquist asked.

"No," Uzvaan said.

"Then how did they die?" Nyquist asked.

"They *failed*," Uzvaan repeated. Then he spoke the Peytin phrase he had used the day before, which Popova had translated as *You can't have a failure in a unit.*

"So it's okay to kill someone if they fail," Nyquist said. "Because you were told it was all right?"

Uzvaan's skin had turned a bluish gray wherever it was visible. Nyquist had never seen anything like it, but he sensed it meant extreme distress. He wondered if he was pushing Uzvaan too hard.

"We were raised," Uzvaan said, "in a controlled environment. Failure was not possible, and that included a failure to follow orders."

"So," Nyquist said. "Murder for you was something you did when ordered."

Uzvaan's color grew even darker.

"Never mind," Nyquist said. "You don't have to answer that because your behavior last week makes the answer obvious. *Of course* you can be ordered to murder someone. You've done it all your life."

"Failures are not 'someone,'" Uzvaan said in a small voice. "They have lost the right to exist."

Nyquist paused. The next logical question—if this were a standard interrogation—would be more of a statement. *But you're a failure now, right? You didn't achieve your goal as destroyer of the Moon.*

But he didn't dare say that. What if he pushed Uzvaan into killing himself, made Uzvaan realize that he should have died because he had done something wrong?

Still, Nyquist couldn't resist one question. Or perhaps it was more of a jab.

"So, you clones are supposed to die if you failed at something," he said slowly, "and to succeed at destroying the Moon, you would have died as well. Does that mean if you succeeded in destroying the Moon, you were a failure? There seems to be no logic to this. It doesn't make sense to me."

"Of course it does, Detective." Uzvaan spoke with great sarcasm, but his expression hadn't altered. Was that what Peyti looked like when they were sad? "It makes sense if one does not think of us as individuals, but as tools. One tosses out tools that do not work. Tools designed for a single purpose only achieve that purpose, often through their own destruction."

"Like bombs," Nyquist said.

"Like bombs," Uzvaan agreed.

Nyquist let the words hang for a moment. They left him shaken. Clearly Uzvaan had thought this through. Why wouldn't he? He'd had a lot of time alone in this place.

"When did you realize you were an individual and not a weapon?" Nyquist asked.

Uzvaan shook his head ever so slightly. "Your question is incorrect, Detective. I was always a weapon."

Nyquist was not going to repeat that question. It showed too much empathy, and that bothered him. So he just waited to see if Uzvaan would answer anyway.

"It is a mistake, in my opinion, not that my opinion is worth much any longer," Uzvaan said, looking down, "to set the timer on a weapon for decades instead of minutes."

Nyquist studied Uzvaan. Uzvaan still wouldn't meet his gaze.

"I had time to contemplate," Uzvaan said. "I learned, when I came to the Moon, when I realized that no one here knew what I was, that I could be seen as something other than a clone. I achieved respect. I achieved position. I achieved a life."

Nyquist swallowed. He was frowning. "Then why did you continue with the plan?"

"You act like I had a choice," Uzvaan said.

"You did," Nyquist snapped. Both words were filled with fury. He couldn't suppress it.

Uzvaan shook his head again. The human movement was, apparently, the best way he could express himself, at least with this.

"I did not think I had a choice," Uzvaan said. "I would contemplate abandoning the mission, and then I would think what fools you all were to believe I was a legitimate Peyti, a real lawyer, someone who was a true individual."

"You were," Nyquist said.

"No." Uzvaan raised his head. His eyes were blue-tinged again. "I have thought on this long and hard, Detective. It is the point that vexes me the most."

He paused. Nyquist wondered if Uzvaan would continue, or if Nyquist should push him. Nyquist had never been this emotionally conflicted in an interview, nor had he felt like so much was at stake.

Apparently, Uzvaan didn't notice Nyquist's conflict.

"I was trained, from the beginning, from the moment of conception—however you measure that—to believe I had no worth. I had a *purpose*, and only in achieving that purpose would I obtain—again, your language does not have the word." Uzvaan said something in Peytin. "This word, it mixes what you call humanity, personhood, a soul, and legitimacy. It is the core of being a Peyti, something that no clone can ever achieve, or so I was raised."

"You just told me you could achieve it," Nyquist said.

"We were taught that we could achieve it through completion of our mission," Uzvaan said. "It was the only way."

Nyquist blinked. He thought about it. He didn't understand Peyti culture. He didn't understand his own culture half the time. He could wander down this side corridor, or he could talk to Popova about it all, maybe get Jin Rastigan to weigh in.

"It is a lie," Uzvaan said. "I know that now."

Nyquist had been so lost in his own thoughts that he wasn't sure what Uzvaan meant. "What's a lie?"

"That we could become—" And again, he used that Peytin word. "I have spent the last week wondering if I could have achieved it without ever doing what was asked of me. I wonder if as a lawyer, as an individual, if I had avoided my training, if I had done something different, would I have achieved this on my own?"

Nyquist let the words hang. He needed the interrogation to move in a different direction, but he didn't want to make Uzvaan more defensive than he already was.

Finally, Nyquist said, "Have you spoken to any of the others about this?"

"We are not allowed to consult," Uzvaan said. "I imagine, however, that they are as shaken by their survival as I am. It is not something we were prepared for. It is not something we ever contemplated."

Nyquist nodded. He wondered if the police could use this before remembering that the police had no access to the clones.

"So," Nyquist said slowly. "This corporation, this so-called *Legal Fiction*. It raised you and you never questioned it."

"Did you question your parents, Detective?" Uzvaan asked.

"They didn't require me to murder people," Nyquist snapped. He regretted the words the moment he spoke them.

Uzvaan tilted his head, acknowledging the statement. The lawyer had returned. The vulnerable being, the one who no longer understood his place in the universe, had vanished.

"For us," Uzvaan said slowly, as if Nyquist were particularly dumb, "such behavior was normal. We did not know differently."

Nyquist felt a flash of irritation. He had always felt that sort of irritation when he interviewed criminals who blamed their crimes on their upbringing. Although part of his mind was telling him that Uzvaan had a point. Uzvaan had been groomed to behave exactly as he had. As if he were a computer, programmed for destruction.

Nyquist tamped down the irritation. Peyti were not computers any more than humans were. And Nyquist believed that every creature had a choice in its behavior—within certain biological limitations, of course.

He asked, "When you went to law school and you learned that killing other Peyti was not only illegal, it was a major crime, when you learned that your original, Uzvekmt, was considered the most foul of all Peyti because he was a mass murderer, how did you reconcile that with your training?"

"I did not know who my original was," Uzvaan said. "Not for decades, and even then, I was not sure I believed it."

Denial. Apparently the Peyti were as good at it as humans. Nyquist threaded his fingers together so that his hands wouldn't form fists.

"As for murder," Uzvaan said. "The first thing we learned in law school, long before we learned any actual law, was that different cultures abide by different rules. What is heinous in one culture is commonplace in another. It is a tenet of the Earth Alliance, no?"

And that was why Nyquist hated talking to lawyers. They answered a question with a question.

"You believed," Nyquist said slowly, "that you were raised in a different culture from other Peyti?"

"I *was* raised in a different culture," Uzvaan said. "It was obvious. I was a boy raised among other boys. The standard Peyti upbringing mixes genders. I was raised in private schools, with special teachers. We were taught that it was akin to what many of the religious upbringings other cultures—including your own—provide. So I believed in our traditions, and felt we were excused for them."

"When did you learn otherwise?" Nyquist asked.

"Anniversary Day," Uzvaan whispered.

Nyquist sat, stunned and silent. He had expected a different answer—law school itself, something, not six months ago.

"Anniversary Day?" He finally managed.

Uzvaan's entire face had turned blue again. "I realize it will seem odd, but when I saw the clones of Frémont, I understood that we were not special. We were merely tools, vessels, *weapons*."

"And still, you put on that bomb. You tried to kill everyone at the police station."

"What choice did I have, Detective?"

Nyquist couldn't stand it any longer. He stood and paced around that tiny bubble. If he had been in the same bubble as Uzvaan, he would have grabbed the bastard by the head and slammed it against the desk, then asked, *What choice did I have, you asshole?*

But he couldn't reach through the walls between them.

Nyquist's stomach churned, and he had to swallow hard to prevent himself from throwing up.

He took a deep, shaky breath. He needed to calm himself.

He had been sent here for answers.

He couldn't get them without asking the questions.

One of the guards flashed a message across its forehead. *Is the interview complete?*

Nyquist shook his head.

It hadn't even begun.

He returned to his chair and steeled himself.

He would get through this.

Somehow.

5

SHE WOKE UP SCREAMING.

Talia Flint-Shindo sat up in her darkened bedroom, throat raw, and hoped her dad hadn't heard. She didn't want to worry him. More than that, she didn't want him tearing in here in the pretend-non-panic mode that he'd been affecting since the Peyti Crisis had begun.

He kept looking at her like she was broken. Maybe she was. She couldn't stop shaking half the time, and tears threatened at the weirdest moments.

She pulled the blankets around herself and scrunched the pillows to support her back. Then she waited, trying to make up a good lie to convince her father that she really was all right.

But he didn't hurry in here like he had on previous nights. Of course, this afternoon she'd been clear-headed enough to hack into her bedroom's security system and make the room soundproof.

Her dad wouldn't approve. He would say, *What if someone broke in and attacked you? How could I protect you?*

But for someone to break into this place, they'd have to actually get in. That meant going through the apartment building's ridiculously tight security system, getting through the doors and windows that she and her dad had enhanced themselves, and getting past her dad—who was an unbelievably light sleeper.

He would probably find it ironic that she had soundproofed the room. She used to be more security minded than he was. Part of that was because of what had happened to her on Valhalla Basin.

A group of hired thugs had imprisoned her in her own bedroom closet before kidnapping and ultimately killing her mother. Not that they actually used a weapon to kill her mother; she had killed herself. But she wouldn't have if the thugs had left her alone.

Talia sighed and eased a bare foot out of bed. The room was cold. She'd turned down the temperature because she had figured out that she slept better in the cold, but that made getting up uncomfortable.

As frigid as the air was, she had to move around. She couldn't stay in bed any longer. Not with the nightmare still lingering.

She took a deep breath and grabbed her robe. She slipped her feet into her furry slippers. If she raised the temperature, the apartment's system (which they weirdly called House, even though this wasn't a house) might alert her father that she was awake, and he'd come in here despite her precautions.

She didn't raise the lights, either. This room had become so familiar to her, she could pace it in the darkness without hitting anything. She'd had a lot of sleepless nights in the past twelve days, and that didn't count how badly she had slept in the years since she moved in with her dad here on the Moon.

When those thugs had broken into her home, they had stolen more than her mother. They had stolen Talia's sense of security, maybe forever.

She sighed and walked in a circle around her bed. One wall had a dressing table with the girly things her father thought she should love. The table had a non-networked master computer, which she really did love, because she could do all kinds of research on it and use it to develop programs. The only person who shared that computer with her was her father. That one thing had been non-negotiable for him, and it was a small price to pay for the freedom to let her brain roam.

There were a couple of chairs, and a full virtual reality/holochamber that had come with the apartment and which she doubted she would ever use.

Reality was tough enough. She didn't want to confuse herself with made-up realities.

She sighed and sat on the edge of the bed. She was exhausted. That was part of the problem. If only she could sleep.

The stupid therapist that her dad insisted on taking her to this week had told her to record the nightmares the moment she woke up.

It'll be like exorcising a ghost, the stupid therapist said. *The more you talk about what you're seeing in your dreams, the less power those dreams will have over you.*

Yeah, right. She'd looked up dream aversion therapy and had seen just how controversial it was.

First, the stupid therapist would get her to talk about the dreams. Then he'd make her use a chip to actually record them. Then he'd play them back in the daylight, in a protected environment.

Only she didn't want her brain to be examined like that.

Her dad told her to cooperate fully with the stupid therapist—that she needed to trust him—but she had her doubts.

He might find out that she was a clone, and right now, in Armstrong, clones were considered evil. She'd actually heard some otherwise intelligent people say that cloning twisted the DNA and made every single clone into a potential psychopath.

Even as a kid, discovering her background for the first time, she'd known enough science to know that wasn't true. The clones were physical copies of the original, nothing more. And maybe not entirely that. Because the originals usually got subjected to a different environment in the womb, one that clones rarely experienced.

Clones were completely different creatures than their original. And, Talia suspected, clones—grown in a controlled environment—were probably more stable, healthier, and saner than any original could be.

She kept that opinion to herself. She hadn't even told her dad that theory.

Talia stood again, because her heart was still pounding. Half her brain was still in the nightmare.

Maybe she could banish it all on her own.

She wouldn't repeat it into any recording device, but she could review it. She'd never tried that before.

The nightmare had started at the Armstrong Wing of the Aristotle Academy, which her dad had enrolled her into because it was the best private school in the city and, he believed, it was the safest. But the school hadn't been safe during the Peyti Crisis.

She covered her face. If she was going to do what the stupid therapist wanted her to do, she couldn't just *review* the nightmare, she had to dive into it.

That wouldn't be hard.

She flopped on her back onto the bed, put her right arm over her eyes, and took a deep breath.

She'd been walking down the hall with Kaleb Lamber. God, he was a jerk. She hated him, but he was the best-looking guy in the school, and he looked at her like she was pretty.

Only he was mean to everybody, including her, and she had yelled at him, and now, he said, he wanted to talk about it, that maybe something else was going on, and she'd seen it. She'd seen it in the way Kaleb's dad treated him, like Kaleb treated everyone else, as if they were idiots in training and not as strong as he was.

She was feeling compassion for Kaleb, and she didn't want to. She didn't want to like him or even feel anything positive for him. For days, she hadn't even looked at his face because he was so handsome, and just thinking that, thinking how handsome he was on the outside and how mean he was on the inside, seemed like thinking something positive.

He asked her to forgive him for being so mean. His face was yellow. At first she thought it was because of the environmental change—Peyti normal, no human could survive that—and then she realized his skin was yellow and black in a pattern of an open human hand.

I don't want to go home, he said. Talia, please. Say you forgive me. Say I belong here. Help me—

She tried to help him. He was in that room now, the room she could see even with her eyes open. Her stomach clenched and the air smelled of onions. The room was the Academy's conference room.

Her links were off; she couldn't reach her dad or Kaleb or Mrs. Rutledge or anyone.

Kaleb was all alone in that room with his dad, who was hitting him, and a Peyti lawyer, who played with its mask. The lawyer looked like every other Peyti to her, gray and long limbed, fingers like sticks. Only its eyes were different. They glowed red.

Your lawyer, *she sent to Kaleb*. He wants to kill you. Get out of there.

Then the Peyti lawyer disassembled part of the mask that covered half his face, squeezed the part in his hand, and the room exploded. She stood there, as debris rained around her like images of Anniversary Day, when nineteen domed cities on the Moon suffered horrible explosions. She felt like she was watching a vid, not experiencing anything.

Kaleb was in pieces now, crying, saying, Talia, I don't want to go home. Say you forgive me—

She put her hands over her ears, a scream building.

I can't, *she sent him, because her links worked now.* I can't forgive you. I can't help you. You're dead.

You're dead.

She sat up, her heart racing. She always woke up at that point. The nightmare wasn't an exact memory. It was wrong in so many ways, but it felt absolutely true.

What was true was this: She had stopped Kaleb from beating up the Chinar twins because he said they were clones (they weren't), and in doing so, she had actually started a big fight in the cafeteria. She and Kaleb had gotten into trouble for it. Her dad got mad at her, but Kaleb's dad—he must have gone way beyond mad. He wanted to pull Kaleb out of school and leave him at home, which Kaleb didn't want.

Because Kaleb had had a bruise on his face that last day, and something about the way he was, something about what he was trying to tell her, made her think that he didn't want to go home because he was scared his dad was going to hurt him.

Her stomach ached. She popped off the bed as if it were causing the nightmares. Kaleb had wanted her to join him in that conference room.

His dad and his dad's lawyers, including a Peyti, were meeting with the headmistress, Mrs. Rutledge, to discuss Kaleb's future at the academy.

Talia had lurked outside because she had felt so confused. Part of her thought maybe she should help him, and part of her thought he was the meanest kid she knew, and he should get what he deserved.

And while she was having that thought, her links shut off, a guard grabbed her, putting his onion-scented hands on her, and dragged her away from the conference area.

But not before she saw the entire conference room's environmental system change to Peyti Normal—a yellowish color. The Peyti lawyer removed his mask and squeezed it. Had the environmental system still been set at Earth Normal, the damn lawyer would have blown up the entire school, maybe even blown a hole in the dome.

But her dad, working with Noelle DeRicci, the Chief of Security for the United Domes of the Moon, had figured out what was going to happen and ordered a change to environmental systems all over the Moon to Peyti Normal, just in time.

The problem was…no human could survive without a mask in Peyti Normal.

Talia watched ten people die.

She watched *Kaleb* die. He screamed and screamed, then collapsed, and twitched. And died.

Talia wiped at her face. It was wet again. Those stupid tears fell no matter what she did. She couldn't stop them.

Her dad, who had left the Security Office to get her out of the Academy, had arrived just after everyone died. He had thought then—he still thought now—that she was upset because she would have been in the room, because she would have *died* if she had been in the room, but that wasn't it.

Her dad didn't seem to understand that if she had *died*, it would have taken a few minutes, and then she'd be done. She wouldn't have known any of this stuff. She'd be okay.

She was upset that *Kaleb* had died. In front of her. When she still didn't know how to feel about him. She didn't like him, but she was beginning to understand him, and she was starting to feel sorry for him, against her better judgment, and she thought maybe—

She shook her head. Her brain always stopped there. Right there, because she didn't want to get past the maybe.

Her dad had asked her, just once, if she was angry at him for the death of those ten people. They were, in the words of the press, collateral damage. If they hadn't died, then every city on the Moon would have suffered dozens, maybe hundreds, of explosions. Millions of people would have died.

Millions *more* would have died, because millions died on Anniversary Day. Her dad said, and Noelle DeRicci said, and everybody said that this was the second attack aimed at the Moon, related, somehow to Anniversary Day, only this time, the good guys managed to stop it.

In the nick of time.

And that was true.

She wasn't angry at her dad for stopping it. She'd helped him with some of the stuff he needed to do to figure out who was hurting everyone, even though she hadn't found the Peyti lawyers. Her dad had done that.

She didn't have to forgive him for that. She was proud of him. Her dad saved lives.

It was just—God, she was stuck. She didn't know how to feel about Kaleb. And she didn't want to be sad about his death.

And she was scared.

Scared of the Peyti lawyers. Not because they were lawyers or because they were Peyti, but because they were clones.

Just like she was.

At her dad's insistence, she had kept her clone identity secret. She didn't have to be told it was a liability, and that had been before twenty clones of PierLuigi Frémont had killed people all over the Moon on Anniversary Day, before these Peyti lawyers (clones of some famous Peyti mass murderer) had tried to kill even more people during the Peyti Crisis.

She knew that regular humans hated clones.

Everyone hated clones even more now.

Her entire face stung. Her skin was chapped, and the tears, flowing down their familiar path, covered the dryness with salt.

She hated it. She hated it all. She hated what the Moon had become, what Armstrong had become.

What she had become.

She wanted to go back, back to Valhalla Basin with her mom (who had lied to her, who hadn't told Talia that Talia was a clone, who had made it sound like Talia's dad hated her when he hadn't even known that Talia existed). Talia wanted to go back to a time when everything seemed simple.

She sank onto the floor.

Nothing would ever seem simple again.

6

THE CUP OF COFFEE WAS WARM IN HIS HAND. TORKILD ZHU STOPPED just outside the building that housed the new offices of S³. He had to pull the door open because the automated building computer hadn't been programmed to accept his codes yet. It was one more thing he had to do, and he had decided to wait until all the new hires were completed.

Privately, he hoped that he'd be able to assign one of them to do this kind of scutwork. He was already growing tired of the details.

Still, he'd been heartened as he finished his walk to the office. He had watched five potential job seekers go into the building ahead of him. That made him smile. He'd been having so much trouble getting anyone to apply, and even more trouble finding qualified candidates.

Most of the unemployed lawyers on the Moon (and there were lots at the moment, since many of the Peyti clones had run law firms) had conflicts that prevented them from representing the clones—provided the attorneys wanted to. Of course, most of them didn't want to.

Zhu wouldn't have either if his colleagues had died in a room where the environmental system had shifted to Peyti Normal because another colleague wanted to blow the entire building to smithereens.

Zhu tried not to be empathetic about that, too. He tried not to think about it at all.

If he had done what he had intended when he traveled all the way back to the Moon a month ago, he might have been one of those attorneys sitting in one of those rooms, dying as the oxygen fled and the poison atmosphere fell around him.

Or he would have lost friends or acquaintances at least. Colleagues. That was the word. He would have lost colleagues.

At least the clones weren't his clients. His client was the government of Peyla, the Peyti home world. Already, in the week since the Crisis, Peyti had been denied admission into Armstrong's port. Each Peyti had had a different reason for being refused, but the pattern was pretty clear. And it was starting to happen all over the Alliance.

Since Peyla was part of the Alliance and had actually been one of the early members of the Alliance, the Peyti government was taking quick action. Even though everyone knew that Peyti lawyers were the best in the business, the Peyti government had hired S^3, a well-known human law firm, to take this case.

The Peyti were incredibly smart. They didn't use their own to fight this battle; they used troops that they knew could win.

Zhu was rather proud to be part of those troops. Or maybe he could attribute his good mood to the fact that he'd walked past Sevryn's and managed to start his day, without bodyguards.

He'd conquered his fear, and that was always the first step toward getting anything done.

Even if he had gotten a bit of mediocre coffee out of it.

He debated tossing away the coffee. The new place simply didn't have as good a brew as Sevryn's—probably because it didn't use Earth-grown beans—and he would miss that. But the cream-cheese-and-orange bagel he'd bought was a delicious new treat, one he'd have as often as he could.

He'd already ordered lunch for the crew upstairs. The new place would deliver.

Yeah, he was proud of himself. He saw that short walk as one of the first steps toward accepting how hard this job would be, and how much intimidation would be built in.

"Torkild Zhu?" a male voice asked behind him.

"Yes?" he asked as he turned, half-expecting to see some young law-yer clutching a tablet loaded with resumes and recommendations. In-stead, he saw half a face and the blur of an arm.

Then something hit him on the side of his head. The sound cracked inside his skull, and his vision went white for a moment. There was no pain, but he knew that would only be temporary. He'd hit his head before and—

A foot hit his stomach, a kick so hard that his breath whooshed out of him. Then another something—an arm? A fist? A weapon—hit his back. His kidneys. This time, he felt the pain, ripping through him.

It would have taken his breath away, had he had any breath left.

He sent something—a scream, maybe?—through his emergency links. Or so he hoped. Because his brain felt odd, warm, and his right eye was closing even though he had been hit on the other side of the face.

He wanted to say, *Don't. Don't hurt me. Stop.* But he couldn't control his mouth. He toppled forward.

Someone kicked his side, and someone else jumped on his back. If he could fall through the sidewalk, he would have, but the ground kept him in place. So his bones gave instead, cracking and snapping.

A hand grabbed his ankle, pulled it toward his head, and more bones snapped.

Voices said something about horrible deaths, about clones, about paying for what he had done, but he hadn't done anything.

His shirt was wet. His entire body was wet with something warm and sticky.

The coffee, probably. It was the only thing he'd been holding.

Coffee. And not very good coffee.

He wanted to say, *Stop, please. I'm only doing my job.* Instead, he coughed out some—coffee? Too thick to be coffee. Tasted of rust or iron or something metallic. And it bubbled up from inside, but he wasn't throwing up, was he?

The very thought made him hurt.

Something landed on his back, but he only knew that because his entire body bounced. He couldn't feel the weight or the ground or anything. He heard more snapping, but didn't know where it came from.

His right eye was completely closed now and his left was pressed against the ground. He couldn't see these attackers. He had no idea who they were. They hadn't been on the street a moment before.

He had watched to make sure he wasn't followed. He hadn't heard any footsteps except his own.

He'd ordered lunch for the staff.

He was a good man.

Really.

Why couldn't they see that?

He didn't deserve this.

He tried to tell them, but they kept kicking him, these anonymous people, these shoed feet, these attackers. They were talking, but he couldn't hear them.

He didn't want to hear them.

If they wouldn't let him talk, he wouldn't listen to them either.

He closed his left eye, feeling the eyelashes scrape against the sidewalk, and heard himself grunt. Another kick, apparently. He was going to ignore it.

It was happening to someone else.

Things always happened to someone else.

That was why lawyers existed. To handle disputes.

Not kickers. Not attackers. These people should have visited the law firm. He could have helped them.

He shuddered, wondering if someone at S^3 would take their case.

Couldn't, though.

Conflict of interest.

Conflict.

Interest.

He sighed, then decided to worry about the legal side of it later.

Later.

After he woke up.

7

Nyquist stared at the Peyti clone across from him. Uzvaan's face was still blue with shame, his hands at his sides. The android guards had returned to their corners.

It almost felt like Nyquist and Uzvaan were alone inside this watery tunnel, linked by their gigantic environmental bubbles.

"Let's go back to law school," Nyquist said, as if Uzvaan hadn't sickened him a moment before. "Who paid for your education?"

"The corporation," Uzvaan said.

"Under what name?" Nyquist asked.

Uzvaan said the Peytin name again.

"No one questioned the name *Legal Fiction,* sending kids who looked alike to law school?" Nyquist asked.

Apparently Uzvaan did not see the irony, because he continued to stare at Nyquist.

"Our schools do not use DNA for identification," Uzvaan said. "It is considered a violation of privacy. And how we appear is our business. Like your enhancements are."

"I was talking about the name," Nyquist said. "Legal Fiction."

"The name has other meanings," Uzvaan said. "I cannot vouch for the schools. I can merely assume that they chose to accept a different meaning for the name."

"Schools," Nyquist said. "They sent you all to different schools?"

"Yes," Uzvaan said. "There are thousands of law schools on Peyla and even more off Peyla that cater to Peyti. All law schools must include an Earth Alliance track."

"You didn't go to school with the other members of your—what do you call it? Team? Unit?"

"No, we did not go to school together," Uzvaan said quietly.

"That must have felt odd," Nyquist said.

"We were prepared for it," Uzvaan said. "We were removed from the compound in our last year, and trained one-on-one."

"In bomb-making?"

"In Peyti standard curriculum," Uzvaan said. "We were tested rigorously in it."

"And if you failed—?"

"I did not fail," Uzvaan said. The lawyer never entirely left him. It was deeply a part of him, perhaps more than he realized. That single sentence, both filled with pride and denial, was legal in its brilliance.

Uzvaan had not failed, so he didn't know what happened to the failures. And he was being trained alone at that point, so he could claim he had no knowledge.

"Did the others you were raised with go to any other school besides law school?" Nyquist asked.

"Not to my knowledge," Uzvaan said. "But law school is a particularly good way for the Peyti to move around within the Earth Alliance."

Nyquist was about to ask his next question when he realized what Uzvaan had just said.

"Are you saying that you weren't all assigned to the Moon?"

"I am, Detective," Uzvaan said. "You know that."

He had suspected it, but he had not had confirmation. DeRicci had warned the Earth Alliance. No one had let her know whether or not more Peyti clones had been found.

"So there are more bombs coming," Nyquist said softly.

"That I do not know," Uzvaan said. "I only know my mission, not the mission of others."

"Your mission," Nyquist said, "was it specific to this date and time? Did it change?"

"No, the date did not change. I have known that date my entire life."

Nyquist froze for a half moment. Uzvaan surprised him. Nyquist had expected this attack to be a Plan B—the kind of attack that would only occur *after* something else failed.

But apparently these masterminds, to use Flint's word, did not plan for failure. DeRicci had been thinking of this all along. She'd been worried another attack would happen. She seemed to understand how this was organized.

Or maybe she had just been planning for a worst case scenario. Maybe she had felt that there would be waves of these attacks until the goal was achieved, whatever that goal was.

"You have known the date your *entire* life," Nyquist repeated.

"Since I could recall." Uzvaan's tone was flat. "I knew I had a creation date and an end date."

That was the second time he had referred to an end date.

"Not a death date?" Nyquist said.

Uzvaan leaned back a little, as if the question surprised him. "No, because death could come at any time."

"So what was the end date?" Nyquist asked.

"The maximum length of my life," Uzvaan said. "We all had maximum dates."

The hair rose on the back of Nyquist's neck. "Were the maximum dates all the same?"

Uzvaan turned blue again. Why would that question embarrass or distress him?

"We were not allowed to talk about our creation dates or our end dates," he said.

"Why not?" Nyquist said.

"Such things are personal," Uzvaan said.

"Would you get killed if you broke that rule?" Nyquist asked.

"I do not know," Uzvaan said. "I did not break it."

The silence hung between them for a moment. Uzvaan had given that answer quickly. Nyquist knew that was a lawyer answer, parsing the question on its face rather than for its meaning.

Nyquist needed to be careful. He didn't have a lot of time to ask Uzvaan questions. Nyquist couldn't play verbal games. He needed to frame his questions as carefully as possible.

"What else weren't you allowed to talk about?" Nyquist asked.

"Our assignments," Uzvaan said.

For a moment, Nyquist thought perhaps he meant study assignments—homework and the like. Then he realized he truly did not know what that word meant.

"Explain assignments," Nyquist said.

"We were told when we were ten what our future would bring. We were sorted and given a life assignment. We could not discuss it with anyone else."

"What was your life assignment?" Nyquist asked.

"I was to become a lawyer in the Earth Alliance," Uzvaan said. "I was told I had an aptitude."

"Were you assigned to the Moon?" Nyquist asked.

"I was to make the Moon my priority," Uzvaan said. "If I did not receive that assignment, I would be considered a failure."

Nyquist shuddered. That failure thing was convenient. Whoever the mastermind was, he could weed out his candidates, leaving very few to do the work.

It was wasteful, if one looked at the clones as tools, like Uzvaan had said. A tool with even the slightest flaw did not move forward.

The amount of money behind this scheme was stupendous.

"You are quiet now," Uzvaan said.

Nyquist looked at him. At least Uzvaan's skin tone had returned to normal.

"Yeah," Nyquist said. "I was just thinking how vast this was. Did you have any idea how many others there were in your—religion or whatever you called it?"

"We knew we were one among many," Uzvaan said. "But if we saw someone else who might have been from our group outside of a group, we were not to talk to them about anything we learned."

"So the lawyers here on the Moon," Nyquist said, "you guys never held a meeting."

"We held many meetings," Uzvaan started, and Nyquist just about exploded with irritation.

"About your upcoming end date or your team or unit or past," he snapped, clarifying before Uzvaan could finish his damn lawyer answer.

"We were forbidden from doing so," Uzvaan said.

"But you did meet," Nyquist said.

"As lawyers, as colleagues," Uzvaan said. "We met the way that all lawyers meet, about cases and clients and our work."

"There's no Secret Society of Peyti Clone Lawyers, huh?" Nyquist asked. He couldn't hold the question back.

"Not that I know of," Uzvaan said, taking the question seriously. "Nor is there a Moon-based organization of Peyti lawyers who are not clones. I know that some of the human lawyers formed one, but the Peyti did not. At least on the Moon."

Nyquist let out a breath. He hadn't expected Uzvaan to volunteer any information so that last was a surprise.

"Because it was forbidden?" Nyquist asked.

Uzvaan looked down. "Because it might be misconstrued."

Nyquist let the words echo for a moment. "Were you being watched?"

Uzvaan looked up at him. Uzvaan's eyes seemed even more liquid than usual.

"I do not know," he whispered.

"They didn't tell you they'd supervise you?" Nyquist asked.

"I assumed they watched," Uzvaan said. "We had been watched our entire lives."

"But you had no proof?" Nyquist asked.

"I had no contact with the people who raised me from the moment I moved to the Moon," Uzvaan said.

"Did you think that unusual?" Nyquist asked.

Uzvaan let out a small sigh. "I tried not to think about it at all."

Nyquist shook his head. "When you did think of it?" he asked, letting his irritation show.

"I assumed they were watching and I was following the rules," Uzvaan said.

"Did other clone lawyers die because they didn't follow the rules?" Nyquist asked.

"I did not know which lawyers had an end date and which ones did not," Uzvaan said.

That was a curious way to state the mission of the clones.

"So, you didn't think that your clone siblings or whatever you called the other clones of Uzvekmt had the same mission you did?" Nyquist asked.

"We were not allowed to discuss our assignments," Uzvaan said.

Nyquist let out a frustrated breath. Now he remembered why he preferring interrogating humans. At least he could *pretend* to understand what they were talking about.

He had no idea what was normal for a Peyti or not, what was normal for *most* Peyti or not, how distinct Peyti culture was—he knew none of it. And he would have thought—just a few hours ago—that he knew a lot about Peyti culture, including how many damn subcultures had spun off of it.

"You didn't assume they had the same assignment that you had?" Nyquist asked.

"It is not advised to assume anything," Uzvaan said.

He'd said that in the past, when Nyquist had been interrogating Uzvaan's clients, and Nyquist had thought the sentence an example of Uzvaan's fussy lawyerly precision.

Now, Nyquist wondered if Uzvaan's unwillingness to assume anything had been simple self-preservation. If Uzvaan had only acted on the facts as he knew them, he would have made fewer mistakes.

Nyquist let out a deep sigh. Normally, in an interrogation like this, he would have brought in specialists. He would have found someone who understood Peyti culture. He would have brought in someone who actually spoke the language and understood the nuance better than a computer program would have—not that he could access one while in here.

"All right," Nyquist said. "Let's be clear. What, exactly, was your assignment?"

Uzvaan closed his eyes. His entire body shivered. He turned from gray to bright blue to gray again.

Normally, Nyquist would have *assumed* that Uzvaan was breaking such an important stricture that the very act of doing so terrified him at a deep level.

But Nyquist was going to take Uzvaan's advice and not assume anything, at the moment, anyway.

"My...assignment..." Uzvaan said, his voice trembling, "was to end twelve days ago at the appointed hour. I could choose my location, as long as my location was occupied by others and was inside an established organization."

Nyquist's face grew warm. He made himself concentrate on the words, but not on their implications. Even though what Uzvaan told him meant that the others probably had the same assignment—and yes, Nyquist was *assuming* that.

"I had to be on the Moon," Uzvaan said. "I could not contact anyone about this assignment. I had to go to my end quietly. I could not complain. Complaining was failure."

And he'd die if he failed. Didn't Uzvaan see the illogic of this? He was going to die anyway, so what was the price he'd pay for not doing the deed?

"I was to use a specially designed mask, which would arrive in my mask-upgrade packet before the end date," Uzvaan said.

Nyquist wanted clarification of that, but he knew better than to interrupt.

"The mask would contain the means to the end, as you humans would say. If I did not understand how to use it, it did not matter. I had to try and risk the failure. There would be no additional instructions. To contact the mask maker or anyone from my past would be to fail."

Good God. Nyquist clenched a fist, mostly for something to concentrate on, so that he wouldn't ask questions.

"I was not to tell anyone what I was assigned. Not at any point," Uzvaan said.

He had said that before, so clearly that instruction got repeated often.

"I was told as a ten-year-old—"

He did not say "child." Nyquist found that revealing.

"—that I would go on to law school for the Earth Alliance. I would qualify for one of three law schools, all the best in the Alliance. To do anything else would be to fail."

Nyquist clenched his other fist.

"I would graduate close to the top of my class, but not at the top of my class. I was not to call unneeded attention to myself," Uzvaan said.

Because, Nyquist knew, to do so would be to fail. But he didn't say that.

"I would become a defense attorney. I would serve at the Impossibles for the minimum amount of time, and then only accept interviews from Moon-based firms. If I did not get any interviews with Moon-based firms, I was to go to the Moon on my own, and apply for work as a law clerk or legal assistant and work my way up to partner, if possible. The timeline was not as certain here, nor as important, as long as I practiced law on the Moon."

Uzvaan met Nyquist's gaze.

"I was not to make attachments outside of work. I was not to spend my money extravagantly. I was not to call attention to myself. To do so would be to fail."

Nyquist hated that repetition, and he wasn't Uzvaan. How deep had that concept been drilled into the clones?

"I was not to leave the Moon in the final year of my existence. I was to proceed to the end moment calmly and without regret. I was to act professionally at all times. I was not to tell anyone that time was nearly up."

Uzvaan closed his eyes again, slowly, as if he could not bear to look at Nyquist.

Then even more slowly, Uzvaan opened his eyes. His skin tone remained the same for the first time in their entire meeting.

"I followed each and every instruction. I did not deviate, even when I wanted to. One could argue that I am breaking the rules now, but one could also argue that the rules no longer apply because I no longer exist. The end date did come. I did not physically die. But I am no longer Uzvaan. I am nothing."

So that was how Uzvaan justified this conversation. Or this series of conversations.

Nyquist waited. He wanted Uzvaan to be done before continuing.

They sat in silence for several minutes. Finally, Uzvaan said, "That is the entire assignment, Detective."

Nyquist wanted to ask the psychological questions. He would have if this were a standard crime. But it wasn't.

"You mentioned a mask upgrade packet," Nyquist said. "I've never heard of that. I thought Peyti got their masks locally, in the various shops here on the Moon."

Uzvaan shifted a little in his seat. "I do not know about other Peyti," he said. "Ever since I left for school, I have received a mask upgrade packet each quarter. I was told I could only use those masks or it would impact my health adversely. The older I got, the more I believed there was some kind of tracking within the mask, something that allowed them to watch over me."

"Them?" Nyquist asked.

"The ones in charge," Uzvaan said.

"Who are they?" Nyquist asked.

Uzvaan closed his eyes again, then tilted his head. "I do not exactly know."

"Someone ran you around," Nyquist said, and instantly regretted the word choice. "Ran you around" was antagonistic.

"Yes." Uzvaan opened his eyes. Their expression seemed more distant. "Many someones. They never told me who they worked for and I never asked. They were simply The Ones In Charge."

"How did you recognize them?" Nyquist asked.

Uzvaan's head tilt grew more pronounced. "What do you mean?"

"Could any Peyti come up to you and tell you that he was in charge of you? Would you have believed that?"

"No," Uzvaan said. "They had to call me by my number."

That stopped Nyquist for a moment. "Your...number?"

"We did not have names for the first ten years of our lives. Some did not have names until we left for school. We were numbered."

"What's your number?" Nyquist asked.

"Private," Uzvaan said.

"It doesn't matter now," Nyquist reminded him. "That person no longer exists."

Another shudder ran through Uzvaan. "I am..." and then he let out a sigh. "I cannot tell you. You could use it to control me."

"In case you hadn't noticed," Nyquist said, "we already control you."

Uzvaan nodded. "I am...." And again, a sigh. "I am not to tell anyone."

"You weren't supposed to live this long either," Nyquist said. He wanted to add, *Overcome the damn training. Get on with this.*

"True enough." Uzvaan shifted. It almost looked as if he were about to stand. Movement reflected in the bubble around Nyquist.

He glanced over his shoulder.

The android guards had also shifted position. Apparently, Uzvaan wasn't supposed to move out of that chair.

"I am," Uzvaan said, not noticing that Nyquist wasn't looking at him. "I am Eighty-Five of Three Hundred."

Nyquist turned, wanted to say, *See, that wasn't so hard, was it?* But the words stuck in his throat as he realized what Uzvaan had said.

Eighty-five of Three Hundred.

It was a clone name, meant to mark the run. Three hundred clones, and Uzvaan was 85th. Or, the three hundredth branch from the Uzvekmt DNA.

"Do you know what that means?" Nyquist asked.

"No," Uzvaan said.

"Were there any others in your group who were 'of Three Hundred'?" Nyquist asked.

"Originally," Uzvaan said. For a moment, Nyquist thought he would continue and give a number. But he said nothing else.

"How many?" Nyquist asked.

"Twenty-five," Uzvaan said.

"And how many survived?" Nyquist asked.

"Survived what?" Uzvaan asked, clearly reverting to lawyer-speak.

"Your childhood," Nyquist said, if what Uzvaan had gone through as a young clone could be called a childhood.

Uzvaan took a deep breath. He shifted for a third time. Finally, he said, "Me."

"Out of twenty-five?" Nyquist asked.

"There were two hundred of us in the compound who received our assignments," Uzvaan said.

Which meant that two hundred of them made it to the age of 10.

"How many of those two hundred went on to school?" Nyquist asked.

"Fifty," Uzvaan said.

Nyquist felt the chill get worse. He couldn't remember exactly how many Peyti clone lawyers had tried to destroy the Moon. That number never stuck in his head. But it wouldn't be hard to find out.

He forced himself to focus.

"Did they all get mask upgrades like you did?" Nyquist asked.

"I do not know," Uzvaan said. "I was not allowed to communicate with them."

And he wasn't going to assume. But Nyquist would.

"Who sent you the upgrade packets?" Nyquist asked.

"They came from *Legal Fiction*," Uzvaan said. "A different branch of it. I had contact information in case the masks were late."

"Do you know what that information is?" Nyquist asked.

"I never had to use it, so I do not have it memorized," Uzvaan said. "I can no longer access my chips or any of my links. If those contacts have not been destroyed, then the information is there."

Nyquist had a hunch the information had been destroyed. It was short-sighted for an investigation, but not as a response to an ongoing threat.

"How did the mask upgrade packets reach you?" he asked.

"Through one of the Moon's delivery services. It varied as to which one," Uzvaan said.

"Where did the packet arrive?" Nyquist asked.

Uzvaan nodded. He understood why Nyquist was asking this. "My office," Uzvaan said. "When I was hired, I gave that as my permanent address. If I lost that job, I would have failed."

"And if you joined a different law firm?" Nyquist asked. "Was that a failure?"

"It was not," Uzvaan said. "I would have had to change my delivery information at the address I had. But I never had to do that."

Still, it was a lead. And like the one from *Legal Fiction*, it was a good lead. It also probably applied to all of the Peyti lawyer clones.

Nyquist finally felt like he had gotten important information, things that would move the investigation forward. Things that would have died with Uzvaan if Uzvaan had succeeded.

Nyquist allowed himself a few seconds of triumph. Then he continued the interrogation, hoping he could stay at least one day ahead of S³.

He was going to find that mastermind, if it was the last thing he ever did.

8

THE MESSAGE THAT CAME THROUGH MELCIA SENG'S LINKS WAS GARBLED. Something about S^3 and a conflict of interest. She thought maybe the message came from Zhu.

Seng stood in the center of the Armstrong Offices of Schnable, Shishani & Salehi, one of the most respected law firms in the known universe. They were opening a branch on the Moon, right after the Peyti Crisis, and, as one of their first cases, they were representing the Peyti government in regard to the Peyti clones who had tried to destroy the Moon.

Yesterday, when she had learned that, her breath had caught, but it hadn't stopped her from taking the job. She wanted work—prestigious work, work that would take her to the upper levels of her profession—and she wasn't finding that kind of work anywhere on Earth.

There were millions of human lawyers on Earth, and outside of the major cultural centers, very few of them were working in human-alien relations. She had majored in human-alien relations in college, then had gone to law school with an eye to interspecies law. She had served at the Impossibles—who hadn't?—and then had returned home to Toronto because her mother had taken ill.

Her mother died last year, and Seng spent six months cleaning up the house, taking her inheritance, and investing it "wisely," as everyone said. That allowed her the time to find the right job, the one that might eventually take her on a road to the Multicultural Tribunals. She wanted to be certified to argue in front of them, and she couldn't get that as a prosecutor, not without a whole new form of training—and more years of school.

She needed to work as a defense attorney, and what better place than at S^3, one of the most famous firms in the Alliance. When she heard about this job opportunity, she took the first shuttle from Earth she could find. She didn't even care when the headhunter warned her that representing a Peyti on the Moon would be a dicey proposition.

Defense attorneys handled bad characters all the time; that was something she learned in the Impossibles. There, she discovered that sometimes what seemed like evil was, in actuality, ignorance. Not that she would say that about these clones.

But she knew there was more to S^3's defense of them than altruism. She had a hunch S^3 had a plan, and she was willing to help with that plan.

Even though the office itself was mostly unfinished.

The furniture had been delivered just before she and the other two dozen potential lawyers arrived. They were interviewed one by one by the only guy in the entire firm at that time, a man named Torkild Zhu.

He looked a little slick in his silk suit. He wore too much cologne. He had broken capillaries on his nose, which made her wonder if he drank too much. Alcoholics often used clearers to remove the alcohol from their system, but it took years for them to realize that they needed enhancements to repair the damage the alcohol had done to their skin and blood vessels.

She'd worked with a lot of alcoholics on Earth, and she would wager that Zhu was one.

But he had seemed pretty together in the interview. And afterwards, he had hired her. He'd even given her an office. It was directly across from the elevator, but the office had a window that overlooked the dome itself. He had apologized, saying the offices were in a part of Armstrong that was being gentrified. He said that was how S^3 managed to get so much space so quickly. He'd even apologized for the view—something about the dome being yellow and scratchy.

She didn't see that. All she saw was the moonscape, gray and bleak, covered with actual sunshine, not the dome-manufactured stuff she had seen since she arrived here.

Of the two dozen people the headhunter had brought, nearly half had walked out when they realized what their first cases would be. Six of the others were the kind of lawyer that Seng wouldn't have hired ever, the kind that had a sleazy vibe that made her think they would cut corners wherever possible.

Apparently Zhu had agreed with her, because the only six people he had hired were the ones she had talked to at the hotel that morning, the ones as interested in the law as in the client, the ones who were looking at life on the Moon as an adventure, while acknowledging how dangerous the place had become.

They had come to work that morning together, dressed to the nines, in their offices an hour before Zhu had told them to arrive. The building had let them in—a little too trustworthy, she thought, even though they did have S^3 clearance—and they were all reviewing the compensation and business packages that Zhu had left for them the night before.

Plus she heard the sound of desks bumping against walls, chairs toppling over, boxes being set down. Grunts as the new team was setting up their offices, one little movement of furniture at a time.

The day before, Zhu had pulled her aside and told her she would double as office manager until he could find a real one. She knew he had given her that job because she had done similar work while in college, and she had received good recommendations from those employers.

Plus, the public defender's office at the Impossibles had given her a recommendation that she saw as both excellent and as a slap in the face: it had said that she was as good at organizing her cases as she was at defending them.

Since no one from the PD's office won cases at the Impossibles, that was the best recommendation she could get. Except for the organization slap.

That part disturbed her more than she wanted to admit.

Still, a job was a job, and she now had a good one with S³.

Which made that whisper through her links so very odd. Why would someone tell her about S³'s conflict of interest? She traced the link, and saw that it had come from Zhu himself. So she tried to contact him directly.

She got nothing. Not even a hint that she had the right link.

She tried again, and this time she got an official discouragement: *You have not been cleared to use this private connection.*

So, she tried to reach him on the S³ link. She was told to wait.

She'd never received that message on a link before.

She thought of contacting the other attorneys, but they were as new as she was. Besides, she'd had weird bosses before. One of the reasons Zhu had put her in charge was that she was organized and knew how to get things done.

She pinged the network and asked if Zhu's location was considered public or private.

For S³, the network responded, *Torkild Zhu's location is available.*

She wanted to impatiently snap, *So where is he?* But she didn't. Instead she searched his location, and was stunned to discover he was near the front of the building.

How long has he been there? She sent, thinking she could just wait until he arrived on their floor.

Ten minutes.

That seemed odd. And it included the moment when she had gotten the weird message. So she pinged him again, and got nothing.

Then she realized she could turn on the building's security system. She asked to see the front sidewalk.

The security feed showed her an empty sidewalk, except for something near the door—which she couldn't really see.

Zoom in, she instructed it.

That something was a pair of shoes, attached to two legs bent at strange angles. Then she realized that liquid was running down the sidewalk toward the next building.

She felt a surge of panic.

The liquid was dark, and there was a toppled cup near the bottom of her screen. Coffee. She had to hope she was looking at coffee.

Zoom in closer to the door, she instructed the feed.

It did. She saw a man sprawled, face down, body twisted and bent in a way that no person's body should be twisted.

Her breath caught.

Are emergency services on the way? She asked the security feed. After all, it should have sent for help if someone had a medical emergency outside the main door.

Emergency services have come and gone, the security feed responded.

She didn't understand that. And she had learned through hard experience that she shouldn't argue with an automated system.

Instead, she sent, *Show me.*

It did. Police officers, faces averted from any security feed, grabbed Zhu, threw him to the ground, and then beat him.

She stopped the feed. It made her hurt in empathy, and terrified her at the same time.

Send for medical personnel, she sent the security feed. And then, in case it had been tampered with, she sent for an ambulance herself.

But she knew better than to sit up here and wait. She sent a message to the other new hires:

Anyone got medical training?

Two people responded, saying that they knew basic health stuff.

Meet me at the front sidewalk, she sent. *Right now.*

Then, without waiting for a response, she got up from her desk and ran to the stairs. She wasn't going to take the elevator, not when she had no idea what was happening.

She thumped down the stairs, her heart pounding, her breath coming in big gasps, regretting the heels she had so proudly put on that morning.

I'm coming, Mr. Zhu, she sent, even though she doubted he could hear her. *I'm coming right now.*

9

MILES FLINT HAD BARRICADED HIS OFFICE IN OLD ARMSTRONG. HE HAD never before used his office's full security package, which he had updated after Anniversary Day. He preferred to do the most delicate computer work on Dome University's Armstrong campus or on the public net at the Brownie Bar.

He liked the anonymity of their systems. The university's had so many users that isolating one would take hours, if not days, and the Brownie Bar had no internal surveillance, so it was impossible to see who was using the system. The Brownie Bar also did not track its customers.

But the research Miles was doing was so dangerous that he didn't want to implicate either of those two places. If he angered the wrong people, then they might go after the locations where the work was done, as well as go after Miles himself.

He couldn't endanger innocent lives like that.

So he hunched on one of the few chairs in the office. He'd spent a fortune for chairs, even though he didn't use them as much as he'd planned. The nanofibers never worked exactly right. They didn't quite sculpt to his body the way he wanted. He got uncomfortable if he sat longer than twenty minutes.

This time, he had arranged half a dozen work stations, some of which allowed him to stand. He was combing for information on a variety of networks, not just the Earth Alliance's network, and he needed to monitor the programs.

He went from station to station, standing or sitting, sometimes looking at information presented holographically, sometimes at a 2-D flat screen that rose above the desk, sometimes on the desktop itself.

The only thing he did not do was let the computers talk to him. He trusted his security only so far. It was easy to track sound. That could be done with the right kind of equipment several meters away—even outside a so-called soundproofed building.

To hack his data streams, though, required extremely sophisticated programs that had to go past his constantly updating security walls. Plus, half the time he used an actual keyboard, which very few people did any longer. A good eighth of his encryption was tied to an existing keyboard, with its quirks. All of the keyboards he had in the office only responded to his DNA combined with the warmth of his fingertips and a measure of the blood flowing through his veins.

No one could cut off his hands and use them to enter his programs. He had to do it, and he had to be alive.

He paced the small room. The floor used to be uneven, but it wasn't any longer. He'd leveled it after his daughter Talia had complained. The building that housed his office was on a list of historic places. He couldn't make a lot of external changes without some committee's approval—or, at least, that was the way it had been in the past.

He had no idea how the regulations would be enforced in this new post-Anniversary-Day, post-Peyti-Crisis Armstrong. He suspected some things might be different.

Flint was a Retrieval Artist. He found humans who had Disappeared—who had vanished, using a service or on their own, rather than face the justice system in the Earth Alliance—which meant he was really good at examining huge amounts of information for the tiniest clue.

In the six-plus years he'd been doing this job, he had gained a healthy dose of paranoia. And he'd been pretty darn paranoid to begin with.

Paranoia was serving him well at the moment, because he was trying to track down the masterminds behind the Peyti Crisis. He was working with—not *for*—the Security Office of the United Domes of the Moon.

In reality, he was working with his old partner Noelle DeRicci. But even then, he was really working for himself, using the systems that her office had.

He had hit a dead-end in his investigation of Anniversary Day—at least for the moment—so he was trying a new tack, one he'd come up with just the day before.

He was going to go after a money trail, like he had done with Anniversary Day. Only the Peyti Crisis trail had threaded through a series of criminal enterprises and ended up, of all things, with the name of a human who had high security clearance in the Earth Alliance.

Even though he'd reported the woman's name to DeRicci, he considered that trail a dead end—at least at the moment. He could hack into the Alliance, but at that high level, there was a good chance he would leave footprints.

He'd been thinking of other ways around that particular problem when he realized he had a prime financial trail to follow.

He needed to track the education of the Peyti clones. Most of them had been lawyers until the day of the bombing. That meant they had gone to reputable Alliance-sanctioned law schools.

And law schools were nothing like the Earth Alliance. The security in the average law school was child's play for a man like him.

He'd been up since Dome Dawn. Ever since the Peyti Crisis, he'd been having trouble sleeping through the night. His brain was too busy. Plus he was worried about Talia. She just wasn't herself.

This morning, she had come out of her room, face blotchy as if she'd been crying. He knew she wasn't sleeping either. But the expensive penthouse apartment they had purchased at Talia's urging had soundproofing between the rooms.

He had to be near her room to hear her cry out, something that worried him. She thought it unimportant. She believed no one would get into the apartment with their level of security.

She didn't think that he'd want to comfort her from a nightmare or simply hold her when she sobbed. She only seemed to believe he wanted to hear if someone attacked her.

The longer her depression lasted after the Peyti Crisis, the more his concern turned from outside attacks to interior ones. Talia was falling apart, and if she called for help in the middle of the night, he wouldn't be able to hear her.

He had taken to staying up for hours after she went to bed, and a couple of times, he had fallen asleep on the couch—a place from which he knew he could hear her if she was in distress.

He had taken her to a psychologist at the urging of DeRicci's assistant Rudra Popova. The therapy felt like a last ditch effort. Besides, Flint wasn't sure how honest Talia could be with the therapists, given that she was a clone.

He told her she could decide whether or not to reveal that information about herself. But he hoped she didn't.

Both major attacks on the Moon—attacks that had destroyed life as all of the residents had known it—had used clones as the primary means of delivery. In many respects, the clones—both Peyti and human—had been weapons in and of themselves.

Now, inhabitants of the Moon—no matter the species—hated clones and saw them all as evil.

Flint didn't care how open-minded the therapists were. He was terrified that they wouldn't be able to get over their gut reactions to Talia's origins.

He ran a hand through his blond curls and felt some dislodge. He looked at his fingers. His hair was starting to fall out. Baldness did not run in his family. He wondered if he was losing hair due to stress.

Then he decided he didn't want to know the answer.

He couldn't think about Talia, at least right now. The best thing he could do for both of them was find out who had financed the Peyti clones and stop another attack.

He had promised himself that whenever he was here working, he could concentrate on work only.

He had left Talia at the United Domes Security Office for just that reason.

If he were being honest with himself, though, he had left her there for other reasons as well. He didn't want her to be on her own. He didn't think she was emotionally stable enough for that.

He decided that if Talia couldn't be with him, then the Security Office was the safest place he knew. He had installed hundreds of extra safeguards after the Anniversary Day attacks, and he had installed a few more after the Peyti Crisis—not that he'd had a lot of time.

He knew that the security staff was also fortifying those offices.

In addition, Popova was there. She understood what Talia was going through, at least on some levels. Popova didn't know that Talia was a clone (hardly anyone did), but she knew some of Talia's history, and knew that these attacks had devastated Talia in ways that nothing else had before.

Popova had lost her lover in a particularly brutal way on Anniversary Day, and the therapists she had sent Talia to had helped Popova overcome the worst of it.

Talia had an appointment with her therapist later that day. Popova said she'd make certain Talia got to the appointment. Flint had asked that some security accompany them.

Yes, he was being overprotective. And at the moment, he didn't care what others thought of that. He needed to keep an eye on his daughter. He was worried.

But he also needed to focus on his work.

He returned to one of the desks and stood in front of it, hands in his back pockets. The information scrolled on the see-through screen faster than he could process it.

But he saw bits and pieces of it—records, documents, forms—all in Standard, even though the language of Peyla was Peytin. He rocked a little. He peered closer and saw shadow documents scrolling with each Standard document. He peered at the shadow documents and realized that his own mind had edited them out.

They were in Peytin, which was a language he couldn't read. It wasn't even recognizable as a language to him. It looked like pen marks on paper, scratches on the surface of a desk, random lines and waves that made no sense to him at all.

Of course the Peyti law schools would require their documentation to be in two languages. Standard was the language of the entire Earth Alliance. If the Alliance certified a school—particularly one that would have graduates that functioned on the Alliance-level, not just some regional level—then the Alliance required all documentation (and anything searchable) to be in Standard.

The Peytin documents had to be for internal use only.

He wondered if he should set up one stream to translate every single Peytin document that his system was sorting through. He walked around the room for a moment, considering it, realizing as he paced just how restless he was.

His job as a Retrieval Artist primarily involved sifting through records. Documents. Histories. Yobibytes of information, more than he cared to think about. He looked for the smallest hint of a fact hidden in large amounts of information.

His greatest skill was combining all of that information in a way that no computer system could.

Even now, even though the networks and links and information streams were all hooked together, and there was more easily accessible information than ever, even though computer systems had gotten so sophisticated that the correct information rose to the surface with a single query, he still outanalyzed the computers. Mostly because even the most modern equipment still couldn't make an intuitive leap that the human brain could.

The error rate in computer intuition was about fifty percent—much too high for someone to rely on.

And he often did the best analysis while he was watching information scroll.

The system was comparing names, backgrounds, applications for the law school, for college, for any public database. It was also looking at financial records, funding, scholarships (and who provided them), grants, and financial aid.

He hoped the Peyti school's financial system was at least similar to the human ones he had encountered in the Alliance.

Because the largest problem he faced now, as he went through all this information, was that he had never analyzed big data from a non-human point of view. He had always searched for Disappeareds or re-searched the backgrounds of potential clients.

Retrieval Artists were a human phenomenon—at least as far as he knew. He always found that a bit ironic. Humans formed the Earth Alliance, primarily, at first, as a trading partnership with other species. But the partnerships would have quickly fallen apart without more compli-cated legal agreements.

As the known universe expanded, so did the need to protect all dif-ferent types of species from each other's laws. Plus, each group needed a treaty to work with the other groups.

And inadvertent crimes, things that seemed small to one group, were often life-and-death to other groups.

Because the original organizers of the Earth Alliance were business types, with very little loyalty to any one form of government, their big-gest focus was on the way that money, business, and trade flowed be-tween species. If a person got crushed by an alien legal system, so be it, as long as a corporation could freely participate.

The Earth Alliance itself nearly collapsed early on, as humans finally realized what they had signed into, and how much risk it put them at in-dividually. The corporations—by then, many of them interstellar—faced losing trillions almost immediately if the Earth Alliance collapsed.

At that moment, the Disappearance services sprang up. Cynics said they were created by the corporations to keep the humans inside the Earth Alli-ance. Legal officials believed that criminal enterprises always filled a vacu-um, and no matter what anyone said, Disappearance services were illegal.

But over the centuries, the evidence showed that the services were a mix of both—criminal enterprises and corporation-formed dodges, as well as good-hearted (originally nonprofit) organizations that attempted to save lives threatened by a single uninformed act.

In doing his due diligence on his potential clients, Flint always started with that uninformed act. He wanted to see if it were truly uninformed. He'd turned down dozens of clients who, he discovered, would deliberately go into alien environments and break their laws for financial gain. They wanted him to let them know when it was safe to return or to test old identities.

He refused to do any of that. Repeatedly.

Researching those uninformed acts had often led him deep into alien databases, but he'd always looked at those databases from a human perspective—could a human being reasonably know that their particular action was against the law? Was this so-called crime a major cultural taboo or was it simply something so local that not even the majority of the culture knew about it? Was the corporation (or the human) educated in the ways of that culture? Or were they venturing into that culture for the very first time?

All fairly easy questions to answer, even with a minimal knowledge of the alien culture.

The questions he had to answer now, with the Peyti, required a more detailed knowledge of the ways that the Peyti culture worked. He was stunned to realize how little he actually knew about the Peyti: They'd been deeply involved in human life and human customs for hundreds of years, but he hadn't realized until this week how little humans had been involved in Peyti life.

It wasn't just Peyti either. Humans seemed to remain uninvolved with all of their alien partners—at least on a day-to-day level. Oh, the experts were involved: those who studied the other cultures or had to work in them for corporate jobs.

But to get as deeply enmeshed in Peyti day-to-day life as the Peyti had become in human day-to-day existence, that didn't happen at all.

And it was already placing him at a disadvantage.

He'd gotten used to having Peyti lawyers, a few Peyti teachers (dealing with Earth Alliance matters), and a lot of Peyti students around, but he'd never done more than interact with them the way one did with people one had no interest in.

His face was flushed, and it wasn't because of the temperature in the office. That hadn't changed. He hadn't realized until now just how human-centered his life and his work were.

If he had been focused on other cultures sooner, he might have figured out how to get the information everyone needed about the Peyti sooner.

He hoped he knew enough about them to find the information now.

He leaned over one of the keyboards and corralled some of the documents that the filters had flagged as important to his search. He would investigate those while more information filled the files.

Then he would examine what he could, looking for patterns.

He hoped he found some sooner rather than later.

He hoped he could find them without asking for help.

Because the more people who got involved, the longer all of this would take.

And he knew, deep down, that the Moon was running out of time.

10

MELCIA SENG REACHED THE FIRST FLOOR OF THE S³ BUILDING, OUT OF breath and slightly nauseous, her feet aching. She had careened down the stairs, hand gripping the metal railing, barely able to keep her balance as she hurried. Then she slammed through the stairwell door, into the lobby—and remembered. It wasn't really a lobby at all.

Just a lot of empty space.

Her stomach cramped, and her heart pounded. Some automated voice on her links told her that an ambulance was on the way. She acknowledged, but didn't speak.

There was movement outside the main doors.

She wanted to run back up the stairs and hide. *Police* had kicked Mr. Zhu. *Police.* And then they had left him on the sidewalk.

All the way down the stairs, she'd been hoping that the river of dark stuff she had seen had been whatever he was drinking (coffee?) and not something else (blood).

She was shaking.

She could see shadowy figures through the opaque doorway. They moved, and it seemed like they were moving near Zhu.

At that moment, she realized that she had called *an ambulance.* Which meant that whoever was outside might be taking care of Zhu rather than harming him.

Or about to harm her.

She owed it to him to see what was going on.

She swallowed and walked toward the door. Behind her, the elevator pinged. She turned, saw—what was his name? Vigfusson. Yeah. That was it, the last name anyway. She could fake the first name. He burst out of the doors and hurry toward her, a small kit in his left hand.

"Where's the injury?" he asked, his pale skin flushed with red.

"Outside," she said. "Be careful."

God, she was a coward. She was going to let him go first. He hurried across the empty lobby, leaving scuff marks on the thin carpet, and slammed the door open.

Then he stopped, and for a brief second, she held her breath. What did he see?

He didn't look at her. Instead, he moved forward, and the door closed behind him.

Whatever he saw obviously hadn't scared him.

Seng squared her shoulders, made herself breathe twice to calm herself, and then she walked to the door. Now there were two moving shadows, and a lump on the ground.

Her people, maybe. Because she had contacted them before heading down here.

She pulled the door open, and stopped just like Vigfusson had. Zhu blocked the door. He was twisted, his legs bent. It took her a second to realize why that looked wrong to her: the legs bent at the upper thigh and the knee. One foot was turned inward and the other outward, but neither position looked natural.

She couldn't see his face or his torso, just his fingers, curved and bruised. The river that ran from him to the street wasn't brown, like coffee. It was thick and dark, with a reddish tint.

Vigfusson knelt beside Zhu, kit open. He was doing some kind of nanowork or something. The other person beside Zhu was one of the other new hires—a man named Rosen. She couldn't remember his first name either. God, she'd only met these people the day before, and there had been two dozen of them, names and faces and eagerness, and she'd been frightened, and oh, God, what was going to happen now?

An ambulance turned onto the street. In her links, the automated voice said, *Your ambulance is arriving now. Be sure to point out the injured party to the attendants.*

Her ambulance. Not the one she'd asked building security to contact. Hers.

She crouched, finally saw Zhu's face, and winced. It was swollen, black and purple, and his mouth was caved inward, blood everywhere. The attack was so savage that the internal repair bots that most people used wouldn't be able to overcome it.

"Is he going to be all right?" she asked, her voice wavering.

Neither man looked at her. They were both tending Zhu. Neither of them answered her.

She was about to repeat the question, louder, when the attendants arrived. They were human, not androids, and all business. They shoved the two men aside and crouched over Zhu.

The first man, a white-and-gold medical cap on his black curls, looked up at her. Did he know she was the one who had sent for them?

"What happened here?" he asked.

"I'll send you the security video," she said. "Do you have a secure link?"

He nodded, and sent it to her on her open links. Then she sent him the information. He leaned back, looked up at her, so startled that his skin turned gray.

"You're certain of this?" he asked aloud.

"I had the security system send for the authorities," she said. "No one has arrived."

The other attendant, who wasn't watching the interaction, said, "We'll need police. This is a crime scene."

"We had police," said Rosen. Apparently he had looked at the security footage too. "They did this."

So much for secure links. Seng wanted to reprimand him, but she wasn't really in charge of him.

"That's a hell of an accusation," the attendant said.

The other attendant touched his arm. "They have footage," he said. "And she's right. I found two separate calls for help from this area, and no one has responded."

"Well, get someone to respond," the first attendant said, "because we can't leave until someone arrives."

"Surely you can take footage of the scene," Seng said. "Get him out of here. He needs medical attention."

Vigfusson stood. He put a hand gently on her arm, and shook his head. He had a compassionate look on his face.

She looked at him, then at Zhu, and then at the attendants. No one was trying to revive Zhu. No one was touching him, not any more. His eyes were slitted, and what she could see of the eyeballs seemed abnormally glassy.

"No," she said. Her stomach turned. She needed this job. And then she felt ashamed that she had thought of herself before she thought of the man who had just hired her, kicked to death by police on the streets of Armstrong.

"I'm sorry, Miss," one of the attendants said. "There's nothing we can do."

He thought she was sad for Zhu. She should have been. He seemed nice enough. But she hadn't known him.

"You can get some authorities here, the coroner, or someone higher up in the police department," she said. "I'm new to this city, but most police departments have an internal affairs division or a complaints department or something. Contact them. *Now.*"

"Already have, ma'am," said the other attendant. "Someone will be here shortly. The coroner if no one else."

They stood, then backed the three attorneys away from Zhu's body, careful not to let them step in the river—which had to be blood. Seng was still shaking.

"The attack was out here, right?" the first attendant asked, and then didn't wait for an answer. "Can you go inside, please? Someone will want to talk with you."

On that last part, he sounded more hopeful than confident.

"Can I have my medical kit?" Vigfusson said.

"Sorry," the second attendant said. "It's part of the crime scene. The coroner will want to examine it."

Vigfusson opened his mouth as if he were going to argue, but this time, Seng stopped him. This time, she saw what was going on.

"Let them take care of it," she said. She almost added that she was certain S³ would reimburse him for the kit, but she wasn't certain of anything.

She led both men back into the building, then propped the door open so that she could watch.

"We're going to record this," she said to the other two lawyers. "Got that? We need to document everything."

"Is that legal?" Rosen asked. He was as new to Armstrong as she was.

"I have no idea," she said. "But we're going to do it anyway."

And then she settled in to watch.

11

NYQUIST COULD FEEL THE SECONDS TICKING AWAY. HE DID NOT LOOK AT his internal clock. He wasn't certain if the systems inside the Reception Center had shut off even the simplest links, and he wasn't sure if he wanted to know.

Instead, he took a deep breath to quell that moment of triumph he'd felt when Uzvaan told him how to track the masks.

Nyquist still had more than twenty-five questions to ask Uzvaan, not counting the things that had come up in this interview.

Nyquist did not look over his shoulder at the android guards. He didn't want to tip them off in any way as to how he was feeling and, more importantly, he didn't want to tip off their handlers that he thought he might be going over his allotted time.

Uzvaan, sitting in the other environmental bubble, blinked at him, skin gray. Uzvaan would shift on that chair ever so slightly, as if the fact that his arms pointed downward hurt him.

Nyquist knew no one in the prison cared what hurt the Peyti clones and what didn't. Nyquist himself should have cared more than he did. After all, he was getting information from this one.

If he could keep himself calm.

"You said you were eighty-five of three hundred," Nyquist said, "and that you weren't exactly sure what that meant. No matter how we interpret your name, it means that there were more clones of Uzvekmt than were in your little team or unit. Do you know what happened to those clones?"

"I do not assume," Uzvaan said.

Nyquist again felt that urge to grab Uzvaan by his little round head and slam it against the table. Nyquist had never felt quite this violent in an interrogation before.

"Let me put it to you this way," Nyquist said. "We thwarted hundreds of Peyti clones from bombing their domes all over the Moon. You only lived with two hundred of them, and by the time you went to law school, only fifty went with you."

"Forty-nine," Uzvaan said. "I was the fiftieth."

Nyquist bit back his irritation. "You don't want to assume, but I will, because law school is notoriously difficult. I'm going to assume that some of your pals failed to meet the grade in their schools—"

"They were not my 'pals,'" Uzvaan said, "and we were already trained against failure."

"I've met lawyers who went through the three best schools in the Alliance who claimed they had professors who flunked everyone the first time they took a class," Nyquist said.

"I avoided those professors," Uzvaan said.

"So you *assume* the other Uzvekmt clones did too."

The edges of Uzvaan's eyes turned blue again. "I did not say that."

"You implied it," Nyquist said.

Uzvaan inclined his head.

"For the sake of argument," Nyquist said, "let's take this out of the realm of law school. You worked in the Impossibles. I'm told that young defense attorneys *always* fail in the Impossibles."

"Unless they have a mentor," Uzvaan said.

That stopped Nyquist short. "A mentor?"

"There are organized ways to avoid cases, sit second or third chair, or to work as a legal researcher, none of which mean losing in court," Uzvaan said. "All of which count as a way of training in the Impossibles."

Nyquist hadn't known that. He would have to check it. "I'm stuck on the mentor thing. Who was your mentor?"

Uzvaan shook his head.

"You promised you would cooperate with me," Nyquist said. "Who was your mentor?"

Uzvaan's face was blue again. "My mentor is not important."

"Maybe not to you," Nyquist said. "To me, however, that name is very important."

Uzvaan lowered his head, and muttered.

Nyquist hoped to hell Uzvaan wasn't speaking Peytin again. "Repeat that louder."

"Mavis Zorn," Uzvaan said.

"That's a human name," Nyquist said before he could stop himself.

Uzvaan bobbed his head once—a single nod.

"You're telling me your mentor was *human*?" Nyquist asked.

"Is that so strange, Detective?" Uzvaan asked, with a hint of his old attitude.

"Yes," Nyquist said. "Were humans running your teams on Peyla?"

"No," Uzvaan said.

"But you accepted a human mentor at the Impossibles."

"You forget," Uzvaan said. "I had graduated from law school. I had attended with humans and I had been taught by humans."

"So a human mentor wasn't that unusual to you," Nyquist said.

"That is correct," Uzvaan said.

"How did this Mavis Zorn contact you?" Nyquist asked.

"I was assigned to her unit," Uzvaan said. "She always took one Peyti. It was considered an honor."

"And she protected you," Nyquist said. "How do you know she was doing her best to keep you from failing?"

"During our first meeting," Uzvaan said, "she called me by my number."

"You were alone," Nyquist said.

"Yes," Uzvaan said.

"Did you ask her questions then?" Nyquist asked.

"I did not," Uzvaan said. "I was to follow her instructions, nothing more."

"And you didn't think this strange?" Nyquist asked.

"What part of it?" Uzvaan said.

"That a human was running you around the Impossibles," Nyquist said.

"To question one's mission is to fail," Uzvaan said.

Nyquist cursed. Those damn lessons were damn convenient. He stood up, fist clenched. The android guards came toward him. Their eyes were flashing yellow. Across the empty space where their mouths should have been, time clocks appeared.

He had one minute to wrap this up, probably because they were monitoring his emotions.

"Did you have other mentors inside the Alliance?" Nyquist asked.

"At what time?" Uzvaan said.

Damn him and his lawyerly twists of phrases. "*Ever*," Nyquist said with too much emphasis.

"I did," Uzvaan said.

"Were they all human?" Nyquist asked.

"No," Uzvaan said.

The time clocks went off, and the android guards' eyes turned red. Nyquist didn't care what the design function for that was, he thought it creepy—creepier than the guards were themselves.

He turned, preparing to shout out one more question at Uzvaan, but the bubbles were separating.

He was done, whether he wanted to be or not.

But he had learned a lot.

He could get both Flint and DeRicci on some of this. He would be able to investigate some of this himself.

He watched Uzvaan's bubble recede into the blueness. Damn, if that Peyti bastard hadn't helped.

Nyquist was trying not to hope. He didn't want to be disappointed.

But for the first time in weeks, maybe months, he actually felt like they had a real chance of not just catching these so-called masterminds, but defeating them as well.

12

HER SECOND VISIT TO THIS PLACE, AND SHE ALREADY HATED IT.

Talia sat on the edge of the stupid blue couch, and looked at the two matching stupid blue chairs. The couch was too soft, but those chairs looked hard. Worse, they looked like no one had ever sat in them, like they wouldn't give at all if someone put their weight on them.

Comfort Center, my ass, she thought, and wondered what her dad would say about that.

Probably nothing. She couldn't imagine him liking this space either. It was too blue—cool colors, he would say—and it had real fake wood or fake real wood or actual real wood, which was just too expensive. Blond wood, like some kind of ash tree or something that she had learned about at the Aristotle Academy, in the botany class.

The class had focused on the importance of different kinds of wood, and how different trees were galaxy-wide, how some trees were considered sentient and couldn't be used for furniture and how some trees weren't sentient at all. And also how certain public places that would cater to aliens from sentient tree planets couldn't have any fake wood at all in them for fear of offending.

Offending, yeah. Right. Offending. Because if they offended aliens, the aliens would fucking bomb the city.

A tear leaked out of her left eye, and she rubbed at it furiously.

The stupid therapist had told her not to shy away from thoughts that made her feel bad. He probably wanted to come into this room and find her sobbing on the couch so that he could feel useful.

She wasn't going to do that.

She wasn't going to sob for anyone, if she could help it.

(She sure as hell hoped that she could help it.)

She had decided that she would ask for a female counselor. Rudra Popova had told her to do that if she felt uncomfortable with Whatsis-name Llewynn ("call me Evando," which she absolutely refused to do).

She didn't want to *be* here. How come no one could figure that out? Her dad said it might be good for her, but she should trust her instincts. And then in the next breath, he said that she needed some kind of help, a kind he clearly couldn't give, and she should give this place a try.

Rudra said that maybe what Talia needed was a Comforter. But Talia remembered that doughy nondescript stupid Comforter lady on Callisto who never listened to her, and who wanted to envelope her in hugs all the time, which, Talia later learned was all about the stupid Comforter because the stupid Comforter had some kind of nano-enhancer that made her *absorb* emotions or something stupid like that.

And if Talia used the word stupid one more time, even though she wasn't saying it out loud, someone would probably call her on it.

Then she shook her head. Too late. She was already calling herself on it.

Critical, critical, critical. She rubbed her eyes again. She was being too critical. She couldn't stop thinking about what a screw-up she was. If only she hadn't started the fight with Kaleb. If only she had kept quiet about the Chinar twins.

If only she hadn't told anyone about how mean Kaleb could be, he wouldn't have been in that room with that Peyti lawyer—that Peyti *clone* lawyer—and Kaleb, at least, would have been okay.

The *school* would have been okay, and she could be there this afternoon.

She'd hated it there in some ways—Dad said it wasn't challenging enough for her, but it was the best they could do—but she liked it, too. She actually felt like she belonged.

She *had* felt like she belonged.

Or at least, belonged more than she had belonged anywhere else since her mom died.

Damn tear. Another one was creeping down her cheek. She wiped it, felt the chapped skin.

This had to stop at some point. A human being (a *clone*, for godssake) didn't have that many tears. She'd have to run out at some point, right?

The door to the waiting room opened, and Whatsisname Llewynn ("call me Evando") was standing there, looking down at her. She popped to her feet so that she was as tall as he was and could look him in the eyes. They had a bit of reflection, and she wondered if he had enhancements so that he seemed more empathetic than he really was.

"Miss Flint," he said.

"Flint-Shindo," she corrected. If he couldn't even get her name right, then how could he understand what was going on with her?

"I thought we'd finish our entry interview," he said, as if she hadn't spoken. "I want to make certain we pair you with the right team."

She glared at him. She could walk right now. The security team that Rudra had sent with her was just outside the building, probably bored and pacing, and they could all get coffee or something before going back up and explaining why Talia left.

And that would be hard enough, because she wasn't sure why she would have left. Because this was all stupid? (There was that word again.) Because she didn't want the help? Because she didn't *need* the help?

Her eyes lined with tears.

Dammit. She didn't want the help and she couldn't stop crying. Maybe some kind of enhancement would be better.

"Talia?" Whatsisname Llewynn ("call me Evando") said in a tone that sounded even more patronizing than the tone he had used a moment ago.

"Talia Flint-*Shindo*," she said, knowing she sounded bitchy, feeling bitchy, knowing she could get even more bitchy, feeling so very bitchy in fact that he had no idea what was coming at him. "That's my name. And I didn't give you permission to call me Talia."

He smiled at her, but the smile didn't reach his eyes. "I get the message," he said. "Your father made you come here. That's all right, Talia, we can work with—"

"No," she said, "'we' can't do anything if you don't respect me. I'm Talia Flint-Shindo, and you need to respect that."

"All right, Miss Flint-Shindo," he said, and to his credit, he didn't put any sarcastic emphasis on her name, "let's go into the back and talk about what we can do to help you."

You can't do anything, she wanted to say. *You can't do anything at all.*

But she didn't say it. Instead, she followed him down the stupid corridor to his stupid office where they had had a stupid discussion just the day before.

He'd get one more day of stupid discussions. One more. And then she was outta here. Because she had no idea how this could help anyone, let alone her.

13

THE POLICE NEVER ARRIVED. THE CORONER DID.

Seng had the prime spot near the door so that she could see Zhu's body. The ambulance attendants had set up a crime scene perimeter, the first time she'd seen one up close. It was made up of a red light beam that could actually burn if an unauthorized someone tried to cross it.

The attendants reminded her of that as they placed the light in front of the door, warning her and Rosen and Vigfusson that they would have to leave via a different exit as long as the lights were there.

She had nodded at that, and hadn't moved. She was recording everything, just like Rosen and Vigfusson were.

Two hours after the call and no police. One attendant had taken the ambulance and left on a new assignment, while the other waited impatiently. He contacted the authorities several times and made a disgruntled sound each time he let his hand fall from his ear.

At one point, his gaze met Seng's and he shook his head. He was angry, too.

She made a note of the name emblazoned across his uniform, the ambulance number (when it was still there), and the licensing information. If this came to some kind of court case, she wanted him as a witness.

Every now and then, she would make sure she recorded his face.

Then she would look down at poor Zhu, his features slack, his skin growing paler and paler by the minute. It just wasn't respectful to leave him there.

Not that it had been respectful to kill him, either.

"What do you think is going on?" Rosen had whispered to her about ten minutes in.

She shook her head. She didn't want to talk about anything, at least not aloud, and she didn't want to have a discussion along links. One of the few motions she had won in the Impossibles had been a motion to download all of someone's logged link contacts. She didn't want any discussion that she had with Rosen or Vigfusson to show up on some court's docket.

The longer she waited, the more her fear decreased. Anger replaced it. She didn't care what this was about. No one deserved this kind of treatment, particularly not from the authorities.

She had just downloaded AutoLearn for Armstrong's local laws when the coroner's van landed where the ambulance had been.

The van was blue and larger than any vehicle she had seen so far on the Moon. The back double doors opened and the coroner emerged. He was a slight man, with curly hair and a petulant lower lip.

He wore a whitish uniform that identified him as Brodeur, so she looked him up while she watched and discovered he was Ethan Brodeur, who had been with the coroner's office for ten years.

That little detail, at least, made her calm down.

"What the hell is this all about?" Brodeur snapped at the attendant. "Where's your vehicle?"

"It left an hour ago." The attendant's voice was calm, but his cheeks were growing red. "And don't yell at me. These good people—*lawyers all*—had called in the emergency over two hours ago. We got here as fast as we could, but no one else is responding."

"What is wrong with the Armstrong PD?" Brodeur asked. He snapped his fingers and a younger man emerged from the back of the van, carrying some equipment.

"Um, that's the issue," the attendant said. "I'm going to send you security footage from this building."

Seng nodded despite herself. That was what the attendant should have done. She hoped he used a secure link, something the Armstrong Police Department couldn't access easily.

But that wasn't her problem, at least, not at the moment.

Brodeur started in shock, gave the attendant a sharp look, and then shook his head once.

"Well," Brodeur said. "That explains it."

"Explains what?" the attendant asked.

"Why I got the call from APD." Brodeur smiled wryly. His gaze swept the area, meeting Seng's for just a moment, as if he wanted her to hear what he was going to say next. "They don't like me in the police department. They actively try to keep me off cases."

Seng let out a small breath.

"What does that mean?" Rosen whispered to her.

She shook her head, trying to silence him. She had an idea. She suspected they didn't like this coroner because his exams didn't hold up in court, the police felt he was doing a sloppy job, or because he had caught the police doing something shady in the past.

She voted for competence. Because the coroner was aware that the police didn't like him, which incompetents usually didn't notice.

Still, she made a note.

"You don't need me anymore, right?" the attendant said. "I mean, I shouldn't have been here anyway, but someone had to keep an eye on this crime scene."

"You did a good job," Brodeur said, then patted the attendant on the arm. The gesture probably hadn't been meant as patronizing, but it was.

Brodeur didn't notice the attendant's grimace. Brodeur was already looking at the body.

He crouched beside it, holding a position that allowed Seng to see what was going on. The ambulance attendant half-walked, half-ran down the sidewalk. He was probably going to catch one of the local trains that ran a few blocks from here.

No one except Seng watched him go. Then she turned her attention back to Brodeur.

"Never seen anything like it," Brodeur was saying to his assistant. "The cops aren't like that in this city."

The assistant, a young man with jug ears and a large nose that could have used some judicious cropping, clearly hadn't seen the footage. He looked confused.

"What are you talking about?" he asked.

Brodeur was taking imagery of the body, passing his hands over it, getting *in situ* stills. Seng hadn't seen a technique like that since she worked in New York, years ago.

"Don't you recognize this guy?" Brodeur's voice rose. He wanted all three lawyers to hear this. What was he about? "He's the one who came to the station, and to our office, with injunctions."

"He works for the *clones*?" The assistant looked down at Zhu as if he had some kind of plague. "Is that why the cops won't come to the murder site?"

"I don't know what they're thinking," Brodeur said, "but this guy sure didn't make any friends in Armstrong."

Then he stood and grabbed something that looked like a pipette from the equipment bag. Seng had no idea what the pipette thing was, only that Brodeur seemed to think it important.

He looked over his shoulder, his gaze meeting hers again.

"Those clones tried to kill everyone in this dome," he said, and it seemed like he was speaking directly to her. To remind her? To warn her? To let her know he was on the side of the cops, even though they didn't like him?

"That's not going to interfere with your work, is it?" Vigfusson snapped, as if he had been part of the conversation all along.

Brodeur looked over at him. "It already interfered with my work. This body wasn't properly handled. Those two hours are going to make any prosecution difficult."

"We recorded everything," Seng said. "Plus the building footage, which I've been routinely downloading, will also show that no one tampered with the body."

Brodeur raised his bushy eyebrows in surprise. "Well, then. Maybe it didn't interfere as much as I thought."

He bent over the body, then used the pipette thing as if it were gathering something. Fluids, maybe? Seng didn't know.

After a few moments, Brodeur looked up and waved his fingers in front of his face. He was obviously looking at some kind of screen through his links. Processing the information? Checking on something?

She threaded her fingers together, then twisted them, feeling the pain echo through her hands. The pain kept her alert.

"Was he alive when you found him?" Brodeur asked them.

Seng and Vigfusson both shook their heads.

"My links said he wasn't breathing," Vigfusson said. "I did everything I could to revive him, but my chips—which, granted, aren't as sophisticated as yours—believed he hadn't been breathing long enough to prevent any kind of revival."

Brodeur's lips thinned, and his eyes narrowed. "What do you use?"

Vigfusson answered with a brand name that Seng didn't recognize.

"Figures," Brodeur said, and returned to his work.

"Hey!" Vigfusson said. "What do you mean, 'figures'?"

Seng's heart was pounding.

"I mean," Brodeur said as he rocked back on his heels, "that you should look at who makes your cheap chips before you actually buy them. Your chip was made by an Earth-based funeral service. Their free-medical-chip business was shut down when it was determined that not only did they fail to revive an injured person, they also notified the funeral service when the person died."

Vigfusson looked at Seng with alarm. Her mouth was dry. She'd heard of things like that, but never paid a lot of attention. This kind of corruption had never concerned her before, so she hadn't felt the need to focus on it.

"I have some emergency medical training," Vigfusson said, sounding defensive. She didn't exactly blame him. "I thought he was gone too."

"Yeah," Brodeur said, his back to them. "There are things that a good bot can do, things a good program can do, while you're waiting for actual medical help that they don't train you in those beginner emergency response classes."

Rosen looked away. Vigfusson leaned closer to the door. Seng unthreaded her fingers and wiped her hands on her skirt. She let out a small breath.

"You're saying he was alive when I called for help?" Seng asked, very gently.

"Not alive, per se," Brodeur said. "But revivable. With the right equipment and knowledgeable people."

Vigfusson bowed his head. Rosen had moved even farther back. But Seng gripped her knees. No wonder this coroner wasn't popular. He was one of the most blunt public employees she had ever encountered.

"So," Seng asked, staring at Zhu's body. "If he had gotten help, he would still be alive."

"Real help," Brodeur said.

Vigfusson winced.

"*Official* help," Seng said.

Brodeur looked at her over his shoulder. He seemed to suddenly understand what she meant. She meant that the public services—the police, emergency responders—had failed Zhu.

Even if the police managed to write off his attack as something that occurred because of rogue cops, the authorities wouldn't be able to get rid of their culpability easily. Someone or someones had blocked the emergency response.

"I didn't say 'official,'" Brodeur said a half minute too late.

This bluntness of his, his ability to put his foot in something, was probably why the police didn't like him. But she was guessing.

"You meant it, though," she said.

Rosen was watching her. Vigfusson had raised his head, the color leaving his cheeks.

"No," Brodeur snapped. "I meant what I said. If he had gotten real help instead of some crappy designer chip, he'd be alive."

"Or if the emergency services hadn't been blocked," Seng said.

"I don't know that they were blocked," Brodeur said, turning away from her. He focused on Zhu.

Brodeur was now covering his ass. She didn't mind. He had given her important information.

It wouldn't bring back Zhu, but it would guarantee a suit against the city.

Clearly, the authorities here already hated S³. So she had nothing to lose for pursuing them for this. And everything else.

Vigfusson, who had seemed so strong an hour ago, hadn't noticed either movement. He seemed lost in his own reflections. He kept staring at his palm, which was probably where the bad chip resided.

She couldn't rely on him. So she put a hand on Rosen's back. He started, then glanced at her, clearly terrified.

Great. Two idiots. Still, she needed one of them, and she would take the seemingly more reliable one.

"Make sure you continue to record this," she said very softly. "I'm going to be right back."

"Where are you going?" he asked.

"Personal," she muttered, letting him think she needed a bathroom or something. What she was going to do wasn't that kind of personal. It wasn't really personal at all.

She was going to get in touch with her new bosses—the real ones, the ones who weren't running a branch on the Moon, but who were running the whole company.

It was time they knew what was going on.

14

NYQUIST WAITED UNTIL HE HAD ARRIVED BACK INSIDE ARMSTRONG'S dome before he tried to contact Flint. In fact, Nyquist went all the way to his apartment first, just because he couldn't shake the dirty feeling he always seemed to get when he talked to Uzvaan.

He showered, changed, and grabbed a Moon-grown apple from the fruit bowl in the kitchen. The apple was turning an alarming shade of dark purple, which meant that it would soon be too pulpy to eat. He didn't care. He was hungry, and he wasn't going to stop.

But he did need to track down Flint.

Nyquist sent a message along his links, hoping to find Flint. Then Nyquist took a bite from the apple, hit a brown part, and picked it out, tossing it away.

He was unbelievably paranoid these days, even for him.

He hadn't wanted to contact Flint from anywhere close to the Reception Center. Nyquist was afraid he was being tracked. In fact, when the prison train transported him to the parking lot inside the dome, the first thing Nyquist did was run a systems diagnostic on all his links to make certain nothing had piggybacked on board from the prison system.

He'd repeated the diagnostic three times so far, each time using a different diagnostic tool and a different method, double-checking his double-checks. And this was just to contact Flint. He wasn't going to share information—not this way, anyhow.

So far, no one at the prison had figured out that Nyquist didn't belong there. They believed his cover story about Uzvaan being the lawyer for Ursula Palmette. Actually, Nyquist believed no one really thought about it.

They didn't care what happened to clones, as long as no one in charge of the prison got in trouble for anything.

He let out a small breath, set the apple on the counter, and ran a hand over his face. He was tired and elated and upset and hopeful, all at the same time. If he took too much time to think about how he felt, he would blame it all on a lack of sleep.

But he knew it was more than that. He was doing his best to keep an emotional distance, and he wasn't an emotionally distant man. At some point, he would have to deal with everything he was feeling.

He just hoped he could postpone it until the crisis—or whatever someone wanted to call all of this—had ended.

He activated his private links, then encoded everything.

Hey, Flint, Nyquist sent. *Where the hell are you?*

Where should I be? The response seemed irritated, but Nyquist couldn't tell. He would probably be irritated if someone contacted him that way, so he was projecting on Flint.

Somewhere that we can talk. Nyquist was feeling so paranoid that he didn't even want to say he had information. He'd gotten warrants on less.

I'm at my office. Is this important? Should we bring in Noelle?

Nyquist shook his head before he remembered that the visuals weren't on. He would talk to DeRicci later. First, he wanted to talk with Flint.

This is just between us, Nyquist sent, then realized how mysterious that sounded. Still, he was going to stick with it.

I'll be waiting for you, Flint sent, and signed off.

Nyquist grabbed the apple. He'd been up for hours, and the apple had shown him just how hungry he was. He would pick up some food on the way to see Flint. No one was eating well lately, and Nyquist was beginning to see it as his mission to make sure that everyone got fed.

He smiled for the first time that day. He never really thought of himself as nurturing, yet there he was, providing meals and worrying about everyone else.

Maybe that was why he had gotten into the protection business. Maybe it was his own gruff way of taking care of the world around him.

Or maybe he just liked police work.

When he was actually doing it, and not making deals with mass murderers in exchange for information.

He finished the apple, tossed the core in the recycler, and rubbed his face one last time. The shower had only helped so much. If only he could scrub the last few hours from his brain, and keep the good things he'd learned.

If only.

15

"So," Mr. Stupid Llewynn ("call me Evando") said as he sat in the captain's chair in front of a fake window with a forest scene on it, "tell me why it's so important to add the 'Shindo' to your name."

As if it were a whim, as if it didn't matter at all, as if Talia was insisting on something stupid.

She sat on the edge of the chair across from Mr. Stupid Llewynn. If she sat back, the chair would try to hug her or something. It had freaked her out yesterday; she wasn't going to make the same mistake today.

Before she tried to answer him, she looked at his office. Browns and creams, warmer tones than the waiting room, but still not real comforting to her. She really didn't like this place, and she wasn't exactly sure why.

Or maybe she just didn't like Mr. Stupid Llewynn. She hated fake people with fake emotions, and he seemed like one of those.

Plus, he wasn't as smart as he thought he was.

"I thought we were finishing the entry interview," she said.

"We are," he said. "But first, let's talk about this insistence on your name. It's different from your father's."

She glared at Mr. Stupid Llewynn. "My mother's name was Rhonda Flint-Shindo. She raised me until she died. She lied to me about my father. She said he didn't want me. Instead, he hadn't even known about me. So I keep the name because it's *mine* now. No one else has that name. Just me."

"And to honor your mother?" he asked.

"My mother 'accidentally' committed a major crime while working for Aleyd Corporation before I was born. When she finally had to face the ones she harmed, she committed suicide rather than take responsibility. She's not someone you honor."

"But you loved her," Mr. Stupid Llewynn said.

"Yeah. When I thought she was just a mom. Then it turns out she's a murderer and a liar and a coward, and I don't love her anymore."

Another tear ran down Talia's cheek. This time, she didn't brush it because she hoped to hell he didn't notice.

His voice was soft. "You found this out three years ago? When you were thirteen?"

"Yeah. So?"

"It's a tough age to find out your mother isn't who you think she is," he said. "How did your dad find you?"

Her breath caught. Jeez. Just in her history alone, there were things she couldn't say.

"He was on a case," she said. "He found me. I can't say more than that."

"Because of his secrets?" Mr. Stupid Llewynn said.

Her dad had explained the conversation they'd had: that Mr. Stupid Llewynn had said that Talia could invoke her dad's secrets for his job, and her own life-threatening secrets whenever she needed to. It was completely up to her.

"He didn't have to take me in," she said. "He did. And he's put up with me."

"Do you think he loves you?" Mr. Stupid Llewynn asked.

She let out a half-exasperated sound, glad it came out first before she called him some kind of name.

"What kind of question is that?" she asked. "I thought this was an entry interview."

"I'm trying to figure out what exactly you will need from us," Mr. Stupid Llewynn said.

And then he waited, as if she remembered the question (she did) and would eventually answer it.

"Me and my dad are a lot better suited than me and my mom ever were. He's as smart as I am, and hardly anyone else is. He really tries, and yes, *God*, he loves me. I don't know why, because I'm a real pain in the ass, particularly right now when I can't even help him—

She burst into tears. She stood up and went to the door. She couldn't pull it open, and she couldn't stop crying. She was actually sobbing, unable to take a breath without big honking sounds, and it felt like her entire body was going to break in half, but she couldn't stop.

She had separated into two people: inside her head, the Real Talia was watching all this drama and standing, arms crossed, urging the What-The-Fuck-Are-You-Doing? Talia to stop crying and to suck it up. Other people have it worse, and she knew that.

A box of tissues floated over to her on a server tray. She glared at it, wishing she had the power to make that tray and those tissues burst into flame, just to prove a point.

But she didn't have that ability. No human did—no species did, as far as she knew.

Then she realized she had stopped sobbing. The anger at the tissues had made the tears stop.

She grabbed a handful of tissues, and wiped off her face.

"Thank you," she said begrudgingly.

She felt like she was at a crossroads now. If she really wanted the high ground, she should leave. But he'd actually gotten her to stop crying.

The last few days, these crying jags would hit her unaware and hold her for about an hour. Her throat was raw from them, her chest ached, and she looked like a mess.

She turned around. He was watching her. This time, the compassion on his face didn't seem fake.

Or maybe she needed it not to be fake.

But he hadn't gotten up to hug her or told her to stop or asked her what was wrong. And she actually appreciated that.

"It sounds like you've been through hell," he said quietly.

She shook her head. "Other people have it a lot worse right now."

"We can't compare pain," he said. "You lost a parent and a way of life. Then you came here to a new way of life, only to have that literally blown up six months ago. And last week, you watched people die. And you lost a friend."

She shook her head again, then blew her nose. When she finished with the tissues, she didn't put them in the recycler—clone caution, she called it once when her dad mentioned it; she didn't want anyone to test her DNA.

She put the tissues in her pocket.

"He wasn't my friend," she said softly. "I told you that yesterday."

"But you had feelings for him," Llewynn said.

"That didn't make him a friend." She moved back toward the chair.

"Which makes his death, and your reaction to it even more complicated," Llewynn said, "because those feelings will forever be unresolved."

She froze. She had been about to sit down again, but she wasn't going to now.

"He wouldn't have been in that room if it weren't for me," she said.

Llewynn threaded his fingers over his stomach. That movement was something that fat people usually did, but he wasn't fat.

"How so?" he asked.

"I was the one who fought him when he called the Chinar twins clones. His hatred of clones really pissed me off. He was playing on prejudice to make them feel bad, and that caused the big fight in the cafeteria, which led to his father trying to pull him out of school and all the meetings with the lawyers, which wouldn't have happened otherwise."

Llewynn sat up slightly. "Did it anger you when his hatred of clones proved to be an accurate reaction to the threats we face?"

Her mouth opened slightly. "What?"

"Clones," he said in a tone that implied she was stupid for not understanding. "We've been attacked by two sets of them now. We're threatened by them. You clearly think the same way, or you wouldn't have defended biological twins against a false accusation."

Her mouth was still open. She couldn't believe he was saying this crap.

"His hatred of clones wasn't reasonable," she said in a small voice.

"Even though they attacked us?" Llewynn said.

"A group of clones attacked us," she said. "It's the same as if a large family came after us. Do we hate the family?"

"Except that it's not the same," Llewynn said. "Clones are manufactured. They were weapons and they ended up killing your friend."

Her stomach turned. What would he do if he realized she was a clone?

For a moment there, she had actually started to think this man—this place—could help her. And now, this.

"You think clones made from a human original aren't human?" she asked, trying to sound neutral.

"I think the answer to that is obvious," he said. "No true human would behave that way."

"Not even PierLuigi Frémont?" she asked.

"He had a different pathology," Llewynn said. "He had a God complex. He also had charisma, so that he could lead followers into places they didn't want to go. That's not the same as attacking an innocent city. That takes a lack of humanity."

"You claim PierLuigi Frémont as human, but not one of his clones?" she asked. She couldn't quite believe what she was hearing.

"It's the difference between a human and an android," he said. Then he peered at her. "Do you disagree?"

The tears were threatening again. Damn him. She had a moment of clarity, and now this—from someone who was supposed to help her. Someone they were paying to help her.

She shook her head. "I'm going to leave. Make sure that door's open."

"But we're not done with the entry interview," he said.

"We are," she said. "My dad said I could leave if I didn't like this. I don't like it."

"I felt like we were starting to make progress," Llewynn said. "Running now won't be good for you."

Like you know what's good for me, she thought but didn't say. She was biting her lower lip so hard it hurt.

"I'm leaving," she said again, and made her way to the door.

She felt hollow inside, as if someone had taken every bit of her, scooped it out, and replaced it with nothing at all. Not even her breath came easily.

"Talia," he said. "Let's finish—"

"Talia Flint-*Shindo*," she snapped as she pulled open the door. "And believe me, we are finished. For good."

16

RAFAEL SALEHI HUNCHED OVER A TABLE IN THE LAW LIBRARY ON BOARD
Schnable, Shishani & Salehi's fastest large space yacht. The law firm
owned dozens of these yachts, but none could travel quite like this one—
and carry as many people.

Over the past week, he'd acquired a lot of company on this ship. In
addition to the thirty human staff members he'd brought—lawyers, legal assistants and researchers—he'd also picked up twenty Peyti lawyers
when the yacht briefly stopped on Peyla.

In addition, he had gathered a large group of legal minds to join
them, from professors and former judges to some of the best legal theo-
rists in the Earth Alliance. He needed a team; what he was trying to do
was something much bigger than a single case or even a group of cases.

He was trying to change clone law forever, and he was going to use
the Peyti Crisis on the Moon to do it.

The law library was his favorite room on this ship. It was one of the
largest public rooms on the ship, with tables everywhere, intermingled
with comfortable chairs. There were networked computers, built into
the ship's system, and a few non-networked computers, known only to
S^3 attorneys.

But what added to the ambience here, besides the soft lighting, were
the shelves and shelves of books—or what appeared to be books, the

old Earth collectible, made-of-paper kind. A simple brush of the fingers revealed that these books were actually holographs, but they still functioned like books.

They were non-networked volumes, which contained everything known on that particular topic—at least everything known when the law library downloaded its latest updates. He had downloaded an update just before leaving on this trip, and when he needed a moment to rest his brain, he would remove one of the books, open it, and watch the information meld with his links.

Mostly, he avoided clone law or Alliance history or treatises on mass murderers. His fingers kept finding the history of the Moon—the ancient history of the Moon—with faint images of the man who had given the Moon's largest city his name and the strange-looking craft that had actually delivered that man, for a few brief hours, to the Moon itself.

Salehi did so to remind himself that to the first man on the Moon, a man named Armstrong, Salehi's quest was unimaginable. There had been no Earth Alliance then, no knowledge of other life in the universe, no real knowledge of the universe outside of the Earth's solar system.

Once upon a time, in a land so far away that no one completely understood it, a group of humans had devised a craft that would enable them to (barely) leave their planet. It had seemed impossible to everyone, according to the millennia of human history before that, and yet these people not only tried it, they succeeded.

Without their risk, his entire culture would not exist. *He* probably would not exist.

They had tried.

Which was more than most people ever did.

He was trying now. The chief Peyti lawyer on board, Uzvuyiten, believed Salehi's quest to change clone law was as impossible as an ancient human finding a way to the Moon. Yet, Uzvuyiten was willing to use Salehi's impossible dream to help all Peyti.

Because right now, after the Peyti Crisis, the Earth Alliance—and particularly the Moon—had become an inhospitable place for all Peyti.

Uzvuyiten was going to stop it somehow, even if he had to use Salehi to do so.

Salehi looked over his shoulder at Uzvuyiten. He sat with his colleagues at a table, its top covered with some kind of chart in Peytin, that they were all studying.

The ship's systems saved all networked computer work, and all of the ship's guests did not have the ability to work on non-networked systems. If Salehi wanted to know exactly what Uzvuyiten was doing without asking Uzvuyiten, then he could have the ship's systems look it up for him.

Uzvuyiten was the most distinctive Peyti that Salehi knew. Most humans had trouble distinguishing the Peyti, primarily because half of their faces were covered in masks when they were in a human environment. But Uzvuyiten was recognizable even with a mask. His skin had turned a whitish gray, unlike the darker gray of most Peyti, and his fingers had been damaged a long time ago. They bent backwards at the tips, where a human's fingernails would be, and the bent ridge glowed an odd blue in the right kind of light.

Salehi could recognize Uzvuyiten from his posture alone, but everyone on the ship could recognize him by his hands or his strangely colored skin.

And everyone knew that Uzvuyiten would be Salehi's co-counsel if any of these cases went to court. Technically, Salehi represented the Government of Peyla, because the government had hired S³. But anyone with brains understood that Peyla was using Uzvuyiten to protect its reputation and its cases.

The door to the law library opened, and Lauren Jiolitti leaned in. She was a slight woman with shoulder-length dark hair and intense eyes. She was on track to make partner, and she worked harder than half the lawyers at S³. That was one reason he had brought her along.

He could trust her.

She scanned the room, then her gaze caught his. She beckoned him. He thought it odd that she didn't even use her links to reach him.

He threaded his way past lawyers and researchers lounging in chairs, working on tablets, and clearly having intense discussions across links.

He slipped out the door into the corridor. It felt like he had left a quiet, safe place and found himself inside a spaceship. The lights were brighter here, and the design all gray and silver.

"What's going on?" he asked.

"We got contacted by a woman named Melcia Seng, who claimed she was with S³ On The Moon."

"I've never heard of her," Salehi said.

"Neither had I." Jiolitti kept her voice down. "So I checked. According to our records, Zhu hired her yesterday."

Salehi didn't like this. "Why did she contact us?"

"Because she says that Zhu can't." Jiolitti's mouth had become a thin line.

"Did she say why?"

Jiolitti let out a long sigh. "I think you need to talk with her."

He frowned. This wasn't any kind of procedure. But then, they were all in strange circumstances.

"All right," he said. "Where's her information coming from?"

"The main S³ links," Jiolitti said. "But you need to go somewhere private."

"Because…?"

"Because," Jiolitti said, swallowing hard, "I don't think anyone else on this ship should hear what she has to say."

17

BARTHOLOMEW NYQUIST LOOKED...*CHEERFUL*.

Miles Flint studied the image of the man he'd always thought of as morose and rumpled. Nyquist stood outside of Flint's office, waiting to be let in.

Even when someone looked right, Flint still went through his security protocols. In fact, he went through them in even more depth than usual. He knew how easily systems could be fooled into assuming one thing when another was actually true.

And Nyquist looking cheerful—especially after the week they'd all had—was just plain strange.

Flint examined everything from the DNA off Nyquist's finger to the shape of his retina. Apparently, that man with a half-smile on his face was Nyquist. Maybe the half-smile was the final clue. Flint couldn't remember if he'd ever seen Nyquist smile fully.

Flint opened the door, and Nyquist slipped in.

"I was beginning to think I was back at the Reception Center," Nyquist said. "That took forever."

Flint shrugged. He wasn't going to defend his security policies. "You sounded mysterious when you contacted me," he said.

"Yeah." Nyquist looked around for a chair. Flint's front office only had one, by design, something he had learned long ago from the woman from whom he'd bought the business. Paloma.

He shook off the thought, and wondered if it had come from Nyquist's presence here. The Bixian assassins that had killed Paloma had nearly killed Nyquist, as well. His face was slightly mismatched because he had never bought the enhancements that would repair all of the damage.

Flint thought of getting the other chair he kept in back for Talia, then changed his mind as Nyquist leaned against one of the desks. The holoscreen that Flint had up reflected light against Nyquist's back and sides.

"I spent the morning with Uzvaan." Nyquist didn't sound as upset about that as Flint would have expected. "He gave me some information that might lead us to the masterminds, as you keep calling them."

Flint raised his eyebrows in surprise. He had been convinced that Nyquist's interviews with Uzvaan would bring nothing to the investigation—but he didn't want to say that to Nyquist. Nyquist hated the interviews already, and Flint hadn't wanted to close off any possibilities.

"The Peyti clones," Nyquist said, "had their masks delivered."

He bounced a bit as he said that.

"The explosive masks?" Flint asked.

"*All* of their masks. From the moment they moved to the Moon. Maybe even before that. They were forbidden from buying the masks here," Nyquist said.

Flint had no idea that the Peyti could buy masks here. That feeling he'd had earlier, about not knowing a culture, grew even stronger.

"I never thought about how any Peyti got their masks," Flint said.

Nyquist nodded. "I knew there were stores—we'd investigated a few over the years, mostly for smuggling operations—but I hadn't thought to trace the masks. The new masks—the explosive ones—are different from all the others."

Flint leaned back. He should have realized that from the start. The clones had to get the masks from somewhere.

"I thought the bombs were an add-on," he said.

"You didn't see them in action, did you?" Nyquist asked. His smile was gone. He looked haunted. Uzvaan had tried to kill Nyquist—everyone at the Detective Division.

"I saw the footage," Flint said. "And the aftermath."

That had been enough. And he hadn't looked at the footage closely. He'd been concentrating on the collateral damage and the faces of the Peyti, not on the method of attack.

"The masks were in two parts. The bomb was on the lower part of the mask," Nyquist said. "The masks looked like a redesign of what we usually saw."

Flint nodded. "And those were delivered."

"*Every mask* that the clones wore, from the moment they got here to the moment of their attack, was delivered."

Flint let out a breath. "And you think we can trace that."

"Easily," Nyquist said. "That's the leak. We can easily trace that. I'm pretty certain your masterminds would never think we would be able to talk to the clones, so we wouldn't know that the masks were delivered."

Flint frowned. They'd know—eventually. Maybe. If the bombs had exploded as planned, there would have been rebuilding, and then investigation. The investigation would have gotten short-changed.

"I think you're right," Flint said.

Nyquist gave him an exasperated look. They weren't easy friends, and Flint knew why—although he didn't try to change it. Both men felt like they had to be the best investigator in the room.

"Even if the bombs had exploded as planned and the investigation started, we wouldn't have found this for months if not years. By then, the information wouldn't lead anywhere." Flint templed his fingers, then tapped the tips against his chin.

He looked at Nyquist, who seemed to be waiting for Flint to catch up to him.

"But it's only been a week," Flint said slowly. "And the masterminds, whoever they are, are probably not thinking about covering up their tracks."

"If they are," Nyquist said, "they're worried about shutting up the clones."

Both men looked at each other. Obviously neither of them had thought of that until now, either.

"I thought S³ gave you all injunctions against harming those clones," Flint said.

"Yeah," Nyquist said. "They enjoined *us*, the authorities. But these masterminds of yours—"

"They're not mine," Flint said, beginning to regret coining the term.

"—they seem to know how every single system we have on the Moon works. They might be able to get someone or something into the Reception Center and take care of the clones."

Flint didn't like the sound of that. He sighed, thinking about it. These masterminds weren't above using bombs and causing a lot of collateral damage.

"They might attack the clones when they get into court, as well."

"If they get into court," Nyquist said. His smile was long gone. "This is a major mess."

"Yeah," Flint said. "But we're making headway. You said you got other information?"

Nyquist half-smiled again. "I did. It turns out that Uzvaan wanted to talk. I didn't get to half my questions before the guards shut me down, but I'll go back."

"What else did he tell you?" Flint asked.

"That's stuff Noelle can investigate or have her pet Earth Alliance investigators look into it," Nyquist said. "I just didn't want them to know about the masks."

"Even Noelle?" Flint asked.

Nyquist let out a small sigh. Then he shrugged. "It bugs me, how many systems these masterminds know," he said. "And how we ignored those damn Peyti clones. We assumed that because they were lawyers, they were going to follow the law."

"They did," Flint said. "Right up until the day they stopped. We had no reason to distrust them."

"I know." Nyquist ran a hand over his face. "I never liked Uzvaan. I thought he was a good lawyer, but I never liked him."

"I'm sure there are a lot of people you don't like who are trustworthy," Flint said.

Nyquist's gaze met his. Flint could read the thought without Nyquist putting it into words. Nyquist wouldn't be here if he thought Flint untrustworthy. The respect between the two men was clear. The friendship—or even the "liking" as Nyquist had put it—wasn't.

"Still," Flint said. "It might be worthwhile to tell me."

"Uzvaan gave me the name of his mentor at the Impossibles. It was a human woman, and she protected him from that failure thing that happens to most attorneys there. It might mean nothing."

"It might mean everything," Flint said.

"The masks are a tangible lead," Nyquist said, taking over the investigation. "The mentor might mean nothing at all—and the information is decades old."

In other words, Nyquist would prefer it if Flint investigated the masks first. Nyquist was trying to direct Flint's investigation, and if Flint were feeling just a little more contrary, he would prevent it.

But he agreed with Nyquist: the masks were a better lead. And combined with the information about the law schools, he might be able to find the masterminds through channels they never even considered.

"And here's the other piece of information that you need to know," Nyquist said. "I'm going to get Popova to double-check it all, but Uzvaan told me the corporation or entity or whatever you want to call it that paid for his law school was some damn Peyti word that means *legal fiction*."

Flint wasn't sure he heard that correctly. "What?"

"That's what I said. Apparently the word has many meanings. But that's the one that Uzvaan, at least, prefers. I asked him if law schools thought it odd that a company called 'legal fiction' paid the bills and he said he had no idea."

Flint let out a long breath, not sure if he believed what Nyquist told him, and not sure he could *dis*believe it.

"I'm going to play you something," Nyquist said. "Record it when I do. Maybe you can use the sound."

Flint recorded everything that transpired in this office, at least when there were verbal conversations, so he didn't have to worry about it being recorded. However, he wasn't sure he wanted Nyquist to know that.

So Flint made a show of setting up a recording.

He nodded when he was ready.

Nyquist touched a chip on his hand. A voice Flint half-recognized said, *Who created us? This I do not know, at least, not exactly. I do know that a corporation titled...* and then a Peytin word resounded in the room, followed by, *The name has many translations, but I believe that the one the corporation's founders intended was a little known meaning for the phrase. It is 'legal fiction.'*

Flint met Nyquist's gaze. "Do you think he's making this up?"

"I don't know what the Peyti are capable of," Nyquist said. "I investigated the meaning myself on the way over here, and got all kinds of translations for the phrase. It's a Peyti idiom that, in some of the southern regions of Peyla used to mean *legal fiction*, decades ago. So he's not lying there. I'm going to play this for Popova when I get to Noelle's office, and see what she says."

"You'll need that other expert of Noelle's—what's her name?—Rastigan?" Flint said.

Nyquist nodded. "I plan to do that. But you might be able to get into some databases with that recorded word, maybe even find how the thing is spelled in Peytin, and scan for that."

"I'm not sure what I'd find," Flint said, "since I don't read Peytin."

"But the system—" Nyquist held up his hands and shook his head. "What do I know? You know how to search for everything, and I don't know how to search for anything. But, I figured, you'd need this for the law school part of the investigation."

Flint smiled at him. Another breakthrough, no matter how they used it.

"Yeah, I will," he said. "Thank you."

And now he had recorded it in some different places. He wondered what he would find when he used it.

He had a lot of work ahead of him, but it was, as Nyquist said, work Flint was uniquely qualified to do.

"Should you let Noelle know about the threat to the clones?" Flint asked.

"I'll tell her in person," Nyquist said. "It's not going to go over well, particularly after that incident with S³."

Flint nodded. His mind was already on the searches he had to do. He leaned over the screen in front of him, and started searching the home addresses of the clones. He began with Uzvaan because that was a name he knew. Once he found it, he searched for delivery information to Uzvaan's home, looking for a regular package.

"How often do the Peyti replace their masks?" he asked.

"Uzvaan said they got the packets quarterly," Nyquist said.

Flint nodded. That made the search even easier. At least for the delivery. He would cross-reference against deliveries to some of the other clones.

"Can I help?" Nyquist asked.

Flint didn't want Nyquist touching his systems. "Maybe, but not here."

Nyquist half-smiled again, as if he had expected that response. "Okay," he said. "Rather than duplicate the effort, you tell me when I need to do the footwork."

"Deal," Flint said, monitoring both screens.

"And if you need my help you say so."

Flint nodded.

"All right," Nyquist said. "I'll wait to hear from you."

Flint nodded. He looked at the various screens, still scrolling the information he had plugged into them earlier. The screen to his left, the one he had searching for deliveries to Uzvaan, had a list that ran hundreds of items long.

Hundreds, instead of millions.

He found himself smiling as well. He had a hunch this was finally going to work.

18

SENG PACED THE TINY OFFICE THAT TORKILD ZHU HAD GIVEN HER BEFORE he died. She had a single window and it overlooked the street, but she still didn't see emergency vehicles or any kind of authority show up.

Her stomach twisted.

She'd managed to reach someone at S³ on Athena Base, who wouldn't really listen to her.

If you want to talk about S³ On The Moon, that idiot had said, *you need to contact Rafael Salehi, and he'll be unavailable for another day or two. Or perhaps you should contact S³ On The Moon directly.*

After too many back-and-forths, she had managed to convince the idiot that she was dealing with an emergency. She wanted to contact Rafael Salehi directly, but all the idiot would give her, besides the contact information for the damn office Seng was standing in, was the public line to the ship that Salehi was traveling on.

Then it had been some crew member, followed by a pilot, followed—finally!—by a junior associate, who seemed to know what she was doing. She promised that Salehi would contact Seng, and then broke the link.

Seng had promised herself that if she didn't hear in the next fifteen minutes, she'd go through the entire rigmarole again.

A holoscreen rose in her office. She hadn't even known that this office had that kind of capability. The screen flicked on, showing an ostentatious S³ logo, followed by a privacy gray background. The privacy background made sure that whoever was looking at the hologram would only see what the sender wanted and nothing more.

A man, slender to the point of gaunt, appeared human-sized where the screen had been. He wore a gray suit, with black highlights that set off his close-cropped black hair and accented the hollowness of his cheekbones.

"Rafael Salehi," he said curtly. "You wanted to speak to me."

Seng's mouth went dry. She licked her lips and almost made herself smile before she remembered that a smile was inappropriate. His manner made her nervous.

Of course it did. He was the head of one of the biggest law firms in the entire Alliance.

"Melcia Seng," she said. "I'm sorry to bother you, but I didn't know where else to turn."

He tilted his head slightly, as if urging her to continue.

"Mr. Zhu is dead," she said. "He was murdered only a couple of hours ago, and we've been running into trouble…."

Salehi's dusky skin grew darker. A frown formed between his eyes. "Murdered?"

"Yes," she said. "Right outside this building. And it's awful, Mr. Salehi. He said that you would be here tomorrow, but we need something today—"

"Murdered by whom?" Salehi's voice was calm, but his eyes weren't. They had grown almost black.

"I can send you the security footage," she said. "It might get hacked along the way, but I can try."

"Try," he said. "Use the connection we have now."

She sent the security vid, knowing he wouldn't even get it for a few minutes, let alone have a chance to see it.

She lowered her voice, even though she doubted anyone else was able to hear. "It was the police," she said. "They beat him and left him for dead, and then no one responded to our distress calls.

The coroner says that if someone had showed up on time, Mr. Zhu would still be alive."

Salehi's chin went up. It was as if the mourning posture he'd had a moment ago faded away, and he became a high powered lawyer, all in one movement.

"The *coroner* said?" he asked.

"Yes," she said. "I recorded it and so did two of the other new hires. They're downstairs recording everything. I made them. I figured if the police are at fault, then we need a record, but I don't know what to do from there, sir. I didn't know Mr. Zhu well, but I can't think what he did to deserve this."

"And you received no hints from the security footage?" Salehi asked.

"The coroner said that Mr. Zhu was hated for the injunctions. The coroner made it sound like it had something to do with the Peyti clones, but Mr. Zhu told me he's from the Moon, and I don't want to jump to any conclusions—"

"Don't worry," Salehi said. "You won't have to jump. I'll take care of that." He sounded grim.

"When will you be here, sir? Because I'm not sure what to do next."

His gaze met hers. His eyes were so dark that she couldn't see any light reflected in them at all. She wondered if that was a trick of the projection or if his eyes really were like that.

"I'll be there tomorrow at the latest," he said. "Will you still be at the office?"

In other words, he was asking her if she was going to stay with S³.

"I don't know about the others," she said, "but I'm staying. I'm pretty mad about this, sir. They shouldn't have treated him like that. Not just the beating—y'know, rogue cops. That stuff has happened throughout time—but it seems like the whole system conspired to let Mr. Zhu bleed out on the pavement."

"You didn't notice him right away?" Salehi asked.

Interesting question at that point. He wanted to know if she was part of the bleed out.

"I—he—I—he sent a message, sir, and it took me a minute to understand he was sending for help. So I searched for him. I found him downstairs ten minutes after I received that message. My colleagues went down with me, and they tell me he was already dead, but the coroner says he could have been revived if an ambulance had arrived on time."

"How long did it take for an ambulance to arrive?"

She shrugged. She hadn't checked the exact time stamp. "I have it all recorded. Every moment of it. We can document it, minute by minute, and add the coroner's comments. I believe him, sir. I think that something's really wrong here."

"Torkild Zhu," Salehi said, his tone soft. "How was he before this? Scared?"

She wasn't prepared for the shift in tone. She frowned. "I just met him yesterday, sir, but he seemed...overworked, a little scattered, glad that a team of us had come on board. We had a lot to do and we were going to get to it this morning, and I have no idea what to do next, sir, I really don't."

Salehi straightened his shoulders as if he were seeing her for the first time.

"Keep recording, keep documenting," he said. "I'll take care of the rest when I get there. Don't give out any materials, even if the police ask for them, and if you have someone who can set up protections on the building's security feeds, have them do so immediately. We don't want any information to disappear, do you understand me?"

She did. He was afraid all evidence of this crime would get covered up before he arrived.

"What are you going to do when you get here?" she asked.

His eyes glinted. He looked dangerous to her, and she almost took a step back.

"I'm going to get justice for Torkild," Salehi said. "No matter what it takes."

19

Surprisingly, his good mood was holding.

Nyquist bounced on his heels as he waited for the elevator to reach the top floor of the United Domes of the Moon Security Office. He wasn't quite smiling—he wasn't sure if it was appropriate to smile these days—but he wasn't frowning either.

The doors slid open and he stepped into the main area, waggled his fingers at Rudra Popova, who seemed startled, and nodded toward De-Ricci's door.

"She in?" he asked.

"Yes, but—"

He didn't wait for DeRicci to finish whatever it was that she was doing. He opened the door, stepped inside, and stopped, as startled by the mess as he had been every single time he had come here since the Peyti Crisis.

DeRicci's office covered most of the top floor of the Security building. Dome Daylight poured in the floor-to-ceiling windows, which would have made the room exceptionally bright and comfortable if it weren't for the mess that surrounded everything else.

Food containers were piled high on a desk near the door. Fortunately, the containers had self-cleaning nanolining so they didn't smell (that badly). Behind them, the weapons cabinet that he insisted she have remained closed. He wondered if she had ever opened it. She could still get to it, despite the mess.

A pile of clothing rose like a mountain from behind DeRicci's desk, explaining why she never seemed to have anything to wear anymore. Desks and computers and chairs were scattered haphazardly around the large plants that had once been decoratively placed, back in the days when an office could be a showroom and a workspace.

But DeRicci spent most of her waking hours here, and since she rarely slept more than four hours per night, this had become her actual home.

He had forgotten to bring her food—something he'd been doing on a regular basis. The moment he realized it, he sent a message through his links to Popova:

If you order us all lunch, I'll pay for it.

She sent back, *Already done, Detective, when I realized you arrived without your customary bag of goodies.*

He wasn't quite sure how to take that, so he smiled and let it pass over him. He was still scanning for DeRicci when she crawled out from under a desk.

"Got it," she muttered.

"Got what?" he asked, and she jumped.

"God, Bartholomew," she said. "You could have warned me."

"And you should have heard your door open and close," he said. "What did you get?"

She held up something between her thumb and forefinger, something so small that he couldn't tell what it was.

"I lost this earring on Anniversary Day," she said. "I finally found it, embedded in the carpet."

So it had been six months at least since this place was properly cleaned. He could believe that. It had a slightly funky locker room smell, despite the abundant nanocleaners that were probably working overtime to keep this place as clean as possible.

DeRicci herself looked as ragged as the office. When he'd met her, she'd been slightly heavier than she probably should have been. She'd had "soft edges," he liked to call it, and now she was all edge. She was so thin that he could see her bones. They were particularly prominent in her shoulders and neck. He had grown used to the sharp contours of her cheeks; they made her eyes seem even bigger.

"I take it you're done with Uzvaan?" she asked.

"For today," he said. "I hope to get back there tomorrow."

It felt like most of the day had gone by, but he realized it was barely noon.

"I got good information," he said. "I think I'll get more tomorrow."

"Why couldn't you stay?" she asked.

"Because," he said, "there seems to be some kind of time limit that the android guards are enforcing."

Besides, it bothered him to be there. But he had already complained about it, and the complaining had embarrassed him, especially given everything that DeRicci had been doing.

She stuck the earring in her pocket. He had a hunch she would lose it again before the day was out. He wanted to run a hand through her hair, guide her to the couch toward the back of the office, and hold her until she fell asleep.

But she wouldn't sleep in the middle of the day. She felt like every minute that she missed was a minute that could cost them.

"Uzvaan gave me the name of the firm that paid his way through law school. He translated it too. I'll work with Popova on that, and maybe you can get Jin Rastigan to do some work as well," he said.

DeRicci nodded, then grabbed a nearby chair. She leaned on it, holding it as it slid slightly across the floor.

"Flint's also looking into it," Nyquist said. "I spoke to him briefly."

And Nyquist didn't tell her about the masks. He didn't want the chance that anyone from this office would investigate those. He was worried about *Legal Fiction* as well, but he figured that would be less of an issue than the masks.

DeRicci nodded. He wasn't even sure she cared that Flint was doing the work on the law schools.

"I have one thing that you or your pet Earth Alliance investigators need to look for," he said.

DeRicci blinked and then rubbed her eyes. She was working to focus. He might have to force her to nap. She was even more exhausted than usual.

"Uzvaan told me he had a mentor in the Impossibles. A human woman named Mavis Zorn. I think we should find her—or someone should—and find out what she knows. And if she's not alive any longer or if she's moved on from the Impossibles, we should see who else she supervised."

"Human?" DeRicci said. "Not Peyti?"

"No," he said, "not Peyti. She protected him from failure, made sure he was second chair on a lot of cases, and kept him out of the courtroom entirely in most instances. I think she was in on it, but that might be my interpretation."

"Human," DeRicci said again. "I didn't expect that."

"Neither did I," Nyquist said. "I asked him to clarify. He did. She was human and she helped him, and he implied that she knew what was going on."

DeRicci shook her head. "How could we have missed all of this going on under our noses?"

He knew she meant the Alliance missing everything, but he understood it. There was some kind of underground, planning nefarious things for reasons he didn't understand, planning those things for *decades*, and it got missed.

"Maybe it didn't get missed," he said. "Maybe the vastness of the scale is what got missed."

DeRicci frowned and didn't say any more. She moved away from the chair, seemingly stronger.

"I'll talk to the Earth Alliance investigators about this Mavis Zorn. And I'll see what else we can track down," she said.

"One last thing," he said. "What happened to the Peyti clones that weren't on the Moon when the Peyti Crisis occurred? Has anyone gotten back to you on that?"

Her cheeks flushed quickly. He saw a flash of temper, wondered if it was directed at him, and then realized she was angry at herself. Before she even answered, he knew what she was going to say.

"I forgot to check," she said, and in her tone was an incredulousness, a *how could I forget something that important?*

"They weren't here," he said. "We have other things to worry about."

She nodded, but he could tell she didn't like that excuse.

"I'll find out," she said, "because we don't want another attack somewhere."

"For all we know, it could have already happened."

She shook her head. "I'm sure we would have heard. The Alliance itself seems to be on alert right now."

She might want to believe that, but Nyquist didn't believe it. Still, he wasn't going to disabuse her of it. She wasn't in charge of the entire Alliance. Technically, she wasn't even in charge of the Moon. Yet she seemed to be taking responsibility for everything.

He decided to change the subject. "I barely touched on that list of questions we had for Uzvaan. I'll go back to those tomorrow, when I see him. But if you think of anything else I should ask him before then, let me know."

She nodded. "I'll see what else we can come up with," she said, but he could tell that her mind was already somewhere else.

He wished he could make all of this easier for her. He wished he could get her to rest.

He wished none of this had ever happened.

But none of those wishes would come true. So instead, he said, "Rudra ordered lunch. I'll bring it in when it arrives."

"Thanks," DeRicci said, and sat at her desk. She called up a holoscreen that he couldn't read.

He felt like he had disappeared from the room.

He told himself he didn't mind.

And as he walked out, he wondered how long he could lie to himself—and how long any of them could maintain this status quo—how long *DeRicci* could maintain this status quo—without completely collapsing.

20

FLINT HAD FOUND AT LEAST A DOZEN REFERENCES TO *LEGAL FICTION*—or whatever that Peyti phrase actually meant. He was surprised he had found so many so quickly. Nyquist had been gone less than an hour.

Flint wandered from screen to screen, plus he was monitoring information on his links as well. His office felt small and stuffy, a feeling he both recognized and welcomed.

He often felt that way when the place was overloaded with information—or rather, when *he* was overloaded with information. That was one reason he used to take some of his dicier research to public, untraceable places like the Brownie Bar.

Here, he felt as if the walls had closed in on him, drowning him inside every single detail.

He welcomed the details now. He was running several searches—not just for *Legal Fiction*, but for information on those masks.

First, he collected all of the addresses of the Peyti clones, stunned that most of those men hadn't changed addresses at all once they had moved to the Moon. Decades in the same place, often in the same job.

He wondered how many of them had turned down promotions that would have required a move or a greater risk of failure. He wondered how hard they had worked at becoming invisible.

They had certainly succeeded—or at least, it seemed that way. But then, he had spent these last two weeks confronting his own blind spot when it came to the Peyti. When it came to all aliens, really. He had seen them as unfamiliar legal systems that imposed incomprehensible punishments for seemingly small crimes; punishments that, as a police officer, he had had to enforce.

He had also seen them as scenery—just part of the Moon itself, varying and colorful, but inconsequential to him once he had left Armstrong's Police Department. If anything, he saw the aliens as something to be understood when he decided to take the case of a Disappeared: he needed to know if that Disappeared had broken what Flint considered a meaningful law or just an incomprehensible one.

He wasn't sure how he felt about that now. What was incomprehensible to him might have been important to them.

No, not *might have been. Was* important to them. Otherwise they wouldn't have made a law forbidding that behavior.

He clasped his hands behind his back, and looked at the hundreds of addresses he had collected. Now, he needed to coordinate that information with the mask shipments, and then find out if the shipments had all come from the same place.

Mr. Flint?

He started. He hadn't thought anyone could contact him through his links.

Then he remembered: he had cleared a handful of people to contact him directly. Everyone involved in the investigation, from Nyquist to DeRicci to Luc Deshin, as well as Talia and the Armstrong Comfort Center.

That was where this contact had come from.

His heart started pounding. Something had gone wrong. He knew he should have accompanied Talia.

Yes? he sent back, hoping none of the fear he felt got added to the link.

Evando Llewynn here. I need to speak with you about your daughter immediately.

Is she all right? Flint sent.

That's what we need to discuss, Llewynn sent.

What's gone wrong? Flint asked. *Have you sent for a doctor?*

There was a pause, and Flint couldn't quite tell what that pause meant.

Then Llewynn sent, *Physically, she was fine when she left here. But I'm very concerned about her mental state, and I do not want to discuss it on links. We need to have this conversation in person. I am deeply troubled.*

If she's physically fine, Flint sent, *why is this so urgent?*

Because, Llewynn sent, *I'm not certain how long she'll be physically fine.*

You said she left, Flint said.

Yes, with those people you have guarding her, Llewynn sent. *That's not the issue. Please, Mr. Flint. Sometimes physical wellbeing is dependent upon emotional wellbeing. Your daughter is fine physically at the moment, but I'm seeing some awful signs that we need to discuss immediately.*

Flint blocked the link for a moment, then ran a hand over his face. His heart was beating triple time. He had been afraid of this. Talia hadn't been well, and he was truly worried that she might do something to harm herself.

He unblocked the links. *I'll be right there*, he sent, and signed off.

Then he looked at his computers, all doing massive searches. If he left them on without monitoring them, he might be vulnerable to hacks and incursions. If he shut off the searches, however, he would lose however much time this was going to take with Llewynn.

Before making a decision, he opened another link.

Talia? He sent. *I'm just checking in. Are you still with Rudra?*

Yes, Talia sent back immediately. *I'll be here until you set me free.*

Her tone had been like that for days. He had to remind himself that it wasn't unusual. She was hostile and angry and upset and frightened—and he didn't blame her.

Let me know if you need anything, he sent, and winced. It sounded so inadequate.

Then, he did something he hadn't done in almost two years. He double-checked his daughter.

Rudra, he sent to Popova. *I trust Talia's with you?*

She just got here, Popova sent. *She just got back from her appointment.*

Is she okay? Flint asked.

I don't know, Popova sent. *She seems the same.*

Somehow that relieved Flint, just a little. The same was okay. He'd hoped she was better, but the same was fine. They'd made it through the same for two weeks now. Surely that could last a few more hours.

He thanked Popova, then stared at the screens.

This investigation was too important to leave anything to chance. One by one, he shut them down.

He would continue the searches when he got back.

A few hours wouldn't make a difference.

He hoped.

21

Nyquist stepped out of DeRicci's office, only to find Flint's daughter Talia sitting at Popova's desk. Talia still looked odd: cheeks red, eyes red, hair a mess, as if she no longer cared about her appearance at all.

"Hi," he said, deciding to pretend he hadn't noticed. "I was looking for Rudra."

"She's getting the food before the guards below completely mess it up." Talia's voice was hoarse.

Nyquist hovered near the desk for a moment. He wasn't sure what to do. He needed to talk with Popova about the translation of *Legal Fiction*, but he didn't want to do that while Talia was here.

He almost asked if Talia could get the food, but he was certain that Popova had already considered that.

He glanced at the elevator doors, as if they would open and he would miraculously be rescued.

"It's okay," Talia said. "I'll tell her you left."

Nyquist shook his head. "I need to talk with her."

"Oh." Talia spoke as if the idea of talking to Popova was a revelation. "I'll go...somewhere else."

"Wait until we've eaten," Nyquist said. The sentence sounded fatuous and parental and all the things that he was not. Or at least he hoped he wasn't. "She's not even here yet."

He wanted to ask Talia why she was here and not with her father. He wanted to ask why she looked so bad. He wanted to ask what was wrong, but knew better, because he really didn't want to *know*.

As he hovered, Wilma Goudkins appeared at the end of the hallway. She spoke over her shoulder to someone behind her, probably Lawrence Ostaka. Sure enough, Ostaka appeared just as Nyquist thought his name.

Goudkins and Ostaka were the Earth Alliance investigators sent by the Earth Alliance Security Division to help investigate Anniversary Day. They'd both been here for the Peyti Crisis. Goudkins had proven useful. Ostaka less so.

Goudkins nodded at Nyquist as she approached. She was a tall woman who had worn her wedge-cut black hair with highlights matched her clothing—at least when she arrived a few weeks ago. Now her highlights were fading and the wedge cut needed a trim. Her fingernails were ragged, and her clothing wasn't nearly as perfect as it had been when Nyquist met her.

Ostaka looked the same. A middle-aged man with some gray, he had a bit of fat around his stomach that he apparently didn't feel like removing. His clothing was rumpled, but it had been rumpled when he first arrived.

Unlike everyone else in the office, he seemed unruffled by the various crises going on around them, as if they didn't touch him personally. Perhaps that was why he had been sent along with Goudkins, because he was one of those personality types who couldn't be bothered with messy emotions.

Goudkins was a dicey choice for investigator, in Nyquist's opinion. She had lost a sister on the Moon on Anniversary Day. While that made Goudkins care, it also put her on par with the investigators here instead of giving her the distance that Earth Alliance investigators often needed.

He didn't mind, though. He liked knowing that Goudkins was personally involved. At least she understood what everyone on the Moon was going through.

"Noelle asked us to join her," Goudkins said as she reached Nyquist.

He nodded as if he were DeRicci's receptionist.

Goudkins passed him and went inside DeRicci's office. Ostaka followed, giving Nyquist a thumbs-up as he went by.

Nyquist had no idea what that thumbs-up meant, if anything. He looked back at Talia.

She shook her head. "I don't know what's going on around here."

At that moment, Popova came off the elevator holding bags of food. The smell of onions preceded her. Nyquist went to her and removed some of the bags.

"Did you order for the Earth Alliance investigators too?" he asked.

"Oh, yeah," she said, "and they're paying. They're on an expense account."

He wished he had thought of that when he'd been buying food. He helped Popova take it to the little kitchen that had gotten a lot more use these last few months than the designers had intended. It was a small room to the right of some of the other offices.

It wasn't as messy as DeRicci's office—it was hard to be that messy—but it wasn't the cleanest room in the building, either.

He swept aside old dishes, put them in the washer, and then washed his own hands. He pulled some clean dishes out of the cupboards and set them on the table.

"We don't need those," Popova said. "Everyone ordered their own individual meal."

She was pulling containers of food out of the bags. The smell of fried meat mixed with the onions. She opened each one, and then labeled it with someone's name.

"Rudra," he said as he placed Goudkins' meal with DeRicci's, "I have another translation for you. This one is really weird."

"All right," she said. "When we finish, I'll take a listen. But you know—"

"That you're not an expert. Right. Uzvaan translated for me. I simply don't trust his translation. After you listen and double-check it, let me know if that's the right name. If it is, will you send it to Jin Rastigan to see if she knows anything else about the corporation he's referring to?"

Popova looked at him over one of the steaming containers. This one contained bright green and red vegetables in some kind of white sauce.

"I can't do that without the Chief's approval," Popova said.

"I'm sure she'll give it," Nyquist said. "Just check with her."

"All right," Popova said. "Then send it to me."

He did. Then he grabbed the mess of plum-covered pork, sautéed spinach, and rice that had somehow gotten all mixed together. He had hoped for a bit of separation in his food, but he would have to settle for this.

"You want me to deliver—"

"I got it," Popova said. "The chief is used to me coming in and out of meetings. She thinks I don't hear anything."

He smiled. "Why don't you send Talia back. It's probably better for her to eat at a table, anyway."

Popova sighed. "Who knows."

And he suspected that was less about where Talia should eat than it was about what was best for her.

He managed one bite of food before his links opened.

Detective Nyquist, I need you back at the station.

The message was from Andrea Gumiela, the chief of detectives. He leaned his head back. He had known this moment was going to come, but he hoped Gumiela would ignore him for a few more days, thinking he was working on something important for the department.

Grabbing lunch, he sent. *I'll be there as soon as I finish.*

Now, Detective, she sent.

Wonderful. He wondered what was so important that he had to report immediately.

The way he felt at the moment, anything that important would have caught the attention of DeRicci's office first.

But he didn't know that for certain.

Still, he shoveled his meal into his mouth, and was nearly half done by the time Talia wandered in.

"Wow," she said as she picked up a fork. "You're an eating machine."

"I'm a man who has been summoned back to work," he said around a mouthful of food he hadn't even been tasting.

"By DeRicci?" Talia asked.

"By my real boss," he said.

She blinked as she tried to put that together. Then she frowned. "I thought crime was on hold in Armstrong during the crisis."

"Don't I wish," he said, and closed the container. He shoved it into the refrigerator that used to be full of fresh food and was now full of more containers just like this one. Only older.

"Hey, Detective," Talia asked as she peered inside her container of food. "Is everything just getting worse?"

He knew the question had more behind it than it seemed. He didn't really have time to reassure her, and he almost said he didn't know.

Then he remembered the good mood he'd had when he arrived here.

"Honestly," he said, "I think we're starting to make some progress."

Her gaze met his, and he could feel the intensity behind it.

"Really?" she asked.

"Yeah," he said, feeling the mood return. "Really."

He left her, hoping he would still feel that way after he talked to Gumiela, and found out what the new crisis was. He was tired of feeling behind. He was tired of being out of control.

He wanted things to return to the way they had been—not necessarily physically, but emotionally. He wanted to be able to predict what was coming next.

And he had a hunch that wouldn't happen for a long, long time.

22

THE CONNECTION SHUT DOWN, AND WITH IT, SALEHI'S BRAVADO DISAPPEARED. He staggered slightly, then sank into the chair behind him. Jiolitti sat across from him.

She had monitored the entire conversation.

"Holy shit," she said softly.

He couldn't agree more. Holy shit indeed. And any other expletive. He ran a hand over his face, trying to get a grip on his emotions.

He was the one who had made Zhu head of S³ On The Moon, he was the one who had made sure that Zhu confirmed those injunctions, he was the one who had sent Zhu into the wilds of an unprotected, angry populace representing murderers and attempted murderers, with no backup and no talk of security.

And of course, Zhu wasn't smart enough to think of hiring security on his own.

Salehi squeezed his forehead. Not fair, he wasn't being fair; Zhu had never had an unpopular case like this, or if he had, he had done so somewhere safe like the Impossibles.

Salehi had had half a dozen cases like this over his career, always away from Athena Base, and—after the first one—with lots of protection.

What an idiot he was. He had been thinking about the legal implications, not the social ones. He hadn't thought about the atmosphere on the Moon because it had been so very long since he'd had a case like this.

Hell, he hadn't thought about it because this wasn't yet a case. It was just a bunch of injunctions.

Against law enforcement.

He'd never had trouble with law enforcement before.

But it sounded like Seng had.

He knew nothing about her except that she had looked rather small and overdressed on that holovid. Her light brown skin, slightly upturned eyes, and tiny nose all gave her a youthful appearance, but he had no idea if she was young, or what kind of experience she had.

Zhu had mentioned he was having trouble finding lawyers on the Moon and that he had interviewed a bunch from Earth. Given Seng's harsh accent, she had spent quite a bit of time on Earth.

And she clearly didn't scare easily.

Salehi couldn't collapse now. He could blame himself later, when he had time. And he needed to blame *himself*, not Zhu, because Zhu had had no idea what he was walking into.

Salehi had simply forgotten because it had been so long.

And because he really hadn't expected lawlessness from those sworn to uphold the law.

Shishani had called him naïve more than once. And he was. He still was.

He took a deep breath, and sat up.

"Were you close to him, sir?" Jiolitti asked.

It took Salehi a moment to focus. Close to Zhu? Maybe in spirit. Zhu had given up sooner than Salehi, though. Zhu had had a lot of idealism as well, and then it had been destroyed a few months ago.

Zhu had represented a clone of PierLuigi Frémont—not one of the clones who had attacked the Moon, an older clone—and had actually gotten him released, hoping the clone could provide background on the Anniversary Day assassins. Before the clone made it a full day, the ship he'd been on, the ship transporting him out of the Alliance, had been destroyed by Alliance battleships.

Destroyed, taking Rafik Fujita with it. Rafik Fujita, one of Salehi's closest friends, whom he'd recommended as transport captain for that mission because he knew Fujita could be trusted.

Fujita, murdered by the Alliance.

Now Zhu, murdered by the Alliance.

That couldn't be a coincidence.

Could it?

"Sir?" Jiolitti asked.

"Sorry," he said, not remembering what she had said before, if she had said anything at all. "I need you to get a team and vet some security firms. *Not* any on the Moon right now, and not any with ties to the Moon. Maybe some from Earth or maybe one of the human-based firms on Mars or something. I want the best."

"Sir?" Jiolitti said, adding that tone people used when they wanted one word to ask a whole host of questions.

"Clearly, we need protection when we get to the Moon, and we're not going to get it nearby. I want a team around that building within the hour, but I doubt that's possible. So I want them on board as fast as you can get them, and someone protecting us when we get to the Moon."

"Human-based?" Jiolitti said. "Because the best firms are—"

"Think it through, Lauren," he snapped. "The Moon is human-oriented and more than a little pissed at aliens right now. Let's minimize trouble, shall we?"

She leaned back slightly, clearly put off by his tone. He didn't blame her. It wasn't her fault that Zhu was dead, that the entire team would walk into a clusterfuck tomorrow.

"I want another team reviewing all the footage that Seng sent. In fact, get back with her, make sure she keeps sending us updates. We need everything she has, and we'll continue to need anything she gets. We're going in there prepared."

"Prepared for what, sir?" Jiolitti asked.

"They murdered one of our own, Lauren, because we chose to represent a group of defendants that they don't approve of. We might not approve of those Peyti clones either, but that doesn't matter. They're entitled to a defense."

He hadn't said that before. He'd been thinking of all clones, of the injustices presented against the Peyti themselves, not about the actual offenders. He was thinking about the offenders now.

"Sir, don't you think that this is too dangerous? We don't know anything about the Moon's government or how this will be handled. We have no allies, and we're going in blind."

He raised his head. He had had hopes for this woman. He wanted to make her partner one day.

"It sounds like this whole thing frightens you," he said so calmly that he almost didn't recognize his own voice.

"Yes, sir," she said. "Doesn't it frighten you?"

He stopped, thought, examined his own emotions. Fear wasn't one of them. Anger, guilt, regret, and loss were all there, but not fear.

"No," he said, and stood. "If you want off this case, let me know. We'll send you back to Athena Base once we arrive on the Moon."

Her mouth opened, then closed slightly. "That's not what I'm saying, sir."

"Then what are you saying?"

"I'm just wondering if this will be worthwhile. I mean, we're going in—"

He held up a hand, silencing her. He didn't want to hear any more. Worthwhile? Schnable thought so: The government of Peyla would pay for this entire defense for years if necessary. That was the money angle.

Shishani thought so: she liked the thought of the money, but she also liked chasing cases that went all the way to the Multicultural Tribunal.

Salehi had thought so: He wanted to change clone law. Or he had.

Now he wanted revenge.

He was going to deal with the clones, the clone law, and with the bastards who murdered Torkild Zhu.

"You do what I tell you or you go home," Salehi said. "It's that simple. You don't get to talk about your feelings. You don't get to talk about whether or not this is worthwhile. You give this work 150 percent or more, or I will find someone who will."

Her mouth was open. He wondered if anyone had ever spoken to her like this.

It took a full minute before she gathered herself.

"Yes, sir," she said. "Security team. Reviewing the footage. I'll have that underway immediately."

"I also want background on this Melcia Seng and all the attorneys that Zhu hired yesterday. I want to know if we can identify the cops who killed Zhu. And I want someone to start investigating local Armstrong law as well as laws for the United Domes. I doubt they have any teeth, but if they do, I'll use them. Or I'll go directly into Alliance law."

Jiolitti nodded, then swallowed hard. "Are we telling the Peyti about this, sir?"

For a moment, he thought she meant the Peyti clones on the Moon. Then he realized she meant all the Peyti lawyers traveling with them.

"Of course we are," he said. "We're a team. And they need to know what we're all facing. It's not just about barring some group's entry to the Moon any longer. It's about sanctioned murder."

And a dozen other things.

"Okay," she said, and headed for the door.

"Lauren," he said, just a little softer. "I'll tell them. I'll tell everyone. You get the security teams in place, and you take care of the footage, and all the other orders I gave you. We need to move fast on this."

"Yes, sir," she said, and left.

He stood for a moment, feeling as if he had been punched in the stomach.

Goddammit, Zhu, he thought. *When did you get to be so very hapless?* It was as if everything Zhu had touched this last year became something worse.

And then Salehi caught himself. He wasn't going to blame Zhu. Zhu was doing exactly what Salehi had asked.

Zhu had been doing his job.

Just like Fujita had been.

Just like Salehi had demanded Jiolitti do.

They'd lost two colleagues so far, and this fight was only beginning.

Before it was over, Salehi suspected, they would lose a hell of a lot more.

23

NOELLE DERICCI STARED AT THE TWO EARTH ALLIANCE INVESTIGATORS SHE had invited into her office, and for a brief moment, she forgot why she had asked them to come.

She was standing behind her desk, thinking about cleaning it up, trying not to think about the worry on Nyquist's face every time he looked at her, and ignoring the sheer exhaustion that made the junk-covered couch against one wall look so very inviting.

She cleaned the sleep out of her eyes—ironic that the stuff in her eyes would be called "sleep" when she wasn't getting any—and made herself concentrate. Three things to discuss with them, two directly with Goudkins, one for both of them.

"Thanks for coming," she said, stalling for a moment. Then she blinked and the thoughts returned, as if someone had programmed them for her.

They hadn't been programmed, of course. Everything in this building was about as secure as a place got these days. That feeling of delay didn't come from outside; it came from within.

At some point, Nyquist's warnings would come true. She would fall asleep on her feet and sleep for days if she didn't get rest.

Goudkins had come farther into the room than Ostaka. Goudkins didn't look as polished as she had two weeks ago. The Peyti Crisis had left shadows under her eyes.

DeRicci had checked up on her, had seen that Goudkins had spent weeks on the Moon after Anniversary Day and had fought to make sure her sister had actually received a funeral.

So many people hadn't.

DeRicci had checked up on Ostaka too. He hadn't been anywhere near the Moon in the days after Anniversary Day. He had been working some other cases in the solar system and, she suspected, he had been brought in to make certain that Goudkins didn't spend all her time chasing the Tycho Crater case.

They were here to coordinate overall efforts. There were lesser ranked Earth Alliance investigators in the other domes, and she had just received information that more would be arriving—non-human investigators. She was told to make certain they would get through the port, as if she had control over what the port did.

She supposed she could try.

The two investigators were staring at her. She wondered how long she'd been silent.

"On the day of the Peyti Crisis," she said, hoping she sounded more authoritarian than she felt, "we sent the information about the Peyti clones to the Earth Alliance, and told them to make certain none of the clones of Uzvekmt were working as lawyers elsewhere in the Alliance. I checked my link. I never heard back from anyone at the Alliance. Did either of you?"

"No," Ostaka said flatly. He hadn't even had a chance to check his links or refresh his memory.

Goudkins looked at him with surprise. "Are you sure?"

"Yeah," he said. "I checked a few days ago. We haven't heard."

At that moment, the door opened. Popova came in, balancing cartons of food. She set them down on the only empty table, in the very center of the room.

"I brought silverware and napkins," she said, looking at DeRicci, as if DeRicci hadn't been using either in the last few weeks.

"Thanks," DeRicci said curtly.

Popova nodded, and left.

DeRicci did not go for the food. It smelled strongly of onions and fried chicken. Her stomach growled. But she'd eat after the investigators left.

"You haven't checked recently, though," she said to Ostaka as if Popova hadn't interrupted them.

"No," he said. "But I would think if there were—"

"Check for me, would you?" she asked. "And I want you to go back several decades, see where these lawyers ended up. It's important or I wouldn't ask."

"Do you have a lead?" Ostaka asked.

"I'm not sure," she said. "I'll tell you if your investigation pans out."

"We don't really work for you," he said unnecessarily.

"Lawrence," Goudkins said, as if he had crossed some kind of line. That was good to hear, because DeRicci couldn't trust her own anger at the moment, and Ostaka usually made her angry.

"We all work together," DeRicci said, grateful for Goudkins' interruption. It gave her just enough time to prevent her from saying something unfortunate. "I'm sure if the Earth Alliance found more of these clones, they're dealing with them, and didn't feel the need to bother us. But I'd like to know. It'll help us in ways that aren't immediately obvious."

"Will you share that information with us?" Ostaka asked.

"Of course," DeRicci lied. She might share it with Goudkins, but if Ostaka kept pissing her off, she doubted she'd share it with him.

"All right," he said. "I'll see what I can find."

"Thanks," DeRicci said. "Have you two found anything?"

"Not really," Ostaka said. "Mostly just chatter. We did discover that the Frémont clones didn't go directly to their target cities. Some of the clones went to nearby domes that weren't blown up. We've sent the information to the investigators there."

"Keep me posted," DeRicci said, and there was enough of a dismissal in her voice that both investigators looked down at the cartons of food, then glanced at the door. "Lawrence, go ahead and take your food. I'd like to have a personal talk with Wilma for a moment. I need to ask her something that I don't think I can ask anyone else."

He frowned, as if trying to understand that. Then he shrugged, as if woman-to-woman stuff was something he wasn't really concerned with.

"Sure thing," he said, and picked up the carton labeled "Ostaka." He walked toward the door. Just before he let himself out, he said to Goudkins, "I think I'll eat in the kitchen today."

"All right," she said, without looking at him. It sounded like she really didn't care what he did.

He let himself out. When the door snicked shut, DeRicci sent a private encoded message to Goudkins. *Are your links with Ostaka off?*

Why? Goudkins sent back.

Because we won't have a discussion if they're on, DeRicci sent. She could have added that it wouldn't take much for her to double-check, but she wanted Goudkins to trust her.

And, deep down, she wanted to trust Goudkins.

They're off, Goudkins sent.

"Good," DeRicci said. "Sit down. Have some lunch."

"What's this woman-to-woman thing?" Goudkins asked.

DeRicci moved to one of the chairs. She picked up the carton labeled "DeRicci" and opened it. The chicken looked a little soggy, but the onion rings (which would probably make Nyquist angry) looked delicious. She took one and bit into it. The onion was thick and sweet, obviously Moon-grown, and the batter was a perfect, buttery compliment.

The food tasted much better than she had expected, and it was all she could do not to devour it.

"I've been really impressed with you," she said, wiping her fingers on one of those napkins that Popova mentioned so pointedly. "I think you truly want to figure out what's going on here. Your partner looks on it more as a job."

"Yeah," Goudkins said. There was a lot of meaning in that single word. Essentially, Goudkins agreed with her and was disappointed in Ostaka.

"We've discovered some things," DeRicci said, "that need to be investigated, but quite honestly, I don't feel comfortable having the inquiries come from any law enforcement organization on the Moon."

"Because?" Goudkins opened her carton. Something steamed, but DeRicci couldn't smell it over her own fatty and unhealthy meal.

"Well, I can't tell you that unless you agree to help us first." DeRicci ate another onion ring.

Goudkins shook her head, and DeRicci felt her heart skip a beat. She had expected Goudkins to help. She really didn't have a plan if Goudkins refused.

"We don't work for you," Goudkins repeated, but without all the attitude that Ostaka had brought to that phrase.

"I know," DeRicci said, "and that's both good and bad."

Goudkins picked up a fork and stirred something in her carton. "You're intriguing me."

"Good," DeRicci said.

"Can I change my mind after I hear what you need?" Goudkins asked.

"No," DeRicci said.

Goudkins scooped up something from her carton. Whatever she had ordered was brown and drippy and completely unidentifiable.

DeRicci ate another onion ring. Her fingers lingered over the chicken leg that sat on top of the entire carton, but she didn't take it yet.

"Will it get me in trouble?" Goudkins asked.

"It might," DeRicci said.

Goudkins set her fork down. "Will it help solve what's been happening on the Moon?"

"Possibly," DeRicci said.

"Will it prevent another attack?" Goudkins asked.

"We don't know," DeRicci said. "We hope so."

"*We?*" Goudkins asked.

DeRicci nodded, then privately gave up and grabbed the leg. It was soggy and she didn't care. She took a bite from it, getting a larger hunk of meat than she planned.

She felt like a primitive throwback, some kind of early human that only ate with its fingers.

The thought was enough to get her to set the leg down.

"I suppose you're not going to tell me who *we* is," Goudkins said.

"I think you're smart enough to figure it out," DeRicci said.

Goudkins smiled. She took another bite of her food. She seemed very dainty compared to DeRicci. But then slight, elegant women always made DeRicci feel like a gigantic oaf, and the feeling intensified when she was tired.

She ate more onion rings. Only a few remained.

"All right," Goudkins said after a moment. "I'm curious enough and I want to know what the hell is going on. Besides, I really want to solve this thing. So I'll help."

DeRicci wiped her mouth, then swallowed the last of the onion rings. Before she could say anything, Goudkins added,

"I suppose I can't tell Ostaka what I'm doing."

"You can't tell anyone," DeRicci said. "You work with me, and no one else."

"So mysterious," Goudkins said.

"Yeah." DeRicci set the carton down. "You'll understand why when I'm done."

24

GUMIELA'S OFFICE WAS A LOT NEATER THAN DERICCI'S, BUT IT WAS A surface neatness. Nyquist had been in this office many times before, and it had been spotless. Now he saw cups behind Gumiela's desk, tablets stacked on top of each other, and a blazer tossed over a chair.

The pre-Anniversary Day Gumiela wouldn't have allowed any of that. The fact that Gumiela's office looked like this now simply meant that as chief of detectives, she had to cope with the occasional media presence here, and she didn't want her office to look as scattered as she probably felt.

If the media ever made it to DeRicci's office, then everyone on the Moon would become even more terrified that things were out of control.

Appearances did matter that much.

And Nyquist was glad that they had little to do with him.

Although, if he were honest with himself, one reason he never got enhancements to get rid of the scars left by the Bixian assassins was simply to let everyone know at first glance that he was a man who *didn't* care about appearances.

(*And*, DeRicci had said to him one afternoon, *the fact that you want to show people at a glance that you* don't *care about appearances means that appearances are a lot more important to you than you're willing to let on.*)

He knew that appearances were important to Gumiela. She always wore a suit jacket over a dress or with a skirt and blouse. Today's skirt showed off her marvelous legs. Her shoes had become practical in the last six months—she'd done a lot of walking and investigating on her own now, and she couldn't wear shoes that accented her look. She had to wear something comfortable.

She wore her hair up, probably because it was easier, and what little makeup she had on merely covered the lines that were forming around her mouth and eyes.

It looked like nothing could cover the shadows beneath those eyes, however.

"You haven't been here since the meeting yesterday," Gumiela said without a hello. "You want to tell me why?"

"Following a lead," he said.

"At the Reception Center?"

He cursed silently. He hadn't wanted her to know where he had been.

"I have some business there," he said.

"You know we've received injunctions from S^3—"

"Yeah," he said, "and I didn't violate them."

"I hope not," she said, and leaned against her desk. It seemed like all the strength leached out of her, "because our relationship with S^3 is about to get even dicier."

He tensed. He had hoped this wouldn't happen when he went to see Uzvaan, but he had known it would be a risk.

"What happened?" he asked, cringing inside. He hoped that reaction didn't show on his face.

She sighed and her dark eyes met his. For once, he couldn't read her mood. Exasperation? Anger? Sadness? Everything mixed together, maybe with a little fear added in?

"The coroner just registered a body," she said quietly. "It's Torkild Zhu."

Nyquist frowned. He didn't know any Torkild Zhu, although the name sounded familiar.

And then the name connected.

It belonged to that overdressed attorney from the day before, the one who had arrived after the division-wide meeting and slapped injunctions against dealing with the Peyti clones all over the department.

"You're kidding, right?" Nyquist said.

She shook her head. Her gaze held his a moment longer.

"Tell me it was natural causes."

"Brodeur says he was beaten to death." She spoke quietly.

Her gaze hadn't left his face. Nyquist let his shock show.

Then he blinked, and realized exactly what she said. "Brodeur was the coroner on this?"

"Yes," she said.

"He's not the best we have," Nyquist said.

"No," she said. "Which he knows, and he believes that someone sent him deliberately."

Nyquist frowned. He wasn't sure what that meant, exactly, but he didn't like the sound of it.

"Why would someone do that?" Nyquist asked.

"Because there's evidence, at least according to Brodeur, that we know the killers."

Nyquist could tell she was choosing her words carefully.

"How well do we know them?" he asked.

"Brodeur thinks they were cops," she said softly.

Nyquist sank into a chair. Now he understood why Gumiela had sent for him. He had warned her just yesterday that the attitude among the detectives was dangerous. But he had thought the danger would be against the Peyti clones—that they would die or be injured in custody, and the investigators would lose their best resources for solving the overall crisis on the Moon.

That had been before S³ had shown up with its injunctions.

Before *Zhu* had shown up with S³'s injunctions.

"You believe him," Nyquist said.

Gumiela's gaze left his, and in that simple movement he saw her answer. Yes, she believed Brodeur.

"I'm going to give you what we have," she said. "I want you to investigate this. I want you to document everything you find, and then I want you to report to me."

"Won't I need a partner?"

"You should have one," Gumiela said, "but if Brodeur is right, then you might end up with an assistant who has a personal interest in this case."

She paused, as if she had an idea that struck her hard.

"You *don't* have a personal interest in this case yourself, do you?"

He let out a half laugh. "You know me better than that, Andrea. I don't kill because I dislike someone or because I hate what they stand for."

Besides, he thought, *I'm the one who warned you about the mood in the division.*

"I know that," she said. "We wouldn't even be having this discussion if I thought you were that kind of man. What I'm asking is this: is there anyone in the division you would bend the rules for? Is there anyone whose involvement you would cover up?"

As Gumiela asked that question, DeRicci's image flashed across his mind. Then, oddly, Flint's. Clearly, there were people he would deal with on his own if he thought they were acting in an extra-judicial manner, but none of them were on the force.

Any longer, anyway.

"In the division," he repeated. "That's what you're asking?"

"What about in life?" Gumiela asked.

He paused. Truthful or not?

He decided on the truth, partly because he wanted Gumiela to deem him unsuitable and assign someone else to this hellish case.

"I think we all have someone in our lives we'd bend the rules for," he said quietly.

She leaned back just a little, then a half smile crossed her face. He thought he recognized the look: Gumiela had just thought of the person *she* would bend the rules for.

"In the division, then," she said. "Is there anyone you would bend the rules for?"

"No," he said, wishing he could convincingly lie about that too. But he couldn't, particularly if Gumiela had asked him to come up with a name of someone he would protect.

She took a deep breath.

"All right then," she said. "You're going to make this your top priority. You will report directly to me and tell no one what you're working on. You will consider me and Brodeur your partners in this, and if you need help, you'll contact one of us."

"He's an incompetent jerk," Nyquist said.

"He's actually not incompetent," Gumiela said. "He's just not as smart as most of our other coroners. And he's an asshole, so no one really gives him a chance. They undercut him whenever they can."

"You want me to take someone who gets undercut as a partner on a case that might have the department facing some high-powered attorney from S³?" Nyquist asked.

"At the moment, we're stuck with Brodeur," Gumiela said. "If you find out that the accusations are true, and if you figure out who the perpetrators are, then we might be able to bring someone else in—someone we trust or someone from outside of Armstrong—to double-check Brodeur's work. But at the moment, we'll make do."

"Can't we put this off until the crisis is over?" Nyquist asked. He really wanted to see Uzvaan again. Nyquist didn't want to waste time on investigating this murder at all.

"I'd love to," Gumiela said. "And you know what? I probably would, if it weren't for S³. They would have been a pain in our behind even if this murder hadn't happened. The fact that it has is just going to make everything worse. I'm hoping to head off the worst of it."

"I think it became too late for that when their representative on the Moon got murdered," Nyquist said.

"You're probably right," Gumiela said. "We just didn't need more on our plate, particularly with S³."

"No matter what, this isn't going to be easy, is it?" Nyquist asked.

"I can't imagine how," she said. "I really can't imagine how."

25

DeRicci let out a long, oniony breath. She didn't care if it grossed Goudkins out. Or maybe she did.

DeRicci stood up.

Once she trusted Goudkins, there was no going back.

Goudkins closed the lid on her food carton and leaned back in the chair in the center of DeRicci's office. DeRicci resisted the urge to look at the door. She hoped Popova wouldn't interrupt them again.

"One of our people," DeRicci said, slowly, giving herself half a minute to back out if she changed her mind, "found a name."

"A name?" Goudkins asked.

DeRicci nodded. She glanced at Goudkins. Goudkins sat primly, legs crossed at the ankles, but her hands had tightened around the food carton. She wanted to know this. She clearly wanted answers as well.

"This name is directly tied to PierLuigi Frémont's DNA. This person isn't selling the DNA, but she's the only person that we have found who has access to something this pure."

"You're being deliberately mysterious," Goudkins said. "Either you trust me or you don't."

DeRicci actually liked the irritation. She decided to ignore it, however, and take her own time on this, tell Goudkins her own way.

"We checked everywhere," DeRicci said. "As one of our sources said, criminal organizations could make a fortune selling Frémont slow-grow DNA right now, only no one has it. No one knows where the clones came from, and no one is offering clones or the DNA for sale."

"You're certain?" Goudkins asked.

"Yes," DeRicci said.

"Why don't you go after this person?" Goudkins asked. "You clearly have resources that are not just Moon-based."

DeRicci had never thought of her "sources" as non-Moon based. In truth, they were Moon-based, just with different access. However, she liked that Goudkins had made that assumption. It made DeRicci's life a little easier.

DeRicci continued, "This woman is high up in the Earth Alliance. She has a security clearance so tight that no one I know can access any information about her."

"Not even the vaunted Miles Flint?" Goudkins asked with just a little sarcasm.

"Not even Miles," DeRicci said. "Not that I would ask him to do so. I'm afraid if any of us here on the Moon start looking at this woman, we're going to unleash something new."

"If she's indeed guilty," Goudkins said.

"Yes," DeRicci said. "And if she is guilty, she'll be expecting inquiries from people based on the Moon."

"But not from within the Alliance?" Goudkins asked.

DeRicci inclined her head. It was a good point, and one she had considered.

"I think you might have the option to hide your search, while we can't," DeRicci said.

Goudkins frowned at her. "What do you mean?"

"Well," DeRicci said, stifling a burp. Great. The delicious onion rings hadn't agreed with her. "I trust that you people have the ability to investigate each other, for promotions and other things, right? Or am I wrong about that?"

Goudkins put her food carton on the table. "You're right. You want me to hide my inquiries as a standard job investigation?"

DeRicci returned to her chair and sat back down. "Or a promotion request. Or a lateral transfer. Find out everything you can about this woman."

"If she works inside the Alliance," Goudkins said, "I doubt her résumé will state that she sells Frémont DNA as a sideline."

"She doesn't," DeRicci said. "Several people have made inquiries of her—"

"From the Moon?" Goudkins asked.

"No," DeRicci said. "All sorts of criminal types, including the Black Fleet and an old partner of hers, have tried to get the DNA from her. It's my understanding that she has rebuffed them all."

Goudkins frowned. "Why would she do that?"

"That's what you get to find out," DeRicci said.

"All right," Goudkins said. "Where does she work?"

"She started in prisons," DeRicci said. "I'm told she was onsite when Frémont died."

Goudkins let out a soft whistle. "That explains a lot."

"It does?" DeRicci asked.

"It explains the timeline," Goudkins said. "Frémont died over fifty years ago."

DeRicci nodded. "All right, that's a start."

"Prisons," Goudkins said. "Is she still in prisons?"

DeRicci shrugged. "This is where it gets interesting. Her job position is high up in the Alliance, and it's classified."

Goudkins let out a sound of disbelief. "I can't investigate someone whose job is classified. That automatically makes her higher ranked than me."

"Are you sure about that?" DeRicci asked. "Because it's my understanding that lots of lower-level positions are classified as a way to keep information contained and controlled."

Goudkins picked up one of the napkins and nervously wiped her hands. When she finished, she kept the napkin clutched in her left hand. "This is going to be very dangerous," she said, more to herself than to DeRicci.

"Yes, it is," DeRicci said, "and that's why I didn't mention it in front of Ostaka. We have a good lead, and we can't track it. But you'll have to be very careful, and you can't consult with anyone in the Alliance."

"Because you think this is Alliance based," Goudkins said.

"I don't make assumptions," DeRicci lied. "Every investigator needs to blaze her own path. But the evidence we find keeps pointing to some Alliance involvement."

"Why would the Alliance try to destroy itself?"

"I don't mean it that way," DeRicci said. "I don't think the Alliance knows what's going on. I think there are things being done with Alliance resources that the Alliance would frown on if it knew."

Goudkins smiled, just a little. "And you want me to do the same thing."

"What?" DeRicci asked. Sometimes, when she was tired, it felt like half her brain had gone on vacation.

"You want me to use Alliance resources without the Alliance finding out," Goudkins said.

DeRicci grinned. She hadn't thought of it that way.

"Yeah," she said quietly. "I guess I do."

26

ETHAN BRODEUR'S CORNER OF THE MASSIVE CITY OF ARMSTRONG CORONER'S
Office was a crabbed little cave that made Nyquist uncomfortable every
time he entered it.

The décor of the coroner's office had never been high on anyone's
list, particularly the architects and interior designers who first built the
place, but over the decades, the entire office had sunk into neglect. It
remained clean and well-lit, but it looked like it belonged to another era.

At least a decade ago, someone had put posters on the wall. The posters advertised concerts or plays, and theoretically, the images changed as
the events changed. But the posters were peeling away from their cheap
frames and several of the images were stuck on events that had happened more than a year ago.

The posters made the entry into the office even less cheerful than it
usually was.

And the smell didn't help. Even though the coroner's office main-
tained the latest environmental systems, there was always a faint tinge
of decay here.

DeRicci said it was psychological: everyone knew what they were
coming into a morgue and expected the smell of death. Once Flint had
mentioned that he wondered if someone had added a bit of eau de decay
into the air filtration system, just to meet the expectations.

Nyquist doubted that, although he thought about it every single time he came down here. That was the other problem: the coroner's office itself was below ground. Not that anyone needed windows here, but no one even tried to dress up the walls with a pretend view.

It felt like a grubby spaceship without the possibility of going somewhere new.

Brodeur had had his cave as long as Nyquist had known him. DeRicci once said that the women in the Armstrong Police Department found Brodeur attractive, but that had to be thousands of smarmy comments and one or two hair enhancements ago. Nyquist had never heard anyone say that they found Brodeur nice or likeable or dateable.

Nyquist knew a lot of detectives who, if Brodeur's name came up in the coroner's office rotation, would do anything they could to bribe another coroner to take the case. No matter what Gumiela thought of him (was she one of the people attracted to him?), Brodeur was difficult to work with at best.

Brodeur's office was dark. A light shown from the work area deep inside. One change this coroner's office had made shortly after Nyquist was promoted to detective (and he didn't like to think about how long ago *that* was) was that each coroner had his own "theater" to do autopsies in. It turned out too many of the coroners claimed the others had left the controls of the theaters set wrong and something failed to record or the temperatures were off or something else had gone wrong.

When each coroner had his own workspace, he also had control of his job quality. Which was probably what tripped Brodeur up.

"Ethan?" Nyquist asked. "You wanted to talk to me?"

He hadn't tried to link with Brodeur. The less Brodeur seemed to be involved with the investigations, the better, at least as far as Nyquist was concerned.

Something crashed to Nyquist's right. He looked over, saw Brodeur standing near a shelf, a pile of tablets scattered on the floor. Nyquist crouched to help Brodeur pick them up.

"Just leave them," Brodeur said. "Each one is a case, and I'm supposed to be the only person reviewing them."

Nyquist wasn't sure he believed that, but he let it go. He had too much to worry about to think about what kinds of things Brodeur might be doing wrong in his lair.

"I caught the Zhu case," Nyquist said. "Gumiela wants a thorough investigation, and she said I have to talk with you about it."

Brodeur looked up at Nyquist. They weren't that different in height, but enough to make Brodeur seem small. Or maybe Nyquist just thought of him as small.

Brodeur sighed and wiped his hands on his lab coat. Nyquist couldn't withhold the wince when he saw that.

Brodeur didn't seem to notice.

"This thing's a mess," Brodeur said. "I don't envy you walking into it. I'll help however I can."

Nyquist felt a bit taken aback. He'd never heard Brodeur say anything like that before.

"Come with me." Brodeur led him into the autopsy theater. Nyquist had watched before, but usually from the outside, so that his presence didn't contaminate the corpse.

"You're done with the autopsy?" Nyquist said.

"Oh, yeah. It's recorded and filed with the various agencies," Brodeur said, "but I left the body out so that the investigating detective could look at what's going on."

Nyquist frowned. This wasn't procedure at all.

The theater was small. It had four gurneys that could rise from the floor and several more that could slip out of the walls. Human corpses were usually stored elsewhere in the building, until they were cremated or dealt with according to the deceased's wishes or religion.

Non-human corpses went to an entirely different wing. When Nyquist met him, Brodeur had been handling non-human deaths. But he'd moved back to human deaths when he received his first—and as far as Nyquist knew, only—promotion.

At the moment, only one body held the room. The body rested on a single table in the center. Lights shone on the corpse from all directions. It was naked and male, but barely recognizable as human.

The bruising made Nyquist's body ache in sympathy. The chest appeared caved in, the face was both swollen and jagged, and one leg seemed shorter than the other.

Even though the arms were at the body's side, they didn't rest properly. One curved upward slightly from the elbow, as if the body were reaching toward the ceiling.

"What the hell…?" Nyquist asked.

Brodeur didn't respond.

Nyquist took a step closer. The stomach and sides were purple from bruising, the back was black with pooled blood.

He couldn't remember what color Zhu's hair had been, but it didn't matter now. Now, matted blood had plastered it against the skull, looking like it had been slapped on.

"Talk to me," Nyquist said.

"My equipment isn't certain what killed him," Brodeur said. "One program believes it was blunt force trauma to the chest, another thinks it was a heart attack induced by severe pain, and a third program thinks he bled out."

Nyquist looked at Brodeur, feeling a bit stunned. Brodeur was *angry*.

"What I know is this, he was beaten badly and when the assailants left, they left him for dead. There's a lot of repairable damage here—if someone had gotten to him with the right equipment within the first twenty minutes."

"Meaning what?" Nyquist said.

"Some idiot lawyer tried to save him with one of those medical programs put out by funeral homes."

Nyquist closed his eyes. He remembered when those things had been banned in Armstrong, and he remembered why they had been banned.

"But that didn't kill him. At least the kid was trying. Zhu had one of those internal programs that repaired damage and did triage so that he could survive longer, at least until he got medical help. But that program was overcome within the first few minutes of the attack."

Nyquist was frowning. He had never heard Brodeur go on like this.

"What I'm telling you is this," Brodeur said. "This attack was so savage that it pretty much took care of every single emergency rescue nano program that we've all purchased."

Nyquist's frown grew deeper. "But he could have survived if he had gotten immediate help."

"Yes. The programs that Zhu had would have stabilized him enough to enable emergency workers to take care of the worst of it before he ever reached a hospital. The problem is that he didn't receive that kind of care."

"Why not?" Nyquist said.

"That's what you're going to figure out," Brodeur said. "It took three separate calls to emergency services to get an ambulance to show up, and I personally think that the only reason the ambulance did show up was that one of the callers was an attorney creative enough to go around the standard systems."

"An S³ attorney?"

"Yes, a new one," Brodeur said. "She's not even a native of the Moon." He waved a hand, as if dismissing that.

"This whole thing is screwed up and would be screwed up even if it weren't for this."

He pinched his fingers together and a gigantic hologram appeared in front of Nyquist, blocking his view of the body.

The hologram showed a street in one of the developing sections of Armstrong. The vid had a view of part of the building and the sidewalk. Zhu showed up, and then three attackers, their faces shielded, kicked his feet out from under him.

They beat him, using hands, feet, and clubs. One man jumped on Zhu's back, then on his head, then on his buttocks, clearly trying to break his spine. While the man was jumping, the woman kicked every single visible area of Zhu's body, and the other man stomped on Zhu's legs.

No one tried to stop the attack. No one even seemed to notice the attack.

The three beat him, then beat him again, and finally, when he was unresponsive, they slapped their hands together as if they had achieved a victory, and left the area as if nothing had happened.

Blood seeped out of Zhu and ran down the sidewalk. It seemed like forever later, but according to the time stamp it was only a few minutes, when a young man burst out the front door, carrying some kind of kit. Another young man and a woman followed.

Nyquist didn't recognize them.

Brodeur flicked his fingers and the image disappeared. "I'm going to give you this. I'm told by the three who tried to rescue Zhu that they recorded everything that happened from the moment they arrived on scene. You have the ambulance attendants who, by the way, did what they could, my arrival, and what I did on site. You also have all the attempted reports to the Armstrong Police Department."

"Attempted," Nyquist said.

"They were rebuffed by our systems. Apparently, someone had tampered with our system so that any calls from that area would be ignored, and anyone who mentioned Torkild Zhu or S³ would be rerouted elsewhere or flagged as a troublemaker who should be ignored."

Nyquist let out a small breath.

"How soon before the attack had that order come in?" he asked.

"That's another thing you get to figure out." Brodeur waved a hand over Zhu's body. "We might not like what S³ is doing here, but I have to tell you, Detective, no one deserves to die like that."

"Painful?" Nyquist asked.

"I don't know," Brodeur said. "Depends on his programs. At first, yes. He might have passed out. His pain receptors might have shut off. Or he might have felt every single blow. I have no idea. But I would guess that, yes, it was awful."

Nyquist stared at the body, nodding. He still had nightmares about that kind of pain. When he'd been attacked by the Bixian assassins, they had cut through his skin, sending terrible, mind-numbing agony through his nervous system. He'd managed to fight them off long enough to get rescued. The man he'd been with hadn't been that lucky.

Whenever anyone mentioned pain, Nyquist thought of those moments—as vivid now as they had been when the assassins attacked him.

"Everything you saw in that footage was police issue," Brodeur said.

"I know," Nyquist said softly.

"Then you should also know that when it became clear to someone here at the department that a coroner would need to go onsite, I was not in the rotation."

Nyquist looked over at him. Brodeur's cheeks were flushed and his eyes flashed.

"There were three more coroners who were slated to get the next deaths ahead of me. I did not jump the line, Detective. Someone jumped me to handle this case."

Nyquist bit his lower lip. Because the department thought Brodeur incompetent.

"I know my reputation," Brodeur said. "I know you people think I'm a screw-up. I know I was brought in to cloud the issues here, so that no one could get charged with this death. So I recorded everything I did, and I asked a friend of mine off-Moon, a respected coroner who has published the definitive book on modern forensics, to supervise me via link. She will testify that I have done the best autopsy she's seen under the circumstances."

Nyquist nodded. He was impressed. He hadn't expected the self-awareness or the creativity from Brodeur.

"We're being manipulated, Detective," Brodeur said. "This man died horribly. If you're not offended by that, then I'll contact Andrea Gumiela myself and get you taken off this case. You need to be outraged, not because Zhu was handling defendants we don't believe in, but because this man was killed for doing his job, a job we need in a civilized society. We may not like what he was doing, but he didn't have to be slaughtered for it, and his death swept under the rug as if he were no more important than a bit of dirt."

"I agree," Nyquist said. "I'll do the best job I can."

"Good," Brodeur said. "I suggest you get an off-Moon shadow, like I did. This case needs to be handled perfectly, and we humans are imperfect creatures."

"Yeah," Nyquist said softly.

He had underestimated Brodeur. It seemed everyone had.

He extended his hand.

"I'll do everything I can, Ethan," Nyquist said. "I promise you that."

"Good," Brodeur said, as he shook once before letting go. "Because I'll hold you to it. I've seen enough senseless death lately. I don't want to see it promulgated by my own colleagues."

"I feel the same way," Nyquist said, looking at that battered body. "Believe me, I feel *exactly* the same way."

27

FLINT WAS BEGINNING TO THINK THE ARMSTRONG COMFORT CENTER WAS misnamed. He certainly didn't feel calm or comfortable whenever he arrived here.

This time, he found himself in a waiting room done in pale lime green with darker wood than the blue waiting room had had. The art was some kind of Impressionistic wannabe thing, done with actual oil and brushes. He could see the imprint of the brush tip on the canvas in varying shades of green, and somehow none of it was coalescing into an image for him.

He wondered if that was on purpose, like those sensory tests done to evaluate someone's mood.

His mood wasn't great. He didn't even sit in the dark green chairs scattered around the room. He paced, which was what he had done the last time he was here.

Pacing and comfort—somehow those didn't go together for him.

Then the door opened, and Llewynn beckoned him. The man actually looked harried, his hair slightly mussed and his eyes darker than they had been before.

He had none of that fake comfort about him today.

Flint followed him through that mazelike corridor, finally ending up at Llewynn's office. Its cream-and-brown coloring didn't calm Flint, either. He glanced at the chair across from Llewynn's captain's chair and wondered what had gone wrong while his daughter was here to cause this kind of concern.

"Thanks for coming on such short notice," Llewynn said as he sat in the captain's chair.

Flint had no real choice but to sit in the other chair. He leaned back, letting the chair conform to his body shape, much as he hated chairs like this.

"You made it sound urgent," Flint said.

Llewynn nodded. "Your daughter cut our session short."

"That doesn't surprise me," Flint said. "I told her she could leave if she wanted to. I didn't want her to feel trapped here."

He didn't add that he wanted to her to protect herself as best she could, and if she couldn't really stop some of Llewynn's probing questions, then she should simply take control of the interview.

Sometimes controlling an interview meant terminating it.

"Look, Mr. Flint, you brought your daughter here because of her deep emotional distress." Llewynn entwined his fingers together, but this time, his thumbs kept moving. He seemed so upset that he couldn't stop fidgeting.

Flint sighed inwardly. He knew why he had brought Talia there, and he didn't like Llewynn's need to recap. But Flint was going to wait it out.

"We both understand that she is not the girl she was six months ago," Llewynn said, as if he had known her. As if he understood her.

Flint almost told him to get to the point. But he was going to give the man one more sentence before he interrupted.

"But after this morning, I'm convinced she's a danger to others."

Flint leaned back in the chair, shocked to his core.

"To *others*?" he repeated. He wouldn't have been surprised if Llewynn said that she was a danger to herself. That was Flint's greatest fear.

But to *others*? How was that possible?

Llewynn took a deep breath. "I'm not sure how to broach this with you, Mr. Flint, so I'm simply going to be blunt. Right now, your daughter is empathizing with the clones."

Flint blinked, unable to make the mental leap. Of course Talia empathized with clones. She *was* a clone.

But Llewynn didn't know that.

"Which clones?" Flint asked.

"All clones," Llewynn said. "Charitably, I'd like to say she doesn't understand how dangerous they are, but honestly, I think she does understand. She still views clones with sympathy and thinks they're misunderstood."

Flint felt his cheeks heat. He wasn't sure how to ask what had transpired in this room.

"And why do you think that makes her dangerous?" he asked.

"She doesn't understand that clones are unthinking weapons," Llewynn said.

Flint was careful not to move.

"She seems to believe that clones have some humanity. She even said that the clones were not as bad as PierLuigi Frémont."

"She did?" Flint asked, because he couldn't believe it. Had Talia been talking about *all* clones while this man had been talking about the Frémont clones?

"Yes," Llewynn said. "She seemed to believe that clones were redeemable creatures, maybe even admirable creatures, and that they weren't weapons at all."

"She knows that clones attacked the Moon twice," Flint said carefully.

"She knows that, and apparently thinks nothing of it." Llewynn's hands were still rubbing together. "I've seen this before, Mr. Flint. Sometimes victims of major trauma absorb the trauma in the wrong way, and it leads to violent acting out, maybe even repeating the trauma on someone less powerful. I'm terrified that your daughter might hurt a lot of people."

"Are you actually saying you think she might blow something up?" Flint asked.

"I don't know," Llewynn said. "It's a possibility. There are a lot of possibilities and none of them good."

Flint was shaking his head. He made himself stop.

Llewynn leaned forward, his hands so tightly clasped now that his knuckles were turning white.

"Under the law," Llewynn said, "it's my responsibility to tell you that she is a danger. If she weren't underage, I would be going directly to the authorities. I'm duty bound to report any threats that I hear that might result in loss of life."

"My daughter threatened someone?" Flint asked, wondering if Talia's temper made her threaten Llewynn.

"No," Llewynn said. "I'll be honest: had she done so, I would have gone directly to the law. But I feel I have a bit of leeway here, since she is underage, and the threat I feel is indirect at the moment."

Flint willed himself to remain calm. This man was going to call the police on Flint's daughter? Because she had defended clones in general?

Then he realized he had no idea what exactly had transpired.

"Perhaps you should tell me what she said," he said calmly.

"I can't, Mr. Flint," Llewynn said. "She didn't sign off on that. You agreed that we wouldn't have to share everything with you. So I would need her permission to tell you exactly what our conversation was."

Wonderful, Flint thought but didn't say.

"Trust me when I tell you that she was positively chilling. To make matters worse, she made it clear she would not return. I'm afraid she's now angrier than she was before and she will harm someone sooner rather than later."

"I see," Flint said. "So what will your next steps be?"

"I am speaking to you. If I feel that you are not taking me seriously, then I will talk to law enforcement. I know they're overburdened at the moment, but I'm sure they will listen about another attack."

"I am a former police detective, Mr. Llewynn," Flint said. "I work closely with the Armstrong Police Department still. Right now, they're understaffed and trying to deal with the attacks that happen on the Moon. I can guarantee that if you report Talia for some vague threat, they won't respond."

"Are you threatening me, Mr. Flint?" Llewynn said.

This man was impossible.

"No," Flint said in his placate-the-crazy-person voice. "I am telling you that from my experiences with the Armstrong PD, going to them right now will not help my daughter or alleviate the threat. Clearly, something happened in your session that chilled you. I take that very seriously. Since the police are overburdened and not an option at the moment, what options do you see that are available to us?"

Llewynn leaned back slowly, unthreaded his hands, and wiped them on his knees. He was obviously trying to assess what Flint was telling him, and how sincere Flint was.

"If you bring her back here, we can find her another counselor—"

"I know my daughter," Flint said. "If she walked out of here in anger, bringing her back will only make her angrier. Are there other therapists you recommend? Maybe a different Comfort Center or perhaps a personal tutor who can assist her?"

Not that Flint would ever hire them, but he wanted Llewynn to believe he was cooperating.

"I'm afraid not," Llewynn said. "Every place in Armstrong is overburdened, to use your word, and there are no places that are as effective as ours."

Flint let out a small sigh. "I can't bring her back here, and I can't have her locked up. Maybe somewhere else on the Moon….?"

"The trauma the Moon has suffered is so deep that some counselors are actually leaving the business right now. They're not equipped for this kind of grief work," Llewynn said. "Many of them believe that the crisis has affected their judgment, and are turning their companies over to guest therapists. Thank heavens Armstrong was untouched, so that we didn't have to do something like that here. My people have been heavily monitored, and they're doing just fine."

Like you? Flint thought but didn't say. Clearly Llewynn wasn't fine, and he was about to sacrifice Flint's daughter on the altar of his post-traumatic stress disorder or whatever the crisis had unleashed inside him.

"I can't bring her back here," Flint said. "I can keep her occupied twenty-four hours per day. I can make sure that someone is watching her. She knows I'm worried about security at the moment."

Llewynn nodded. "That's good until she stops being watched. And then she'll do some kind of harm."

"Perhaps there's some place on Earth that I can send her? Surely, there has to be some other counseling center that you would recommend." Flint kept his voice calm. He had separated himself from his emotions. He had to: otherwise, he might harm this asshole.

"I can send you a list," Llewynn said, sounding a little less agitated. "The therapeutic tradition began on Earth and continues to thrive there."

He frowned, then looked down at his hands, still clutching his knees.

Flint waited. The man was still not thinking clearly.

Then Llewynn lifted his head. "I think it's wise to take your daughter from the Moon. A change of venue might calm her and it'll certainly get rid of the daily reminders of her trauma. That, plus the assistance of one of the counselors I recommend, might help her heal."

If only that were true, Flint thought. He wished things could have been different. But he had gone for the traditional solution, even though his intuition had told him Talia was the wrong candidate for it.

He was disappointed that this gamble hadn't worked; he wanted to help his daughter. But if Llewynn hadn't contacted Flint, things might have gotten a lot worse.

If Llewynn believed that Flint wasn't going to take his advice, things could still get a lot worse.

Flint stood and extended his hand, even though he didn't really want to touch Llewynn. "Thank you. I promise I will get this resolved."

Llewynn stood as well. He took Flint's hand and shook it with some kind of weird emphasis.

"I'm so relieved you're listening to me on this," Llewynn said. "Often I have to convince parents to go past their instincts."

"I'm a former police officer," Flint said, removing his hand from the shake ever so gently. He resisted the urge to wipe his palm on his pants. "I've seen what happens when parents don't listen to warnings."

"I'm sure you have," Llewynn said. "I'll send you a heavily notated list later this afternoon. Good luck, Mr. Flint."

"Thank you," Flint said sincerely. He would need the luck. He had no idea how he could help his daughter. He did know that Llewynn was right about one thing: he had to keep trying.

Or he might lose Talia forever.

28

Nyquist took Brodeur's warning seriously. As Nyquist made his way to the crime scene, he thought about bringing on an investigator to shadow him.

And he couldn't come up with any name at all.

Everyone he knew and trusted on the Moon was already working on the bigger picture—solving the crimes that were destroying Nyquist's home. He didn't want to take anyone he knew away from that.

He knew of others off-Moon, but no one he really trusted. Besides, if he had to share links—even encrypted ones—given what was happening on the Moon, he was afraid the investigation might become *more* compromised, not less.

Gumiela trusted him to handle this.

He would document everything, make fantastic backups, and keep them at the security office—and maybe even ask Flint to store some backups.

That way, if things got too dicey or too corrupt, Nyquist had options besides his own department.

A few years ago, he might have been as saddened as Brodeur over the corruption in the department. But Nyquist didn't feel as idealistic as he once had. After all, he had barely avoided dying in a bomb blast instigated by a lawyer he had once recommended to people. He had investigated the assassination of the Mayor and seen more footage of destruction than he ever wanted to see again.

He had also seen the good-hearted people he knew get crushed by exhaustion and emotional overload as they tried to cope with this crisis.

Yes, he wished what was happening in the Armstrong Police Department wasn't happening, but he would have been naïve if he expected the PD to go about its work unaffected.

In some respects, it was a miracle that so few officers had gone off—at least in the short term.

Even he didn't want to investigate this crime. He felt it was not as important as anything else he had to do right now.

Bartholomew Nyquist, the detective who occasionally made that fatuous speech, the one about each life being worth something. The detective who had done his best to avoid dealing with crimes involving aliens because he might have to make the kinds of choices that had driven Miles Flint from the department.

That Nyquist had now actually evaluated a life and deemed it less worthy of investigation than other lives.

He wondered if Torkild Zhu's family would understand.

Nyquist bet that families of the Peyti Crisis and Anniversary Day victims *would* understand.

He also knew that Gumiela was right: S³ would be all over this. It was amazing they weren't already.

And he really wished that motivated him enough to do a good job on this investigation.

In actuality, all he wanted to do was wrap up this case and return to the bombings. On the drive to S³'s offices, he considered resigning from the department so that he could help DeRicci full time.

But the only access he had to Uzvaan and the prison had come through his police ties.

And besides, he was a detective first. Before his world literally exploded, he had realized that working for the Armstrong PD was the center of his identity, something he did not want to give up.

He wasn't sure that was true any longer, but he had to factor in one other aspect of his life now: his identity as an Armstrong PD detective was one of the last things remaining from the old world. He wasn't sure he wanted to give that up.

Somehow he had talked himself into focusing on this investigation by the time he got to the area near S³'s offices.

He parked several blocks from the crime scene. He had noted on the footage that Zhu had walked a few blocks to get to the S³ offices. Zhu was carrying a disposable coffee mug with the name of a deli on the side.

The deli was open and doing a brisk business, but not as brisk as the deli next door. The scent of coffee and baked bread would have normally enticed Nyquist to enter one or the other place, but he wasn't hungry at the moment.

At some point, he would interview the staff of both delis to see if they witnessed anything. Right now, however, it was more important for him to retrace Zhu's steps and make certain that everything on that footage Brodeur had given him seemed accurate. The last thing Nyquist wanted to do was interview people at the deli only to discover that Zhu had been using the same disposable cup for days.

The walk to S³ was short. The street was empty, and the buildings had that neglected look much of Armstrong had these days. A check on his networks showed that there were a lot of low-level legal services available in this neighborhood, and quite a few law-related businesses.

Almost every single law firm and law-related business had been shut down since the Peyti Crisis. In some cases, the firms were shut down because they'd lost staff. In others, they were shut down because one of their lawyers had tried to attack Armstrong.

The entire Moon-based legal community was in complete disarray. Which made S³'s arrival a few days ago seem even more astounding.

Nyquist hadn't liked Zhu, and he had been offended that Zhu slapped injunctions on law enforcement. Zhu's firm was, in its own way, guaranteeing that these massive crimes would not get solved.

Anyone with half a brain would know that killing Zhu wouldn't prevent the machinations of S^3. If anything, S^3 would probably become more determined in its war against law enforcement because of Zhu's death.

But thinking didn't seem to be anyone's strong suit this week. That meeting with all the detectives the day before had left Nyquist unsettled. Most of them hadn't been interested in solving the Peyti Crisis; they'd been interested in getting revenge.

And clearly, someone had taken revenge on Zhu.

Nyquist sighed and looked down the long block that led to the brand new offices of S^3 On The Moon. The building looked a little rundown. A human security guard stood at the door, arms crossed.

He hadn't been on the footage, at least that Nyquist had seen.

And if he had been around, then Zhu's attack made no sense.

Nyquist ignored the guard for a moment, and scanned the rest of the area. There were no crime scene lasers, nothing to block off the sidewalk where Zhu died, even though Brodeur had set the lasers up.

He had left everything in the best shape possible for the crime scene techs and he had waited until they arrived before leaving with Zhu's body.

That meant that the scene should have remained off-limits for at least 24-hours.

Nyquist's stomach turned.

No one was following the rules here, and that would just make his job harder.

He crossed the street, and approached the guard. The sidewalk still had a long, black stain running down it—Zhu's blood mixed with coffee, as it flowed away from the building. There was even a bit of a body-shaped depression in the thin layer of Moon dust that every public place in Armstrong seemed to attract.

The guard watched him approach. The guard was a tall, burly man with broad shoulders and large muscles straining against his clothing. The muscles looked real and not enhanced.

He was cradling a laser rifle, which flashed its registration on a police link as Nyquist approached.

The guard was with one of the biggest security firms on the Moon.

Nyquist raised his right palm as if he were going to take an oath in court. He made the badge embedded into his skin flare so brightly that it would show up on security vids.

The guard stopped cradling the rifle. He moved his hands along it, so that he could aim it at Nyquist if necessary.

In all his years on the force, he'd never had this response to his approach before.

He supposed it made sense, though, since it was clear that Zhu's murderers were cops.

"I'm no threat to you," Nyquist said, keeping his hand up. "I'm investigating Torkild Zhu's murder."

"Go back to your office," the guard said. "The killer's there."

"I know," Nyquist said. "But I couldn't see any faces on the security vid I had. So I know what type of person did the crime. I just don't know *who*."

"So?" the guard asked.

"So, I need to do a thorough and accurate investigation. I'm sure that S³ would want the killers to be punished, and that means I have to go by the book."

The guard grunted, and shifted his hands slightly. "What do you gotta do?"

Nyquist came closer, palm still up. He felt a little ridiculous, but he also knew that he was on security vid. So he wanted to make sure that everything he did was correct.

"My name is Bartholomew Nyquist," he said. "I'm a detective with the Armstrong Police Department, and I had nothing to do with what happened here this morning. In fact, I wasn't even inside the dome when it happened."

"Good for you," the guard said in a tone that implied he didn't care.

"Were you here this morning?" Nyquist asked.

"You're kidding, right?" the guard asked.

"No." Nyquist kept his tone calm.

"My firm got hired after this poor guy died. I came as quickly as I could. We'll have more security here starting in a few hours."

So it was good that Nyquist arrived when he had.

"I'd like to investigate the scene," he said, "and then I'd like to talk with anyone who was here at the time of the death."

"You can't pin this murder on S³." That was a different voice. It was female, and it broadcast over the building's security link.

Nyquist couldn't see the speaker. Obviously she was inside somewhere.

He looked up, scanning for the camera. He knew roughly where it was, based on the footage he had seen, but he didn't know exactly.

"I'm not trying to pin it on anyone here," he said to the woman, whoever she was. "It's clear that Torkild Zhu died outside the building and no one from S³ had anything to do with his murder. As I told the guard here—"

"I know," the woman said. "You need to follow the book. Too bad your colleagues didn't."

"Yes," Nyquist said. "It is."

"It's unusual that a cop shows up without a partner, isn't it?" she asked.

He wished he could see her. "I'll tell you why face-to-face," he said. "I'm not going to shout to the entire street."

"The entire *empty* street," she said, and then went silent.

The guard had raised his eyebrows, as if he were impressed by her forcefulness.

Nyquist wasn't. He had known he would encounter resistance here. He just hadn't expected it right away.

Maybe he still was a bit of an innocent.

He looked at the guard.

"I'm going to walk the scene," Nyquist said. "I'll be recording my every move, and I'll be backing this up outside of my internal system."

"So the police can delete it?" the guard asked.

"I'm not that dumb," Nyquist said. "I was just letting you know what I was doing and why, so that you don't interrupt me."

The guard let out a snide half-laugh. "If you think it'll do any good."

Of course it wouldn't do any good. Torkild Zhu was already dead. S^3 had already declared war on law enforcement here in Armstrong, and Armstrong's law enforcement community had struck back. Ill advisedly, but they had.

Now, Nyquist had to straddle the two, and make it all work.

On top of everything else.

He nodded at the guard, and began to record.

29

GOUDKINS STUDIED DERICCI FOR A MOMENT. DERICCI STIFLED ANOTHER burp. She surreptitiously brushed a chip on her stomach with her thumb. The chip released a soother to calm her stomach. If she used the damn chip too much, it would notify a doctor or stop working, and she wondered if she had reached that level yet. She really hadn't been taking care of herself at all. She glanced at the couch, and thought of the way it tempted her with a nap.

"You weren't kidding when you said this would be dangerous," Goudkins said.

"I meant it would be dangerous on a lot of levels," DeRicci said. She really hadn't thought of the personal danger to Goudkins. DeRicci didn't care if someone got harmed getting information, at least, not at the moment. Maybe she would have six months ago.

Goudkins was frowning.

"To be frank," DeRicci said, "I'm a lot more concerned about increasing the danger to the Moon than I am about either of us."

Blunt, as always. It had gotten her in trouble from the beginning of her career, and now that she was the last person standing, it was probably going to prevent Goudkins from working with her.

"Yeah." Goudkins nodded. "I'm being stupid. There's so much at stake here and I'm worried what'll happen to me if I get caught. As if the universe was the same place it had always been."

DeRicci's gaze met hers. The sad truth was that the universe *was* the same place it had always been. The Moon was different. *They* were different. Maybe the Alliance was different.

But probably not.

"You haven't given me the name," Goudkins said.

"I'm only giving it to you if you're actually going to help us."

"Of course I'm going to help, Chief DeRicci. I lost..." Then Goudkins shook her head. "I know how serious this is. I know how dangerous it is. I told you I'd help."

"Then you have to be cautious," DeRicci said. "You can't tell Ostaka, you can't work with our links here in the office, you have to work somewhere that looks like a non-Moon based location. Can you do that?"

"Of course," Goudkins said.

"All right." DeRicci took a deep breath. Trust didn't come easily to her, especially on something that had this kind of stakes. "You're looking for a woman named Jhena Andre. She initially worked in a lower-level position at the prison that housed PierLuigi Frémont. She was there on the night he died, and according to our source, she took some of Frémont's DNA. She's never tried to sell it, and we don't know what happened to it."

Goudkins was frowning. "How do you know she still has it?"

"We don't," DeRicci said. "We're on the thinnest of threads here. But every time she gets contacted about the DNA by the person who helped her steal it, she tells that person not to contact her again."

"She doesn't deny that she has any?" Goudkins asked.

DeRicci shook her head. "She's also not defensive about being contacted. Now, that might be because she's one of those completely unflappable people who has worked so long in the underbelly of the Alliance that she really doesn't care what other people think. But the folks I've been talking to think that she has it, and isn't surprised when she's asked about it, and she's playing every angle she can think of."

"What do you think?" Goudkins asked softly.

DeRicci liked the question. It was the kind of question a good investigator asked to get a sense of the person she was talking to.

DeRicci could have avoided it, and let Goudkins make her own conclusion. But she didn't.

"I think we've hit a pattern," DeRicci said. "Every time we get a lead, it takes us to someone in the Alliance, and we either shut down or assume that this person couldn't be involved."

Goudkins folded her hands together. She tilted her head slightly in a sympathetic listening posture.

Also good.

"I think right now, we have to rule out Andre as a source of the DNA. She might have sold it decades ago. She might have disposed of it that night. Or she might be using it herself. But," DeRicci said, "we need to know."

Her words hung in the air for a moment.

"All right," Goudkins said. Not *I agree*, not *that makes sense*, but *all right*, as if there were nothing more to add.

She started to stand.

"Wait," DeRicci said. "We have one other lead for you to check out."

She hadn't meant to use the word "we," but it was out there now. She guessed there was a "we." Her, Nyquist, Flint, maybe even (although she didn't like it) Deshin.

Goudkins sat back down, and looked expectant, so DeRicci launched into it.

"We've been investigating the clones," DeRicci said, deliberately not being specific about the Peyti clones or Uzvaan. "And one of the things that we've discovered is that they were raised to believe failure caused death."

"I'm not sure what that means," Goudkins said.

"They were raised in groups, and if someone failed, that person was killed." DeRicci didn't add that the clone was killed by the other clones.

"Harsh," Goudkins said.

"Yes," DeRicci said. "Here's the thing: the Peyti clones became lawyers, many of them defense attorneys, which meant that a goodly number of them went through the Impossibles."

Goudkins frowned. "I thought the point of the Impossibles was to teach that many cases were unwinnable."

"Something like that," DeRicci said. She had never given the Impossibles a lot of thought. "Since these Peyti clones couldn't handle failure, we decided to find out how they managed to survive the Impossibles. One clone mentioned that he had a mentor—"

"You spoke to a Peyti clone?" Goudkins asked. "I thought we were enjoined against it."

"We are," DeRicci said, "and I didn't. I got this information from someone else."

Goudkins had a slightly incredulous smile on her face. "You have a source."

"You could say that," DeRicci said, not willing to give up any more information on Uzvaan. "We don't know how many Peyti clones this mentor handled or protected at the Impossibles. All we have is a name, and the fact that she was there several decades ago."

"Another woman," Goudkins said.

DeRicci nodded. She hadn't thought of that and wondered if it was significant. She would let Goudkins figure that out.

"Her name is—or was—Mavis Zorn. She's human. I'd like you to track her down, maybe even talk to her if you can, and figure out what she does or doesn't know. But be discrete."

"I got that part," Goudkins said. "She might have been a pawn, you know."

"Yes, I do," DeRicci said. "If I understood the Impossibles, I could say for certain. But I don't know, and I have no idea how all this works."

"I'll investigate both of these," Goudkins said. "But which do you think is the one I should focus on first?"

"Andre," DeRicci said. "If we can find the source of that DNA, we might be able to trace everything."

"All right," Goudkins said. "How often do you want me to report to you?"

"Every few days if you don't have anything," DeRicci said. "And immediately if you do."

"Got it."

Goudkins stood. Then she bowed her head, just a little.

"Thank you," she said. "I value your trust."

I hope it wasn't misplaced, DeRicci thought but didn't say. She stood too.

"Let's hope one of these investigations pays off," she said—and wished she knew exactly what that meant.

30

As a young detective, Nyquist had learned to walk the grid of a crime scene. Ironically, the old timers who trained him told him to use bots and crime scene cleaners to find whatever had been left behind— from tiny trace evidence of all types to almost invisible DNA.

Bots were useful. They got all kinds of evidence human beings could not see. But humans often noted things at a crime scene that no bot would ever catch. And a dedicated detective with a trained eye saw even more.

It wouldn't have taken much to sneak up on Zhu. If people were tailing him, they could have walked softly and jumped him. Nyquist's standard-issue shoes made almost no sound on the sidewalk.

He walked back and forth, stopping to pick up several small things and placing them in evidence bags that he always carried. He used to think he was obsessive about evidence bags, but this habit had often turned out to be a very useful one, and it was useful now.

He found what looked like a decorative button, a small swatch of silk— maybe from Zhu's suit—and a plastic toothpick. He found some spatter that he made sure he recorded. He found a splash of liquid along the sidewalk heading toward the door (the bulk of the liquid had gone toward the street).

At the edge of his grid, as he turned the corner to start back toward the building's door, he found a light brown heel of a shoe, curved just a little with only a little lift.

He used the bag itself to pick that one up. The heel of the shoe looked awfully similar to heels on his shoes.

He found half a dozen other small items that seemed less promising.

He stood over that body shape in the light film of Moon dust, noted the other footprints around it, wondered if anyone had recorded this during the crisis. This was the kind of detail that Brodeur often overlooked.

Nyquist made sure he didn't.

Then he peered at the drying liquid trail that flowed toward the street. A stir stick was in the middle of it all, but it seemed to be the only non-expected item in that little river of liquid.

He recorded all of it, then removed the stir stick, careful to keep the blood/coffee mix on it.

He placed the bags in his pockets, then glanced down the street. Technically, he should place everything in his car, but he didn't want to leave the area—not yet, anyway.

"Stealing from a crime scene?" That voice belonged to the woman again.

He turned, only because it was instinct to turn in the direct of a voice, fully expecting to be talking to the speakers again.

Instead, a slight woman stood behind him. She had light brown skin, a small nose, and lovely, dark eyes. She wore a dress covered with a long jacket, which would have looked stunning if it weren't for the grime on her knees and the front of her shoes. She'd been crouching or kneeling, perhaps in the light coating of Moon dust that he was currently standing in.

She had her hands on her hips, and her mouth was turned downward, negating some of the impact of those dramatic eyes.

"First," he said in his most patient voice, "a police officer assigned to a crime scene can't steal from it, although he can violate procedure, which I am not. Second, this is not an official crime scene."

"Yes, it is," she said quickly.

"There are no crime scene lasers, and there weren't when I arrived. I have footage to prove that."

She lifted her chin slightly. She knew he was telling the truth about that.

He decided to go for a long shot. "Did you remove the lasers that the coroner set up?"

"No," she said flatly.

"Who did?" he asked.

Her gaze flicked toward the guard. *She* hadn't removed the lasers, but the guard had.

When he saw her react to a technicality, Nyquist knew he was talking to a lawyer, probably someone from S³.

"I'm Bartholomew Nyquist," he said.

"I know," she said flatly.

"The customary response is to introduce yourself in turn," he said.

She took a deep breath, then released it slowly, as if he irritated her. He probably did.

"Melcia Seng," she said. "I work at S³."

"I figured," he said. "You're the one who called in the ambulance."

"Among other things," she said.

"And you let your new employee here take down our crime scene? That was strange."

Her lips thinned. She did not respond, which was probably a good thing. It might protect some of the integrity of what Nyquist found.

"Ethan Brodeur is working with me," Nyquist said, figuring she knew the coroner's name from all Brodeur had said. "He told me that you have more footage of what happened today. I'd like a copy."

"So you can destroy it?" she asked.

It was Nyquist's turn to sigh. "You need to pay attention to detail," he said. "I asked for *a copy*. You get to keep the originals."

At least for now. But he wasn't going to add that. He didn't want to alienate her any more than necessary.

"We have more," she said. "A lot more."

He nodded. "Good. I'd like it all. I will be taking the security video from this building as well. I have a warrant for that. If you want copies of that, I suggest you contact someone right now to copy it for you."

"No need," she said. "We've been copying and archiving all day."

Excellent. She told him more than he had asked for, without him posing the question directly.

In other words, they had footage of everything that happened from the moment Zhu showed up on the security footage, carrying his coffee. Nyquist could think of that as a problem—which, considering it was S³, he would have thought a few months ago—or he could look at it as a way of protecting his investigation.

Brodeur had told him to get a shadow. He had one, at least on the important information.

It was S³ itself.

She was studying him. "How do I know that you'll investigate this case? How do I know you won't just make it disappear?"

"You don't," Nyquist said. "You have no reason to trust the police right now. I saw the same footage you did. It's clear that whoever killed Torkild Zhu was either a group of police officers or someone who had access to regulation police equipment. Normally, I would be investigating theft of regulation equipment. But I don't think this case is normal."

"Why not?" she asked, sounding intrigued even though it was clear she didn't want to.

"Because Zhu had, in a few short days, become the public face of S³. And you folks are interfering not just with a police investigation, but with solving the biggest crimes to ever occur on the Moon."

"That's your opinion," Seng said.

"That's not just my opinion," he said. "I think everyone in law enforcement here and off-Moon believes it."

She squared her shoulders. "What does that matter?"

"Emotions are high here right now. We've lost a lot of friends. We've been under a lot of strain. We've been betrayed by people we trust."

"Such excuses," she said.

Anger flashed through him. He did his best to keep it under control. He hoped he didn't show just how deeply she had gotten to him.

"I'm not making excuses," he said as calmly as he could. "I'm stating facts. The fact is that S³ has provoked an already volatile community. Which is why the chief of detectives put me in charge of this investigation."

"So you can sweep it under the rug?" Seng asked.

"Because I'm the only person she knows who won't," Nyquist said.

Seng studied him for a moment, as if she could see through him and know whether or not he was speaking the truth.

Finally, she said, "It's wrong for the police to murder anyone."

"I agree," Nyquist said.

"I don't feel right cooperating with you," she said.

"I know," he said. He wanted to add that she should anyway—it was the only way to figure out who exactly killed Torkild Zhu.

"If you find those cops," she said, "what'll happen to them?"

"They'll be arrested," he said.

"So?" she asked. "Then what?"

"They'll be treated like any other murderer," he said.

She looked away at that moment, and he wondered if he lost her. Then she glanced at the ground where Zhu had been.

"Shouldn't they be treated worse?" she asked quietly.

"If you believe that," Nyquist said, "then you believe that the Peyti clones should be treated worse than other murderers as well."

"Do you believe that?"

"Intellectually or emotionally?" he asked.

She grinned. The look surprised him. Then she shook her head.

"Touché, Detective."

He nodded once. "Let me have your footage. I'd also like to interview everyone who saw or responded to the attack. Can you do that?"

She crossed her arms tightly, almost as if she were hugging herself. "You can interview me," she said, "and I'll give you the footage. As for the others, they have to decide for themselves."

"Fair enough," Nyquist said. "Fair enough."

31

NERVES JUMPED IN GOUDKINS' STOMACH AS SHE HEADED BACK TO THE room everyone called the central conference room, but which she privately referred to as her office. She and Ostaka had been working in this place ever since Popova banned them from reception before the Peyti Crisis.

Since then, they had taken over the entire room.

It was comfortable, with windows on all four sides. The windows opened onto the corridors, but that didn't matter. It made Goudkins feel like she was in the center of everything.

Apparently, the room had initially been designed for Popova, but she hadn't been able to see the elevators from here, so she moved into what Goudkins would have called the hallway. Popova had to control everything when it came to who was on the floor and where they were going.

In the offices where Goudkins usually worked, some kind of android handled reception.

Popova was too important for reception—she was DeRicci's right hand (and more)—but she needed to know everything happening on the floor, maybe even in Armstrong, and she felt that this room was simply too isolated.

It was a little isolated, which was why Goudkins relaxed a little here. She could get work done without being bothered.

Although after the meeting with DeRicci, Goudkins knew that her days in this particular office were numbered. She couldn't do the kind of research that DeRicci wanted from here. It would be traced back to the Moon.

Goudkins would have to do the research from her ship, which was dicey all by itself. She had sworn she wouldn't let Ostaka know what she was doing. They didn't share a ship; they had arrived at different times from different places, but because they were partners on this case, they had access to each other's ships.

And, in theory, both partners kept track of each other.

Ostaka was hunched over a screen, a steaming cup of coffee beside him. He was the only person in the building who looked like he hadn't missed a meal or a night's sleep. He said that was because he'd been through a lot of tight situations before, and he was used to them.

Goudkins believed he looked—and stayed—calm because he had nothing to care about here. He hadn't lost anyone on the Moon during Anniversary Day, like she had, and he counted the Peyti Crisis as a win, even though there had been a lot of collateral damage.

He really hadn't been that involved on the day of the crisis either, so he hadn't seen everything in real time.

She wondered if it would have affected him; she had no idea. Even after weeks of working with him, she didn't know what he did or didn't feel passionate about. He had no real family anywhere, although she had no idea if he had had a family once, and he was tight-lipped about his friends.

He was one of those people who had become all about the job and, in her opinion, it showed.

"Did you find out what happened to the Peyti clones off-Moon?" she asked as she slid a screen toward her. She would probably do some preliminary set up here, then claim she needed to investigate with their secure systems…if she told him what she was doing at all.

He looked up at her, a frown on his face. "Why would I do that?"

"Because it's important," Goudkins said.

He shrugged. "The presence of those clones off Moon got reported up the food chain. I'm sure that someone took care of it. We don't need to double-check everyone's work."

Her breath caught. "I think we do. Other people could die if there's going to be a second attack with those clones, and people off the Moon don't seem to understand how serious this all is."

You don't seem to understand how serious this all is, she almost added, but didn't. It was hard to keep quiet about his attitude. She didn't want to alienate him further.

"It's not our job," he said, looking down. "We're investigating here."

"The chief asked us—

"And we don't work for her," Ostaka snapped. "You might do well to remember that."

Goudkins cheeks warmed. "I thought we decided to work together so we wouldn't duplicate investigations," she said after a moment.

He shrugged again. Whatever was on the screen seemed a lot more important to him than this conversation.

"Lawrence," she said. "We agreed—"

"You're too emotionally involved." He didn't even look up as he said that. "I've already reported that to headquarters. You really are paying attention to the wrong things."

She crossed her arms. "You want to tell me what you're doing? What you've discovered? Because as far as I can tell, you haven't made a single breakthrough in any of these cases."

"I'm reviewing entry logs for the port," he said. "I'm tracking the Frémont clones."

"Back to where?" she asked, even though she knew the answer. She had tracked them on the way here. The ships had come from a variety of places, and the Frémont clones had met here. What he was investigating had already led Goudkins nowhere.

"I figure we look at how they paid for their transport."

"I already did that," she said. "So did the Port of Armstrong. We've come up with nothing. You're duplicating a five-month-old investigation."

He raised his head, looking at her over the screen. "Reviewing old work for missed information is a legitimate investigation tactic. In fact, it should be done on cases like this where the initial investigators were too tired, too stressed, and too emotional to do a good job."

She let out a small breath. "You're serious."

He nodded.

"The Moon's been attacked twice, and all you can think to do is repeat investigations that are closed. You're not following new leads and you're not doing anything of value."

"That's your opinion," he said, "and as I noted when I reported to headquarters, you're too emotionally involved to have any clear-eyed view of any investigation."

She remained quiet for a long moment, not trusting herself to speak. If she said anything, she would sound as emotionally off the beam as he accused her of being.

When she could trust her voice, she said, "No wonder you're always available for the next job. You have no ability to see beyond your own ego. You're one of those little men who are so insecure about their own abilities that the only way you can succeed is by tearing down others."

His eyebrows went up. Had no one spoken to him like this before?

"Well," she said, "a person like you might do well in standard investigations. But this one isn't standard. It involves millions of lost lives, and a lot of work to prevent another attack. You pride yourself on being the only one who sees everything clearly, but you see nothing. You only want the next promotion."

His mouth twisted into a condescending smile. "You have no control over my career. We're colleagues. You're not my boss."

"No," she said. "I'm not, so I'm not going to worry about the way you waste your time. I'll just request another partner. Excuse me."

She left the room and made herself breathe deeply. And then she smiled.

A real smile.

She had recorded their entire conversation, which would help in her request to replace him. Even if he had been reporting bad things on her, it didn't matter. His contempt would get him taken off this job.

But all of that mattered even less than the gift he had just given her. His ego had just enabled her to work on her ship with the secure connection, and not explain why she needed to.

He would think she was doing it just to tattle on him—and, truth be told, she was. But she would stay there and investigate all the things that DeRicci had asked for, because, unlike Ostaka, Goudkins believed in cooperation.

She and DeRicci wanted the same thing.

They wanted to solve these attacks on the Moon.

They wanted to prevent another attack on the Moon.

And they wanted to keep the Alliance stable.

Ostaka might say he wanted those things, but it would only be lip service. He really wanted to keep moving up in the bureaucracy—and he didn't care who he stepped on to do it.

He might have stepped on her these last few weeks, but he had picked the wrong target.

She would get him out of this investigation, and she would figure out what was going on here, if that were the last thing she ever did.

32

SENG DIDN'T KNOW WHAT TO THINK OF THE RUMPLED DETECTIVE STANDING before her. Bartholomew Nyquist's clothing needed tailoring, and his face seemed mismatched.

Halfway through their conversation, Seng realized that Nyquist's face was horribly scarred, and he hadn't used any enhancements to fix it. Which meant that the gray threading his hair was probably natural as well.

He looked tired and sadder than anyone had a right to. But he seemed sincere.

She had watched him from the moment he arrived. After she had shouted at him through the building's security system, he had paced the area where Zhu had died, picking up little things, and putting them in evidence bags. She made sure that the guard had recorded all of his actions, although she knew everything was on the security feed as well.

When Salehi got here, he would have to deal with the guard and the security firm he had hired. The guard had said that the crime scene lasers were no longer necessary, that they interfered with his work, and that they needed to be taken down.

If Nyquist was to be believed, then the guard had made a huge error, one that could have an impact on Zhu's murder case. If there ever was a murder case.

She wasn't sure she believed Nyquist on that.

She wasn't sure she believed him on anything.

Still, he had come here—alone—and he seemed sincere. She particularly liked his answer to the question about justice for the Peyti clones. He had delineated between an intellectual response and an emotional one.

She was having the same sort of response to Zhu's death.

She had a hunch that Nyquist knew it.

"I'll send you the footage," she said, her heart hammering against her chest. She wasn't sure if she was reacting that way because she was afraid of Nyquist, afraid of what he would do with the information, or afraid of what might happen to her if Salehi found out she was cooperating with the local police. "Do you have a secure link?"

This is it, he sent her. *Send the footage on this link.*

She had about a half a second in which to back out. She ignored that half second and sent the footage—all of the footage—from the entire day.

Her mouth had gone dry.

Thank you, Nyquist sent.

She nodded.

"Now," he said aloud. "Can I ask you some questions?"

She glanced at the guard. She didn't want him to hear anything.

"We probably should go inside," Nyquist said.

"No," she said firmly. She knew Salehi wouldn't approve of that. Zhu wouldn't have either. Neither of them would want the police to know how very new this law firm was. Nor would they want the police to know how inexperienced the lawyers were—at least with Armstrong law.

"It looks like you want to talk in private," Nyquist said. "I just thought…"

"Here's fine," she said, arms still crossed.

"All right," he said quietly. He glanced at the guard too, as if the guard's presence bothered him as well. "Let's start at the beginning."

She almost said, "You have the footage. You've seen the beginning."

But she didn't. Instead she waited, trying to keep her legal mind alert to any traps that Nyquist might be setting.

"First I need some background," Nyquist said. "I need a sense of Zhu. All I know about him is the legal connection to the Peyti clones. How long have you known him?"

Here it was: the beginning of the trial of Torkild Zhu. Maybe it hadn't been police officers, someone might say. Maybe it had been a disgruntled client, or an old friend with some tougher friends brought along for assistance.

"Ms. Seng?" Nyquist asked a little more pointedly. "How long have you known Zhu?"

She swallowed hard.

"Twenty-four hours," she said. "I just met him yesterday."

33

GOUDKINS USED HER PALM TO OPEN THE LAST LOCK ON THE SMALL SHIP the Earth Alliance had assigned her. She stepped inside. The air smelled slightly stale.

"Ship," she said. "Refresh."

A wisp of air touched her black hair, and sent a shiver through her. The air felt cool. It probably was colder in here than it was in the conference room in the Moon's security offices. She had forgotten how warm she had felt when she first arrived, only weeks ago.

It seemed like she'd been involved in these investigations for a hundred years.

The ship had narrow corridors that led to the small pilot's bay, the three private rooms, and the large investigative area. The ship wasn't really designed for travel; it was designed for an on-site investigation, with set results.

The ship's cargo level, underneath this one, had a small cargo bay and two large cells, complete with android guards. Right now, the android guards were off and stored in the bay, but should Goudkins need them, she could activate them with three very simple codes.

Ostaka didn't know she was here. She had shut off the protocols that notified him of any entry into the ship before she left the Security Office. That way, if Ostaka investigated the change in ship's status, he would find nothing.

But the records of Space Traffic Control here in the Port of Armstrong confirmed what Goudkins' investigation told her as well: Ostaka hadn't responded to the notification of the change in the protocols. She doubted he had noticed.

Goudkins sighed, then changed the access passwords on the ship. Not to bar his entry: he could get in if he believed that she was injured, but only if he got clearance from headquarters.

She made sure the alarms were activated so she would hear if anyone entered the ship. Then she went into the investigation room.

The networks here had fifteen levels of security built in, not counting the security tied to the ship itself. The ship created its own system wherever it went, so that it never used the systems developed by local governments.

So many of Goudkins' colleagues spent their entire careers investigating local governments within the Earth Alliance that trusting those governmental systems was foolhardy in the extreme.

She slipped into the chair in front of the system she always used for investigations. That way, if there were any questions about the conduct of the investigators, the trail would be easy to retrace. The ship itself backed up every keystroke, every vocal command, every thought-link connection, so that no one could change the information on the various systems—at least, not without some serious skills.

Neither she nor Ostaka had those skills.

She ran a hand through her hair.

This was the moment at which she took control of the investigation.

She opened a secure channel to Ava Huỳnh, her immediate supervisor. Then she used a special encrypted link.

It would take a moment for the contact to reach Huỳnh.

Goudkins pulled another console toward her. She would investigate while she waited. She had a lot to look into, and she would do it whether Huỳnh approved or not.

As if summoned by that thought, a hologram of Huỳnh appeared on top of the second console. She was wearing all pink, including a touch in her bangs, and the outfit only made her seem ridiculous.

Huỳnh was a tiny woman anyway, and for that reason people often underestimated her. Her clothing didn't help.

What she lacked in fashion sense, however, she had in brains. She was the most intelligent investigator Goudkins had ever worked with. And she was a compassionate boss.

"I was wondering if I'd hear from you," Huỳnh said.

Goudkins decided to play coy. "Why?"

"Because Ostaka says you've been co-opted by the natives. He's filed a detailed report about all the stuff you're doing to help them." Huỳnh appeared to be standing in her office, but her image was so tiny that Goudkins couldn't tell.

She thought of expanding the image, but that would make Huỳnh too real. Goudkins wanted to keep some measure of control, at least in her own mind.

"We're not getting along," Goudkins said.

"Obviously," Huỳnh replied dryly.

"He's not investigating," Goudkins said. "He's just double-checking everyone's work. I don't think he's left the Security Office for the United Domes of the Moon except to sleep for days."

"Because of his investigation?" Huỳnh asked.

"Because—I don't know. He doesn't interact with anyone there, and he is pretty hostile to me. I recorded our last interaction, if you want to see it."

"I do," Huỳnh said. "Send it to me."

She didn't ask Goudkins if he had done the same. On the way to the port, Goudkins had gone over every recent interaction she'd had with Ostaka. She couldn't think of anything a supervisor would find amiss in her behavior with Ostaka.

But then, she wasn't a supervisor.

Still, she sent the last conversation to Huỳnh. Goudkins knew that Huỳnh wouldn't go over it until this meeting ended.

"Was that it?" Huỳnh asked.

"No," Goudkins said with surprise. "Not at all. I planned to contact you before I had that little altercation with Ostaka."

"All right." Huỳnh shifted slightly as if her feet hurt. And if she wore the pointed, high-heeled shoes that she often wore when she was trying out new fashion, then her feet probably did hurt. "What's up?"

"A couple things," Goudkins said. "First, I've been working closely with the Chief of Moon Security, Noelle DeRicci. She's the closest thing the Moon has to a leader right now."

"Closely?" Huỳnh asked.

"She would like me to investigate a few things through the Alliance servers rather than the Moon servers. She's worried that someone might monitor Moon investigations and block them."

"Do you share that worry?" Huỳnh asked.

"I have no idea what we're dealing with here," Goudkins said. "So I think caution is wise. Ostaka thinks I shouldn't work with her at all. Since I'm here at your direction, I figured I would ask you."

"You don't think the Moon's government was behind any of these attacks, do you?"

"The United Domes of the Moon barely exists right now," Goudkins said. "I doubt they would have set up something that so completely destroyed their growing structure. Do I think another Moon government might be involved? I would if the domes hadn't been so hard hit in the first attack. I can follow every lead I have, but I'd rather work smart than repeatedly go over the work that everyone else has done. And I think part of working smart is working with some very good investigators here."

"I have teams in every dome," Huỳnh said. "They've found nothing to suggest a Moon-based attack. I'm sending in Peyti and some other non-human investigators as well. I think we're covered if there is some kind of Moon-based attack."

Goudkins hadn't expected any of that. She frowned, trying to parse Huỳnh's comment. Then realized that she didn't understand most of it.

"So, you're saying you're okay with me working closely with No-elle DeRicci?"

"As long as you report regularly to me, I'm fine with it," Huỳnh said. "The moment you believe working with them compromises your investigation rather than strengthens it, pull out."

"I will," Goudkins said. "Should I tell Ostaka?"

Huỳnh sighed. "No. I'll deal with him. It wouldn't hurt to have an old-fashioned anti-government investigation as well."

Was that what Huỳnh thought Ostaka did well? Because Goudkins had seen no evidence of it. But that didn't mean anything. Ostaka might be good at a certain type of investigation and bad at others. If he stayed with his strength, and Goudkins worked from hers, they might discover something.

And Moon might miraculously rebuild everything next week.

She tamped down the internal sarcasm.

"DeRicci had a question," Goudkins asked, "and since I'm talking with you, I thought I'd ask it. If you don't know, I'll see what I can find."

"What's that?" Huỳnh asked.

Goudkins swiveled her chair slightly so she wasn't twisted oddly as she faced Huỳnh.

"In the middle of the Peyti Crisis, as they're calling that day here, DeRicci's office discovered that the Peyti clones were all of Uzvekmt."

"I'm aware of that," Huỳnh said in a tone that urged Goudkins to get to the point.

"There was, and continues to be, a lot of evidence that the Uzvekmt clones developed off-Moon, and DeRicci was concerned that they might attack places other than the Moon. She sent all of that information to the Alliance, and I'm not sure if that information ever got to you."

"It got to me," Huỳnh said. "Late, but it got to me."

Late. That wasn't good.

"Were there other attacks?" Goudkins asked.

"Not that we've found," Huỳnh said.

"Were there more clones of Uzvekmt?"

Huỳnh shifted again. Then she inclined her head sideways. "We found hundreds of them."

Something in her tone was off. Goudkins wished she had increased the hologram's size after all so that she could see Huỳnh's face more clearly.

"And what did you do?" Goudkins asked.

"We didn't have to do anything," Huỳnh said. "They did it all."

Goudkins frowned. "What do you mean?"

Huỳnh shook her head, then looked down. She took such a deep breath that even through the small hologram, Goudkins could see Huỳnh's shoulders rise and fall.

"They died, Wilma," Huỳnh said. "All of them. The same day as your Peyti Crisis."

"Died?" Goudkins asked. "They just…died?"

Huỳnh shook her head again. "I said that wrong. At the exact same hour that your attacks began, every clone of Uzvekmt that we found, *every single one*, killed himself."

Goudkins put a hand to her mouth. She didn't mean to show shock; she had done it before she even registered her own action.

"How?" she asked.

"Different methods," Huỳnh said. "Not what you'd expect."

"No bomb, then," Goudkins said. "Did they take anyone else out with them?"

"Most of them, no. A few managed to. Those were the ones who did use bombs. And they were in Earth environments. They had the same masks. But they were isolated, usually on a space station or a space yacht or, in one case, in a remote resort. Not something other governments would have even noticed if Chief DeRicci hadn't alerted us to the clones' existence."

Goudkins' heart was pounding. "Don't you find that odd?" she asked. "Wouldn't you think that they would all use the masks the way the clones here did, as well?"

"I find this whole thing odd," Huỳnh said. "We're investigating on the Peyti side. We have some leads. I'll keep you apprised."

And then she winked out.

Goudkins wanted to slam a hand on the console. She wasn't done talking with Huỳnh. But Huỳnh was done.

Still, Goudkins had gotten through the important part of the discussion. She had tentative approval to work with DeRicci and, Goudkins hadn't had to admit what DeRicci wanted her to investigate.

Then she stood up, unsettled by what Huỳnh had told her.

Only the clones on the Moon had deliberately gone to a place filled with people and tried to blow it up at the appointed hour. A few others had, but not enough to notice.

Everyone else died here.

DeRicci was right: the attacks definitely targeted the Moon.

That piece of information was a lot more important than Huỳnh seemed to think it was.

Goudkins relaxed a little.

They were on the right track. *She* was on the right track.

Solve the problem on the Moon, and maybe, just maybe, they would solve the problem everywhere.

She nodded to herself, feeling better about helping DeRicci, feeling better about the investigation, and finally, *finally*, feeling like she could do something to avenge her sister's death.

34

AND SO THE INVESTIGATIVE FRUSTRATION BEGAN. WHAT SEEMED LIKE A straightforward case of retaliatory murder now looked a bit more complicated.

Nyquist left the crime scene feeling more unsettled than he had when he arrived. He had interviewed more than a dozen attorneys. None of them had known Torkild Zhu longer than a few days. Some had spent less than an hour with the man.

They were all shocked—*shocked!*—that he was dead, but they weren't heartbroken and they were a bit too calm about it. Not that they could have killed him. Or at least, they couldn't have for reasons that were obvious.

None of them felt anything about him, except maybe a bit of irritation that he had died before completing their work documentation.

Most of the lawyers were from Earth, and had answered some kind of S^3 help-wanted ad. None of them seemed to know anything about Armstrong, and very few of them had been to the Moon before.

Maybe Nyquist's imagination was lacking, but he couldn't figure out why any of these people would want Zhu dead. He was their boss and their contact to S^3. A few of these young lawyers speculated that the jobs might be gone entirely now, and one young man (very young) had almost burst into tears.

That was the only threat of tears that Nyquist had seen all afternoon. And those tears had nothing to do with Zhu.

The dozen S³ staffers didn't even know if Zhu was married or had children or had been in Armstrong long. They didn't know when someone would replace Zhu from S³'s hierarchy, although Seng noted that one of the partners was on his way from Athena Base.

That kind of trip could take a week or more, so Nyquist wasn't sure what would happen to the Peyti clones case in the meantime.

He knew he wasn't supposed to worry about that, but he felt like it was a small clue. Because someone might have known that Zhu had no backup here. Even a short delay in dealing with the Peyti clones would keep the door open for investigations like the one Nyquist was running with Uzvaan.

Then he mentally corrected himself. *Had been running* with Uzvaan. Because right now, he was enmeshed in this case.

The only bit of personal information he could get from the S³ staff about Zhu was small, and it had come from his very first interview.

Melcia Seng mentioned that she was pretty sure Zhu was an alcoholic.

Nyquist asked her how she knew that.

"Broken capillaries in his face," she had said. "And a general disheveled air. I've worked with alcoholics. They're often really good attorneys because they see the dark side of everything, but they usually cope with it by mixing hard booze with clearers, and it does something to their skin."

Nyquist had nodded. He had seen that as well.

As soon as he left her, and while he was waiting for one of the other lawyers to visit him in the front of the building, he asked Brodeur to check the state of Zhu's liver.

If you're asking whether or not he was an alcoholic, Brodeur had sent, *it was impossible to tell. There were signs that he'd been drinking a lot, but it looked like recent behavior. And he hadn't done anything in about a week.*

Nyquist sighed. He was afraid nothing about this case would be easy.

Although he was leaving the crime scene with bags of evidence, several dozen hours of footage from various points of view of the crime and its aftermath, and two hours of (mostly) worthless interviews.

He was already tired and he'd only started on this case.

He was nearly to his car when he passed the two delis. One, Sevryn's, turned the closed sign on as he approached.

The other had the door open as a young man inside cleaned the floor himself. Apparently both delis closed after the lunch crowd left.

"Excuse me," Nyquist said, leaning in and holding up his palm with the badge on it. "I'm Detective Bartholomew Nyquist. Do you have a moment?"

"Sure," the young guy said. He ran a hand over his face. He looked exhausted.

"Did you know there was a murder near here this morning?" Nyquist asked.

"No." The young man seemed surprised.

"The man who died was carrying a to-go cup from your deli. Do you recognize him?"

Nyquist opened a small hologram between him and the young man. The hologram was from the police station when Zhu had entered to serve those injunctions.

The young man blinked, then looked at Nyquist, clearly shocked.

"Yeah, yeah, I know him. Is he the victim or did he hurt someone?"

"Do you think he could have hurt someone?" Nyquist asked.

"Hell, no," the young man said. "He was one of those wimpy guys, you know? He came in here yesterday after they poured soup all over him at Sevryn's, and he pretended like nothing had happened. He promised me a lot of business. He's *dead?*"

"Yeah," Nyquist said. He hadn't heard about the soup, and he'd follow up on that in a moment. "When did you last see him?"

"This morning," the young man said. "He bought coffee, and said he would contact me with a lunch order. He didn't though, and I thought maybe—well, the thoughts weren't charitable."

"Why not?" Nyquist asked. "Wouldn't it have been normal to assume he had forgotten?"

"They *poured soup* over him," the young man said as if Nyquist hadn't heard him. "You gotta think a guy like that isn't real likeable."

Nyquist almost smiled. "Yes, you do. I see. Did you find him likeable?"

"I didn't know him. But he seemed friendly enough." The young guy leaned on his broom.

Nyquist looked at it, saw that it had an automated switch so that it could have done the cleaning itself. He wondered why anyone would chose to sweep when the tools did the work for them.

"Do you know what caused the soup incident?" Nyquist asked.

"No," the young guy said. "I don't get involved in my customers' lives. Safer that way."

Nyquist nodded, feeling some disappointment. "Do you have security footage?"

"From this morning?" the young guy asked.

"Yeah," Nyquist said. "And from the soup incident."

"I might," the young guy said. "I definitely have this morning. I'm not real good about keeping daily logs. You want me to get them for you?"

"Please," Nyquist said. "While I'm waiting, I'm going to go next door and see if they'll tell me anything."

"Good luck," the young guy said. "Old Man Sevryn, he's a real son of a bitch."

Nyquist smiled. He liked this guy. "I'll keep that in mind," he said, and let himself out the door.

35

HER DAD TRUSTED DETECTIVE NYQUIST.

Talia stood in the kitchen at the United Domes Security Office, hands on the carton of food that she hadn't opened yet. She was staring after Detective Nyquist, who seemed unusually cheerful.

She hadn't expected it of him. His mood seemed so discordant with everyone else's moods these days that she'd been staring after him for some time. He'd left a while ago, looking a bit distracted, but optimistic too.

She should have asked him why he was. He said something about progress.

Progress. She wasn't sure what that meant. She took all of the boxes of food that were scattered around the kitchen and put them in the recycler. Then she paused to look at her work.

The place seemed cleaner. It certainly felt better. The clutter actually bothered her.

Everything bothered her. Only the degree of bother differed.

And that damn therapist bothered her the most.

She grabbed some dishes and put them in the cleaner. Then she added more until the thing was full. She turned it on.

Suddenly, the kitchen looked like it used to.

She opened the door to the refrigerator, saw the cartons of old food, and turned them on with a single touch. They told her, one at a time, if the food was still edible.

Most of the cartons had been in there so long that the food was actually gone, recycled by the nanobots. The cartons themselves needed to be tossed away, and she did that too.

Her own food was probably cold, but she didn't care.

She really wasn't hungry.

That meeting with the therapist disturbed her on such a deep level that she wasn't sure she wanted to eat at all.

She washed her hands, then sat in one of the chairs, suddenly tired.

He hated her without even knowing what she was. She was going to have to tell her dad that she couldn't go back. She was so glad she hadn't trusted the therapist with any more details of her life.

She hoped he wouldn't investigate her relationship with her mother. She hoped it wasn't in Valhalla Basin's records that she was a clone. And it could be in their records. Valhalla Basin was run by Aleyd Corporation, and Aleyd had found out she was a clone.

They wanted to own her—would have claimed her as their own if her father hadn't shown up.

"You okay?" Popova brought her carton back into the kitchen and then stopped. "What hell happened here?"

Talia shrugged one shoulder, unable to tell if Popova was pleased or not.

"*You* did this?" Popova asked.

"It was bothering me," Talia said.

Popova grinned at her. "The therapy's working, then. See? I told you they were good."

Talia bit her lower lip. She wanted to tell Popova that the therapy hadn't worked at all, that the man who ran everything, Mr. Stupid Llewynn, was a bigot and an idiot, but he had helped Popova and Talia didn't want to disappoint her. Popova thought they could be of assistance to Talia and she tried, she really did.

There was just no way she could stay at a place whose managing partner or whatever Mr. Stupid Llewynn called himself was so incredibly and harmfully ignorant.

Talia had been going over every single bit of conversation they'd had, making sure she hadn't let anything slip. She was proud of herself: she hadn't screamed at him or told him she was a clone or did anything to reveal herself—that she could tell.

She had just left, and she wasn't going back.

"I'm so glad they helped you," Popova said. "You keep going, and you'll feel a lot better. I guarantee it."

Talia smiled at her. She wished it could be that simple.

But this was the first time in more than a week that she hadn't felt like crying. So something had changed.

"If you need to talk," Popova said, "I'm right here."

"Thank you," Talia said. But after that interaction with Mr. Stupid Llewynn, she wasn't going to trust anyone with her secrets. No one except her dad.

He wouldn't like what had happened either.

Popova looked at the carton of food still on the counter.

"You haven't eaten anything," she said. "I'll reheat this and you're going to choke down a few bites, okay?"

Talia's stomach growled, surprising her. She hadn't felt hungry—or so she thought—but apparently she just hadn't been paying attention.

"Okay," she said.

Popova hit the reheat button on the carton. It glowed red for a moment. Then she handed the carton and a fork to Talia.

"Eat," Popova said. "I'm not going to hover, but I am going to trust that you'll take care of yourself."

"I will," Talia said, and opened the carton. The stir-fry chicken and vegetables steamed. The jasmine rice actually looked appetizing.

She took a bite and savored the delicate flavors in the sauce.

Popova smiled at her again, and then left.

Popova was right: something had changed in that meeting with the therapist, and it wasn't just because Talia had stood up for herself.

It was because of something Mr. Stupid Llewynn had said before he went all crazy on her.

But you had feelings for him.
Those feelings will forever be unresolved.
Forever unresolved.
Forever.
Exactly.

She couldn't figure out how she felt about Kaleb, because she'd never really known him. She couldn't ask him questions, she couldn't find out if he was bullying the other kids because that was all he knew or because he enjoyed it or both. She couldn't figure out why she felt drawn to him and why she felt like fighting him.

Because he was just a construct in her memory now.

Like her mother.

Talia balled her hand into a fist, feeling anger surge through her. Her mother had lied to her, over and over again. Her mother had turned their entire life into a lie, and then, when Talia found out, her mother killed herself.

Not that her mother ever knew that Talia had found out. By then, her mother had been kidnapped to face justice for her actual crimes, and Talia had to deal with all of her mother's lies alone.

Oh, her dad helped. But her mother had lied to him too. Repeatedly. And he couldn't do anything about it either.

Both of them had unresolved feelings for Talia's mother. Feelings just lingered, like a bad smell. Only she couldn't open a window and make them go away.

She got up, and got herself some water. Then she leaned on the sink for a few minutes.

Unresolved.
Forever.

She'd lost so much. Her mother. Kaleb. Her safe haven—on Valhalla Basin and here, in Armstrong.

Her identity.

Tell me why it's so important to add the 'Shindo' to your name.
I keep the name because it's mine now. No one else has that name. Just me.

And, she thought, *I am alone.*

That was the core of it all. She had to deal with all of these unre-solved emotions on her own. She wasn't who she had thought she was. Her mother hadn't been who anyone thought she was. And Kaleb—well, Talia never did figure out who he was.

Plus…those Peyti lawyers. They weren't what anyone thought they were either.

And clones. Everyone thought they knew clones now, and they didn't.

Especially not Mr. Stupid Llewynn.

Talia went back to the table, and picked up her fork.

Weird how putting things into perspective actually made her feel better.

Weirder still how some idiot like Mr. Stupid Llewynn could help her put things into perspective.

Maybe he would have been a good therapist—for a non-clone.

He'd been good for Popova, after all.

Talia ate slowly, savoring each bite. The food finally had flavor again, and she knew the difference was her. She felt a little more like herself for a change.

Her new self.

Talia, Miles Flint's daughter. The straight-A student at Aristotle Academy. The girl who didn't make friends easily and occasionally pissed people off. The girl who was so smart that people in the Security Office wanted her help.

The girl who had somehow managed to build a life for herself after her other one imploded.

She set her fork down.

She was tired.

But it wasn't the exhaustion of depression. It was the exhaustion that came after a long run, after some hard work, after too many late nights.

She pushed the carton aside, and rested her forehead on her arms.

Just a little sleep and she'd be better.

Maybe Detective Nyquist was right.

Maybe they were starting to make progress.

Maybe she was.

And it was about time.

36

THE YOUNG GUY NEXT DOOR WAS WRONG ABOUT ONE THING: "OLD MAN Sevryn" wasn't old. But he was a son of a bitch.

Nyquist had to put his badge against the door before Sevryn would open the door.

"We're closed," Sevryn said. "And I'm out of everything."

Nyquist pushed his way in. The deli was small. It had four tables near the window up front, a display cabinet that was now empty, and a rotating holographic display that still showed slices of various sausages and lunch meats.

The place smelled faintly of coffee, rye bread, and cheese.

"I know you're closed," Nyquist said, thinking Sevryn's statements were a little odd.

"Well, I'm not giving leftovers to the department," Sevryn said, shaking his head as he closed the door. He didn't move, though, remaining near the entrance. "My business is down since the Peyti Crisis. I can't afford to give away stuff."

Nyquist let out a small breath. Someone in the police department was extorting food from Sevryn? Nyquist would look into that.

But first, he wanted to talk about Zhu.

"I'm not here about food," Nyquist said, although as he spoke, his stomach made a liar out of him. It growled.

Sevryn rolled his eyes.

Nyquist ignored the reaction.

"I'm here," Nyquist said, "because a man was murdered not too far from here."

"That lawyer?" Sevryn said.

That was interesting. The young guy next door hadn't known what Zhu was—or hadn't said he knew. But this man, he knew.

"Figured something would happen to him," Sevryn was saying.

Nyquist frowned. "Why?"

"Nobody liked him," Sevryn said. "He was representing them clones, you know?"

"Enlighten me," Nyquist said.

"The Peyti lawyers. The ones that nearly killed us. How stupid is that?" Sevryn asked.

"Well," Nyquist said, deciding to play along. Not that it was hard to do so, "no one at the station was happy about it."

"No kidding," Sevryn said. "I heard you guys bitch about it ever since he dropped those documents on everybody. Then he has the nerve to show up here."

"I hear there was an incident," Nyquist said.

"I wouldn't call it no incident. Considering how angry everybody was, he got off pretty lucky." Sevryn glanced at the counter, as if remembering.

Nyquist knew that Sevryn was talking about the soup incident and not the murder. If Sevryn had been hostile, Nyquist would have challenged him over his choice of words.

Instead, Nyquist asked, "How was he lucky?"

"Oh, man," Sevryn said. "Everyone, they wanted to hurt him something awful. I talked them out of it."

I'll bet you did, Nyquist thought but didn't say. "How did you do that?"

"Honest?" Sevryn asked. "I didn't want my place known for violence. I said so."

"Yet something happened," Nyquist said.

"Not nothing, really," Sevryn said. "A couple of cops bumped him. Nothing major. Spilled a drink on him, a little hot soup, and then he looks at me for sympathy."

He sounded indignant.

"And you didn't give it to him," Nyquist said.

"Would you? That idiot clone lawyer."

"I was at the precinct when he came in," Nyquist said truthfully. "I wasn't happy with him at all."

"Me neither, and I didn't want him stinking up the joint. I hear he went next door. Like getting his business was a real coup."

"You don't think it was?" Nyquist asked.

"I serve you guys," Sevryn said. "I'm not helping someone who's trying to hurt the Armstrong PD."

Nyquist nodded. He understood the attitude, and even empathized with it. He hadn't liked Zhu either. But Seng had been right; the man hadn't had to die for doing his job.

Nyquist nodded toward the rotating holographic display. "I assume you have good security here."

"Yeah, so?" Sevryn crossed his arms. Apparently he thought that Nyquist wanted to get some free food out of him.

Considering that Nyquist had skipped lunch, he wouldn't have minded. But that wasn't what he was asking. "Do you have security footage of the soup incident?"

"Sure," Sevryn said. "I keep everything. When I opened this place, this was a bad neighborhood. I learned it wasn't one incident that made a criminal, it was several. So I would make sure I had footage on those thieves, you know, the ones who would pocket something and you wouldn't notice the first or second time, but when you went back, you'd find it? I caught a lot of people for you guys. That's how I ended up with so many cops who come here every day. They'd stop in, they'd buy something after arresting someone, they'd come back."

He peered at Nyquist, and Nyquist finally understood.

"If you weren't closed, I'd buy a sandwich. I haven't eaten all day."

"I can make you something while you look at the footage, see if it's something you want."

"I'd like that," Nyquist said.

"I don't got a lot of choice at the end of the day. Pastrami on rye okay? Maybe with some real Earth cheddar?"

Nyquist's mouth watered just at the mention of it all. "I'd love some. How much?"

"I don't usually charge cops," Sevryn said.

"I'm investigating a crime here," Nyquist said. "I have to pay or the investigation's compromised. So charge your regular rate."

Sevryn sighed. "I gotta reopen my register."

"Sorry," Nyquist said. "We can skip the sandwich if it's too much trouble."

Sevryn studied him. At that moment, Nyquist realized the entire payment conversation had been a test—and he'd done something Sevryn hadn't expected.

"It's not too much trouble," Sevryn said. "I'll set up the footage on that table over there, holographic. You need sound too?"

"Please," Nyquist said. "I'll get some coffee too, if it's not too much trouble. I can serve myself."

The coffee pot sat on a small burner not too far from the counter. There was still some dark liquid inside.

"That ain't so good," Sevryn said.

Nyquist smiled. "I drink precinct coffee. *Everything's* good in comparison."

Sevryn nodded, as if he'd heard that before. "I'll set up the footage and get your sandwich. You gonna need anything else?"

"Not to eat," Nyquist said. "But I'd like to see any other time the lawyer was here. Particularly this morning."

"He wasn't here this morning," Sevryn said. "I kicked him out. I didn't need his type here."

"Still," Nyquist said. "I'd like to see this morning."

"There ain't nothing," Sevryn said a little too quickly.

Nyquist pretended not to notice. "I'm sure there isn't. I'm collecting all the footage from every business between here and the law offices to see what shows up."

"Most businesses are closed right now," Sevryn said. "That's what's been eating into my profits, no pun intended."

"I know," Nyquist said. "I'll probably need a warrant for most of the others."

He kept his voice level, but he wanted Sevryn to know that he would do whatever it took to get the necessary information. Especially since Sevryn was suddenly quite nervous.

The man knew something, maybe even overheard something being discussed. And he was worried.

Because he overheard friends? Or because he was afraid of retaliation by police?

Nyquist decided to play a bit stupid, not ask Sevryn at all, and let the footage tell him what he needed to know.

"I appreciate all your help," he said, and took the table nearest the window. He looked out on the street, while he waited for Sevryn to set up the security footage.

Nyquist tried not to have any expectations. But he already did.

He had a hunch he knew exactly what he would find.

37

GOUDKINS HAD SOME STANDARD PROCEDURES THAT SHE FOLLOWED whenever she started an investigation. They were simple, but they were usually something that the other investigators overlooked.

She did a scan of public documents to find any mention of the person she was investigating.

She set up the screen to her right to look for information on Jhena Andre, the first name that DeRicci had given her. DeRicci expected Goudkins to look surreptitiously to discover Andre's history—and Goudkins would, eventually. But public records searches were common for a variety of reasons, and never got noticed or flagged within the system.

So Goudkins always did those first.

She did the same on the screen to her left for the other name that DeRicci had given her: Mavis Zorn.

And then she stood up. She paced this level of the ship, double-checking the security.

Her interaction with Ostaka had bothered her enough that she worried he might try to sneak in. And while she had been tricky with the security codes, she knew just as well that he could be tricky with codes.

She ran a hand through her hair, then went into the ship's galley and removed a bottle of water from the small fridge. She put the cool bottle against her forehead. It felt like the day was almost over and she had just begun.

The stress had made her uncomfortable. She felt like she was doing something illicit, and she wasn't.

Ostaka was.

Her eyes opened.

She hadn't thought it through. They had been ordered *not* to investigate the Frémont clones, something that had bothered both her and Ostaka when it happened.

She had promptly forgotten that order when the Peyti Crisis happened—not that she had violated the order. She hadn't. But her attention had moved to the Peyti clones and everything that they had done.

The fact that Ostaka was piggy-backing on the port's and the Security Office's investigations of the Frémont clones was just a sneaky way for him to get around the order to not investigate the clones.

She felt both a bit of admiration for what he was doing—violating the order—and a bit of worry. She had sent that information directly to Huỳnh, who might shut him down completely.

Goudkins rolled the bottle against her skin, feeling it sooth a budding headache.

If Ostaka got sidetracked on this investigation, it would be his own damn fault. He was the one who had started the war with Goudkins.

She had just retaliated.

She brought the bottle down, then twisted the top and took a swig. The water was delicious. She had been thirsty and not even realized it.

She wished those thoughts had calmed her down. She was the one who had felt they needed to work together, and they hadn't. But if he was actually double-checking the Frémont information as a way of conducting his investigation—smartly doing it from the Security Office's system—then he was finding a way around the order.

She should have supported that.

If she had been thinking clearly.

If he hadn't been such an asshole.

She wandered back to the consoles, feeling vaguely guilty.

Well, she couldn't undo what she had done. She had to live with it now.

She took another drink of water, then looked at the screens. The screen on the right was still gathering and compiling data.

The screen on the left was done.

Mavis Zorn had died ten years before. She had passed out in her office at the Impossibles. If someone had found her, she might have survived. But no one had, and she died, alone, at her desk, of something the death certificate called "natural causes."

Apparently there was no autopsy. Mavis Zorn had been older than she looked, employed at the Impossibles *after* she retired from teaching. She had worked at the Impossibles for forty years.

She left no family and very few (if any) friends.

Goudkins studied her biography.

Zorn had taught all over the sector, usually at one of those domed communities that arose near some kind of mining operation or agricultural development at the edge of the known universe. An entire cadre of traveling teachers went from short-lived community to short-lived community, educating young people, and moving on when the operation near the domed community shut down.

She was nearly seventy when she decided that teaching and traveling were too much for her. She went to law school, got her degree, and was one of the few people who got stuck permanently at the Impossibles.

Or so it seemed.

Goudkins frowned at the limited information. How had this Zorn woman ended up with enough power to not only mentor young lawyers like Uzvaan, but to prevent them from handling cases that would harm their delicate sensibilities?

She couldn't tell with a simple glance, and she knew she would need to do more digging to find out.

So she turned her attention to the screen on her other side.

It had finished scrolling as well.

Jhena Andre had had a standard career in the prison system before moving into administration decades ago. Then her work became classified to anyone who looked it up.

The first thing Goudkins did as she opened the classified file was cross-reference Andre's name with any existing investigations.

And what crossed Goudkins' screen made her sit back in surprise.

The order that had given her the most trouble since she arrived on the Moon—the one that prevented Goudkins and Ostaka from doing any investigation of the Frémont clones—had originated from Andre's desk.

And it hadn't just gone to lower-level investigators like Goudkins and Ostaka. It had gone system-wide.

No one was to investigate those clones without Andre's permission.

Goudkins felt cold. Her heart started to race. She was onto something.

It was something big.

It was something that could cost her job.

She didn't care.

Because, if she could track this all down, she might actually find out who ordered these attacks.

And she might be able to stop them.

38

NYQUIST ALREADY HAD HIS SANDWICH BY THE TIME THE HOLOGRAPHIC
security footage rose on the table top. The sandwich itself was a work of
art—the pastrami the best he'd ever had, topped with crispy lettuce, a
sweet tomato, and sharp cheddar. The bread even had a bite to it. He had
no idea what kind of sauce covered everything, but it made his eyes water.

Sevryn started up the footage twice, and each time, it collapsed.
Nyquist knew this game: he'd express impatience, and Sevryn would
tell him that the playback wasn't working. He'd fix it and give it to Nyquist later.

Then, later, Sevryn would tell him that the footage got destroyed in
the machine malfunction.

Nyquist enjoyed his sandwich, let Sevryn monkey with everything,
and planned to charge the man with obstruction if anything got destroyed while Nyquist was sitting there.

Finally, when he had finished half the sandwich, he leaned back.

"You know," he said, "I know a lot about security systems. I could get
that working or we can just download the footage on one of my chips
and I can look at it back at the precinct."

He wiped off his mouth and stood.

"In fact," he said, trying not to sound too dramatic. "Why don't we
do that? It'll be easier."

Sevryn gave him a panicked look, and Nyquist tried not to smile. Clearly Sevryn didn't know much about security systems at all. He had been trying to make it appear like he couldn't make it work, when he actually could.

Erasing something from the system was nearly impossible if you were new to it all.

"I got it," Sevryn said. "Finish your sandwich."

A hologram appeared on the table top, half over the remaining bits of sandwich. The entire front of the restaurant showed in the footage.

A line went out the door.

The four tables had well-dressed customers, cramming their mouths with sandwiches similar to the one that Nyquist was eating. The low hum of conversation almost sounded like it was live.

The line included several uniformed police officers. None were looking directly at any of the cameras that created this three-dimensional image.

Still, Nyquist's stomach clenched, and he suddenly regretted eating the meal.

He recognized about six of the dozen cops in line. Most of them were detectives, even though they were wearing their uniforms. Many detectives had started wearing uniforms after the Peyti Crisis, partly because headquarters thought a uniformed presence made the streets seem safer and partly because uniforms were durable and almost impossible to mess up.

They also stored trace evidence as a matter of course. Most police officers thought that a good thing—it made sure their prosecutions were easier.

But if they were the perpetrators…

"Everything okay?" Sevryn asked.

"Great," Nyquist said, and hoped his response sounded genuine.

"I still got some cheesecake," Sevryn said.

"I—this sandwich will be more than enough, thank you," Nyquist said, still staring at the images moving before him. He recorded everything, in case Sevryn decided to destroy it after all.

Nyquist swallowed hard. The sandwich was threatening to return. He still hadn't seen any faces straight on—at least of the police—but he thought he could identify several of them.

He hoped he was wrong.

Then one of the cops turned, and Nyquist saw his entire face. Lucien Gaetjens. His flat nose and broad cheekbones made him readily identifiable. Nyquist had never worked with him, but had dealt with him a lot when Gaetjens was trying and failing to pass his detective exams. Gumiela had even suggested that Nyquist take him into the field and train him, and Nyquist had respectfully (he hoped) said no.

Not because of Gaetjens, but because Nyquist had enough trouble with partners. He didn't need to mentor someone already having problems.

Beside him, another cop, whose face Nyquist recognized but name he didn't know, leaned over and whispered something. Nyquist reluctantly turned on his department identification program. Pedro Federline. He was still a beat cop, who had been with the department nearly ten years.

Which meant he either had attitude problems or he didn't have the patience (or the smarts) to move up in the ranks. Usually, failure to move meant someone was in the wrong job.

Although Nyquist had known several beat cops who were perfectly content where they were.

Zhu came through the door. His suit appeared to be silk, but Nyquist couldn't tell. Several of the cops looked at Zhu, but he didn't seem to notice.

A few of the cops whispered with each other, and one laughed.

Nyquist's heart was pounding, as if he were seeing all of this in real time.

Zhu was staring at the menu, clearly oblivious to everything going on around him.

The female cop had just gotten two things from the counter, one a gigantic container of soup. She turned.

And Nyquist closed his eyes, just for a moment.

Exactly what he had been afraid of.

Savita Romey.

He thought he recognized her posture and her form. He had worked with her on more than one case, flirted with her more than he liked to think about, and had gotten angry with her the morning of the detectives meeting.

She had suggested that they torture the Peyti clones to find out what they knew. Or maybe just hurt them on general principles.

Nyquist had moved away from her then, feeling deeply disappointed.

Her gaze was on Zhu, and her lips thinned.

Nyquist had seen that look before. It was Romey's version of disgust. She hated Zhu.

She usually used that hate to solve cases. She'd been one of the first responders to Mayor Soseki's assassination site on Anniversary Day, and she'd done as good a job as could be expected.

Nyquist always kept her on his rotation, because he knew she could get the job done.

He pushed the sandwich away, watching as Zhu made his way up the line.

Romey handed off the soup to Gaetjens. He nodded and grinned. Then Romey took the lid off her coffee and walked directly into Zhu.

"Savita," Nyquist whispered.

Zhu saw her at the last minute and moved out of the way as coffee, so hot that it steamed, splattered on the floor. A few other patrons moved back, alarmed, clearly burned. They said something that Nyquist couldn't make out.

But he could make out what Romey said.

Sorry, she said to Zhu in a tone that was equal parts sarcasm and intent.

Gaetjens bumped Zhu from behind and poured the soup on him. That had to burn.

Yeah, Gaetjens said in the same tone that Romey had used. *I'm sorry, too.*

Then a third cop came in from the side and dumped some kind of liquid on Zhu.

Oh, my, the cop said. *Lookie what a mess you made.*

Nyquist did a search for that cop's face, and found it belonged to Omar Nettles. Nyquist had never seen him before, but that wasn't as odd as it sounded. There were thousands of police officers in the Armstrong Police Department; he couldn't be expected to know them all.

Zhu looked at Nettles in surprise. Nyquist was surprised as well. Nettles made it clear that this little interaction really *wasn't* an accident.

Zhu held up his hands in protest. *Look, guys, I didn't mean—*

Guys? Romey asked, waving her coffee cup around and deliberately spilling more on the floor. *Do I look like a guy to you?*

And that was when Sevryn stepped in, yelling at everyone. He threw the four police officers out first. Then Zhu thanked him, which also seemed like a mistake.

Sevryn snapped, *Don't think I don't know who you are. I didn't lose nobody last week, but on Anniversary Day, I lost a son, two uncles, and my Aunt Marie. So I don't need your kind here.*

Zhu actually seemed offended. Deeply offended. That caught Nyquist's attention. Why would a man who represented the Peyti Clones be upset by a link to Anniversary Day?

I'm not doing anything connected with Anniversary Day, Zhu said. *I'm—*

The hell you're not. Sevryn had started yelling. Everyone in the deli was looking at Zhu, not just the cops. Zhu had taken a step backwards, as if distancing himself from Sevryn.

Sevryn continued, louder, *Those clones, they were working with them other clones, and they're all trying to destroy us. Now you're out there, recruiting soulless lawyers to save their asses. You have every right to conduct your business as you see fit, and so do I. And I don't see fit to feed the likes of you. Now get out.*

Zhu looked at the people around him as if he expected a defense. The cops just stared at him. Everyone else looked down.

He sighed, and for a moment, Nyquist thought he was close to tears. That seemed odd.

Then he apologized, and sloshed toward the door, leaving soggy footprints behind. People moved aside as they saw him coming.

Shadows moved outside the windows.

Nyquist looked at them. He would have to make the footage larger when he viewed it at the precinct, which he would do. He couldn't just let this go, especially with Romey's involvement. Gumiela—hell, every-one on the force—might think him biased.

Then, to Nyquist's surprise, Zhu stopped in front of the door. He raised his chin and squared his shoulders, like a man who had found his courage.

He said, *For the record, we're hiring more than a hundred people. They'll need someplace to eat. You just screwed yourself out of a lot of business, old man.*

Nyquist winced. He had just told everyone in the building that he worked nearby. And that they would have to put up with hated lawyers and the Peyti clones for a long time.

A couple of the cops whispered to each other as Sevryn let out a bitter laugh.

I don't need your kinda business, he said. *Have you looked around?*

Zhu pointed a finger at him, clearly not paying attention to anyone else in the place. If he had been, he would have left quickly.

Instead, Zhu said, *You pissed off a lawyer, buddy, who is hiring a bunch of other lawyers from off-Moon. Think it through.*

Nyquist's breath caught. Zhu had been oblivious. He truly had not known the impact of his own behavior on the people around him.

Are you threatening him? a woman asked on the footage asked just as Nyquist had wondered the same thing.

Zhu grinned at her, and ran a hand over his soggy suit. *Do I look like a man who can make a credible threat?*

And then he left.

He was clearly visible through the window, stopping just outside, then proceeding forward—to the deli next door, according to its owner.

Zhu had had balls. Not a lot of people sense, but balls.

Nyquist would normally have admired that, except this time, it had probably gotten Zhu killed.

On the footage, everyone talked about him, gesturing and shaking their heads. Sevryn had gone back to serving people.

But the cops—the cops watched Zhu, long after he disappeared from view, at least on this small hologram.

Nyquist let out a long sigh.

He leaned back in the chair, and saw Sevryn watching him.

"I'm going to need this," Nyquist said.

"I know." Sevryn sounded sad.

"Is there anything you want to tell me before I watch the rest of the footage?"

"There's nothing else that day," Sevryn said.

"But there was something this morning, wasn't there?" Nyquist asked.

Sevryn ran his hand on the countertop. His fingers were shaking.

"This is my business," he said. "My life, my livelihood, everything I am, everything I do."

Nyquist waited. The man was clearly deeply terrified.

"I don't want to get in trouble," Sevryn said softly.

"You won't get in trouble from me," Nyquist said.

"It's not you I'm afraid of," Sevryn said, and then he sighed and closed his eyes, as if he'd said something wrong. He probably had. He just admitted intimidation.

"You're afraid that someone will figure out that you said something?" Nyquist asked.

Sevryn kept his head down. He nodded, like a child who was being chastised.

"You're going to give me the footage from today," Nyquist said. "I'll have footage from every business within a five-block radius before the day is over. If whatever happened occurred in public, then no one will know you spoke up at all."

"Except the idiot next door," Sevryn said bitterly.

"I spoke to him too," Nyquist said.

Sevryn raised his head. "What'd he say?"

"He wasn't a fan of Zhu either. But he would take his money."

"He'll take money from anyone. Just like he'll use Moon flour to save a little, not caring about the taste." Sevryn shook his head.

"So," Nyquist said, not willing to let this go. "What are you failing to tell me?"

Sevryn ran a hand over his mouth, then spoke through his fingers—or started to. When he realized what he was doing, he let his hand drop.

"Those three, the ones who threw food on him?"

"Yeah," Nyquist said, wishing he didn't have to hear this.

"This morning, they saw him next door." Sevryn's gaze met Nyquist's. "They decided to teach him a lesson."

Nyquist went cold. "Is that what they said?"

"No," Sevryn said. "They decided he needed to empathize with victims."

Nyquist didn't move.

"They said they'd teach him how it feels to be attacked." Sevryn's face had gone pale. "They said they'd make it a lesson no one at S³ would ever forget."

39

DeRicci's source had been right. Jhena Andre was involved in this entire mess, somehow.

Goudkins pulled her hands away from her console and stood up again.

If Andre had enough power to order every investigator in the Alliance to ignore the Frémont clones, then she had a lot of power indeed.

Goudkins' heart was racing. She had to be very, very careful now. Those sideways means of investigating that she had discussed with DeRicci were probably irrelevant.

If Andre could direct an entire investigation from wherever she was, then she would clearly monitor anyone accessing any information associated with the Frémont clones.

Which meant that Ostaka was in trouble, no matter how careful he had been.

Goudkins actually thought of warning him, even though he had been such an ass with her. Then she nodded once to herself. Of course, she would warn him, when she returned to the Security Office—and not before.

She paced for a few moments, weaving in and out of the bolted-down chairs and consoles, thinking. If Andre was powerful enough to control investigations system wide, then she had the ability to monitor investigations as well.

It didn't matter how Goudkins approached her investigation: Andre would know about it.

So Goudkins needed to make her investigation about Andre, not about the clones—any clones—and then weave whatever information she got together, not using some system, but using some deductive reasoning.

She would have to hope that would be enough to get her to one of the lower-level Alliance courts that would give her secret access to internal files.

If she needed that.

First, she needed to see if Andre was the one pulling strings, or if she was acting in someone else's stead.

And that would be harder to determine than Goudkins wanted.

But she could do it.

She returned to her chair, and brought up a third screen. All she wanted here was Andre's work history.

Normally, Goudkins would have searched through bank records, but that would probably notify Andre that someone was interested in her.

Goudkins was just going to do a "who is?" search, the kind that a reporter, a job interviewer—as DeRicci mentioned—or someone looking to promote might do.

She had to be very, very careful.

Her hands were trembling as she brought up Andre's complete work history.

Andre started in the prison system over fifty-five years ago. She had an entry-level job in the maximum security prison that housed PierLuigi Frémont in the last days of his life. Frémont managed to kill himself rather than face the punishments ahead of him, which meant that everyone in that prison was investigated for collusion with Frémont.

Eventually, a lower-level guard was charged with negligence in taking care of Frémont, and removed from the system with a serious reprimand; but oddly, no one who had been on duty when Frémont actually died was found guilty of anything, including stealing Frémont's DNA.

Goudkins did not linger over the investigation. She didn't even download it for later use, worried that it was being monitored. She would look at it if she needed to, but not on this day.

On this day, she was pretending to be interested in Andre, the person.

Andre worked her way from an entry-level position at a difficult prison to administration at one of the prisons that housed rich humans. More of a resort than a place that punished prisoners, the prison also gave perks to those who worked there—from high-end housing to fantastic food to all sorts of exercise and entertainment options.

That prison—and others like it—were considered rewards for employees who did fantastic work elsewhere.

Nothing in Andre's easily accessed files showed her to be anything but a model employee. She married, had two children, and then divorced. Her husband raised the children on Earth, insisting that she use her short vacation every year to visit them somewhere inside Earth's solar system, and far away from any prison.

She did not dispute that.

Goudkins found it odd that such a detail would be in Andre's job record, and then, as she dug deeper, she realized why.

That file had been attached when the children were young, and it showed simply that Andre was willing to work anywhere in the Alliance because she had no "regular" ties to hold her in one place.

As long as she got enough vacation time to see her children once a year, she was willing to work anywhere—which wasn't a common attitude for any employee.

The children grew, Andre's trips inside the center of the Alliance stopped, and if she visited her adult children, there was no record of it in her work history.

Not that there needed to be. By the time the children were grown, they would no longer be considered a factor in her employment anywhere.

Goudkins saw no record of grandchildren, and nothing that would tie Andre anywhere.

Her jobs reflected that.

She was promoted higher and higher in prison administration, working her way from the ritzy prison to the assistant in charge of the Human Division of the Earth Alliance Prison System. Eventually, she took over the Human Division, and was offered a position in the Joint Division, where she could work her way farther up the food chain.

That was the only job she turned down.

No explanation was given.

But Goudkins knew that operating a Joint Division, where humans and aliens had to work together, was one of the hardest jobs in the Earth Alliance. Some humans weren't suited for it, and usually found out when they were fired.

Andre probably knew she wasn't the kind of employee who could handle that stress.

Or maybe she had a different career path in mind.

She remained head of the Human Division of the Earth Alliance Prison System for almost a decade when she was promoted to a position in Earth Alliance Security.

And that was where her jobs started to become classified.

She had apparently taken classes in security and undercover work. She became one of those employees who investigated other employees, making certain whether complaints against them were justified or not.

She spent five years in that division.

Goudkins couldn't see what Andre had worked on without the proper clearance, and Goudkins saw no reason to get that clearance.

The more she dug, the more confused she got.

Why would a woman who investigated other Earth Alliance employees try to destroy the Alliance?

If, indeed, she did want to destroy the Alliance.

Right now, Goudkins was operating on speculation.

Eventually, Andre rose to the head of the division that investigated other members of the Security Team. She focused on humans-only, and generally operated in Investigations and Prisons. Occasionally, she would cross into the Business side of the Security Division, but not that often. And once she'd been asked to help out in the Political Section, and again, she turned the job down, claiming she wasn't qualified.

In the past three years, she had risen to a deputy of an important deputy of another deputy inside the main office of Earth Alliance Security Division—the entire division that went over all of the various security departments.

She was handling thousands of human employees and not batting an eye. The Division handled hundreds of thousands of employees of all Earth Alliance species, and Goudkins had no idea how anyone kept everything straight.

Just thinking about it made her head hurt.

But it did answer one question: How one woman could manage to shut down an entire investigation into the clones of PierLuigi Frémont. She had the ability to do so—at least in the human division.

Goudkins wondered if the non-human investigators could look into the clones. She wasn't even certain how she would get an answer to that question. If Andre's office was monitoring all traffic concerning the Frémont clones, then even posing that question to Huỳnh would be nearly impossible. She couldn't think how to do it.

If it weren't for the coincidences—Andre present when Frémont died, Andre having access (possibly) to Frémont's DNA, DeRicci's source saying that Andre had some of the DNA, and Andre limiting the Frémont investigation—then Goudkins wouldn't have believed this woman would have been involved in something so big that it could harm the entire Alliance.

But Goudkins' investigator's gut told her that Andre was in the middle of all of it, and that there was something here, even in her sparse work history, that explained why—or at least how.

Goudkins would have to think about that.

She would also have to report what she had learned to DeRicci.

But Goudkins wasn't going to communicate with anyone inside the Alliance about this, particularly over links.

Too risky—and too dangerous.

At least at this stage.

She was just starting, after all. And if she got into a hurry, she would screw up.

So she made herself take time.

She made herself turn her attention back to Mavis Zorn. That seemed safer. At least for the moment.

At least until Goudkins could bounce what she had learned off someone else, and invite them to worry about it as much as she did.

40

NYQUIST LEFT THE AREA WITH HOURS AND HOURS OF FOOTAGE FROM Sevryn's. He would have to comb through all of it, but he had enough information to talk to Romey, Gaetjens, and Nettles. As he drove back to the precinct, he tried to decide how he wanted to handle this.

Did he go to Gumiela right away with the three names? Or did he match up everything?

He also needed to find out from her if she wanted to handle the arrests herself.

Not that he was ready to arrest anyone yet.

Which told him how he wanted to handle this.

He needed to make sure everything was in place before he did anything. He needed as much evidence as possible, and everything ready to go.

He needed to evaluate the trace collected from the scene, figure out who had blocked all of the emergency calls, and satisfy for himself whether the three had planned to kill Zhu or simply give him a lesson that had gotten out of hand. Nyquist had his suspicions, but with something this big, he couldn't act on a suspicion. He needed firm facts.

But first, he needed to talk to Gumiela.

He let the car drive itself to the precinct. He set up the interior so that everything coming in or out was encrypted. He didn't pay any attention to the streets around him.

He sent a message to Gumiela: *I have one very important question.*

She appeared on his dashboard, tiny, tired, and well dressed. "What?"

Are you alone? he sent.

"For the moment." She looked annoyed.

He said, aloud, because he needed to say this out loud, not send it through his links.

"I know who killed Zhu."

"That didn't take long," she said.

"They didn't try to cover their tracks," he said.

She sighed. He had a hunch she knew that already. But he couldn't be certain.

"Do you want their names?" he asked. "Or do you want a case we can present in court? Because those are two different things."

"Can you make a court case?" she asked.

"Yes," he said.

She cursed.

He hadn't expected that. She had clearly hoped he wouldn't find enough evidence.

"Witnesses?" she asked.

"Yes," he said.

"Civilians?"

"Yes," he said.

She nodded, then tilted her head back, as she often did when she was thinking about something.

"And," he said, "you need to know that everyone at S³ will make a big stink about this."

"I'm not sure I care about S³," she said.

"You might want to. All the lawyers working there right now are from off-Moon." He wasn't arguing for a court case. A court case kept him away from Uzvaan and finding out what happened during the Peyti Crisis. A court case kept him from helping DeRicci.

A court case was just a distraction. And yet, if he really thought about it, a court case was the only thing that would keep law and order on the Moon.

"Why are there no easy choices?" Gumiela asked.

Nyquist let out a bitter laugh. "You're asking the wrong guy."

She brought her head down. Even tiny, she looked more powerful than all the people had in the footage from Sevryn's deli.

"Make a court case," she said softly. "And make it stick."

41

FLINT PARKED SEVERAL BLOCKS AWAY FROM THE SECURITY OFFICE. HE needed to calm down before he saw Talia, and he figured a walk would help.

It didn't help as much as he wanted it to. Sure, it stretched his legs, but all the empty buildings and the quiet streets made him realize just how different Armstrong had become since the Peyti Crisis began.

How different they all were.

He wasn't sure how to approach his daughter; he needed to make certain she was all right after the interaction with the therapist, but he also couldn't alarm her unduly.

The fact that he was alarmed wasn't helping.

So, by the time he had reached the top floor of the security building, he was as disturbed as he had been when he left the Armstrong Comfort Center. (If ever a place was misnamed, that place was.)

He got off the elevator. The first person he saw was Popova.

She was standing near her desk, holding some kind of drink in her hand. She was smiling—which surprised the heck out of him.

"If you need to see the chief," Popova said, "she might be free for a moment."

"Thanks," Flint said, hoping his confusion didn't show. He had been afraid that, by leaving Talia here, the entire office had been taking care of her.

Clearly, that wasn't the case.

"Actually," he said. "I'm looking for my daughter. Do you know where she's at?"

"She's in the kitchen," Popova said. "And before you go, I have to tell you that whatever the Comfort Center is doing, it helped. She cleaned the kitchen today, and she hasn't cried at all. She seems a lot better."

His confusion got worse. She *cleaned* the kitchen? She had been neat before all this started, but she hadn't been since the Peyti Crisis. Her bed was unmade, her clothes strewn everywhere. It seemed like all she could do to shower and occasionally put food in her mouth.

The fact that she actually cleaned something sounded like his Talia had returned.

He wasn't sure how to reconcile that with the disturbing meeting he'd had with Llewynn.

Especially if it meant Flint had to send Talia back there. He wasn't sure it was safe for her. In fact, he was convinced that it wasn't safe.

But if it was helping…

He gave Popova a perfunctory smile, then walked back to the kitchen. Talia was sitting at the table in the middle of a room that looked nothing like it had the day before. No dishes were stacked on the counter, no food cartons littered the table. The recycler was chewing through a pile of material, but that was its job, and it was doing so somewhat silently.

Talia had her head down, her face turned sideways, eyes closed. She was asleep, and she looked peaceful.

He didn't want to disturb her.

A nearly empty food carton sat beside her, a fork still in it. It smelled faintly of chicken and jasmine rice.

Popova was right. Talia seemed to be a lot better.

He glanced at the refrigerator and tried to decide if he should open it and see if there was some fruit inside, like there usually was.

Then he decided even that might be too noisy. He didn't want to wake his daughter.

He had taken one step backward when Talia yawned.

"Dad?"

She lifted her head. Her right cheek had a red impression from her shirt, slashing across her skin.

She rubbed her eyes, then blinked at him. "Everything okay?"

"That's what I came to see," he said. He decided he wasn't going to say anything more until she told him what happened at the Comfort Center.

"I've been a big baby," she said.

"No," he said. "What you've gone through—"

"Dad, listen," she said. "I'm sorry. I—"

"Talia, you've been through hell, and—"

"*Dad*." She spoke with such force that he stopped talking altogether. "I can't go back to that place."

He let out a relieved sigh. They had been talking at cross purposes, probably because of the way she had started the conversation.

"The Comfort Center?" he said, just to be clear, because he had already misunderstood her once.

She nodded, then glanced at the door. When she seemed reassured that no one was outside, she beckoned him forward and kicked one of the chairs out for him to sit in.

He sat down and leaned toward her. They could probably have done this on their links, but he was going to let her dictate the conversation.

"Don't tell Rudra that I can't go back," Talia said softly. "I *hated* it there, Dad. That guy who does the entry interviews, he—"

and at that moment she switched to their private link.

—*hates clones.*

—*I know,* Flint sent back. *He asked me to talk with him today, worried that your attitude about clones was harmful.*

Harmful how?

Flint shrugged. No way was he going to tell his daughter what the man had actually said.

Rudra thinks he helped me, Talia sent. *I don't want to lie to her, but—*

"—you know." She had switched back to a verbal conversation.

"I do know," he said. "And it looks like you had some kind of break-through today."

"He did say something," Talia said. "I thought about it. I'm still think-ing about it, and it actually helped."

"Should we find you someone else, then?" Flint asked quietly. "May-be someone not on the Moon?"

She blinked up at him, as if she hadn't considered that. "We'd leave here?"

He hadn't planned for that. He'd actually been thinking only of her. He didn't want to leave. He wanted to resolve this.

But maybe leaving would be the best thing for her.

"Maybe it's something we should consider," he said.

She was already shaking her head. "If we leave and something hap-pens and you could have stopped it—"

"I'm not all-powerful, Talia," he said.

"But you're important," she said. "And what kind of people would we be if we left, just because we can afford to, and everyone else has to solve this on their own? I'll tell you. We'll be exactly what that stupid bigot thought I was. Something not worth anyone's time."

Flint put his hand on one of hers. It was warm, which was also a first for the past week.

"Sometimes," he said quietly, "people have to take care of themselves before they can help others."

"Yeah, I get that," Talia said. "But I don't believe in running away. That's what Mom did."

The words hung between them. Flint knew what she meant. Rhonda hadn't run away from Valhalla Basin. She'd been kidnapped. But rather than face what she had done and what was coming, she killed herself.

He and Talia could argue as to whether that had been a good choice for Rhonda, but clearly, his daughter thought less of her because of it.

"Sometimes," he said carefully, "leaving is the best option."

"Do you want to get out of here?" she snapped.

"If it's the best thing for you," he said, "I'll do it at a moment's notice."

She stared at him. Then she teared up. His breath caught. He didn't want to send her on another crying jag.

She blinked once, the tears fading. And she smiled at him.

"That stupid bigot asked me if I thought you loved me," she said. "He was such an asshole."

"I do love you, Talia," Flint said. He probably didn't say it enough, either.

"I know," she said. Then her smile turned into a grin. "Imagine his surprise if he found out what I really am."

Flint put his other hand on her wrist, wishing he could pull her into a hug.

"You're not a 'what,' Talia," he said. "You're as human as he is. More so. Let's forget him. Because you're right. He's an idiot. And so is everyone else who shares his opinion."

That's a lot of people, Talia sent. *More every day, it seems.*

I know, Flint sent back. *We'll have to figure out how to handle that. But not today. Today, we take care of you.*

She shook her head. "I'm better, Dad. It's like arguing with him pulled me out of some deep sleep and gave me a focus. I'm not one hundred percent, but I can deal better."

Flint couldn't restrain himself any longer. He pulled her against him and held her tight.

You tell me if you need us to do something different, he sent.

I will, she promised. *Believe me, I will.*

She was warm against him, her hair smelling faintly of her shampoo. He felt more relieved than he had expected.

Talia was back. He had missed her.

He wasn't going to stop worrying about her, but he had her beside him now.

Together, they could fight this thing.

Even if she did nothing, he felt free to work on the future.

For both of them—

And for everyone else they knew.

The thrilling adventure continues with the seventh book
in the Anniversary Day Saga, *Starbase Human.*

Can the fate of a forgotten starbase hold the key to the Moon's survival?

Long before the Anniversary Day bombings brought the Moon to its knees, a far-flung starbase became the testing ground for a diabolical plan: the annihilation of every human inhabitant by an army of clones.

Every lead to the masterminds behind the bombings uncovered by criminal kingpin Luc Deshin dead ended in an Earth Alliance connection.

Undercover operative Iniko Zagrando refused to play patsy for the Earth Alliance Military Division Intelligence Service, and now he's fleeing for his life from his old bosses.

And Frontier Marshall Judita Gomez puts her own life and the lives of her team on the line when her search for the origins of the Anniversary Day assassins leads to an Earth Alliance cloning factory.

From the quiet courage of a Disappeared who struggles to decide whether to come out of hiding to the potent fury of a master criminal who puts a plan in motion to strike back at an overwhelming enemy, *Starbase Human* brings readers one step closer to the exciting conclusion of the Anniversary Day saga.

Turn the page for the first chapter of *Starbase Human.*

OVER THIRTY-FIVE
YEARS AGO

1

Takara Hamasaki crouched behind the half-open door, her heart pounding. She stared into the corridor, saw more boots go by. Good God, they made such a horrible thudding noise.

Her mouth tasted of metal, and her eyes stung. The environmental system had to be compromised. Which didn't surprise her, given the explosion that had happened not three minutes before.

The entire starbase rocked from it. The explosion had to have been huge. The base's exterior was compensating—that had come through her desk just before she left—but she didn't know how long it would compensate.

That wasn't true; she knew it could compensate forever if nothing else went wrong. But she had a hunch a lot of other things would go wrong. Terribly wrong.

She'd had that feeling for months now. It had grown daily, until she woke up every morning, wondering why the hell she hadn't left yet.

Three weeks ago, she had started stocking her tiny ship, the crap-ass thing that had brought her here half her life ago. She would have left then, except for one thing:

She had no money.

Yeah, she had a job, and yeah, she got paid, but it cost a small fortune to live this far out. The base was in the middle of nowhere, barely in what the Earth Alliance called the Frontier, and a week's food alone cost as

243

much as her rent in the last Alliance place she had stayed. She got paid well, but every single bit of that money went back into living.

Dammit. She should have started sleeping in her ship. She'd been thinking of it, letting the one-room apartment go, but she kinda liked the privacy, and she really liked the amenities—entertainment on demand, a bed that wrapped itself around her and helped her sleep, and a view of the entire public district from above.

She liked to think it was that view that kept her in the apartment, but if she was honest with herself, it was that view and the bed and the entertainment, maybe not in that order.

And she was cursing herself now.

While the men—they were all men—wearing boots and weird uniforms marched toward the center of the base. Thousands of people lived or stayed here, but there wasn't much security. Not enough to deal with those men. She would hear that drumbeat of their stupid boots in her sleep for the rest of her life.

If the rest of her life wasn't measured in hours. If she ever got a chance to sleep again.

Her traitorous heart was beating in time to those boots. She was breathing through her mouth, hating the taste of the air.

If nothing else, she had to get out of here just to get some good clean oxygen. She had no idea what was causing that burned-rubber stench, but something was, and it was getting worse.

More boots stomped by, and she realized she couldn't tell the difference between the sound of the boots that had already passed her and those that were coming up the corridor.

She only had fifty meters to go to get to the docking ring, but that fifty meters seemed like a light-year.

And she wouldn't even be here, if it weren't for her damn survival instinct. She had looked up—before the explosion—saw twenty blond-haired men, all of whom looked like twins. Ten sets of twins—two sets of decaplets?—she had no idea what twenty identical people, the same age, and clearly monozygotic, were called. She supposed there was some name for them, but she wasn't sure. And, as usual, her brain was busy solving that, instead of trying to save her own single individual untwinned life.

She had scurried through the starbase, utterly terrified. The moment she saw those men enter the base, she left her office through the service corridors. When that seemed too dangerous, she crawled through the bot holes. Thank the universe she was tiny. She usually hated the fact that she was the size of an eleven-year-old girl and didn't quite weigh 100 pounds.

At this moment, she figured her tiny size might just save her life.

That, and her prodigious brain. If she could keep it focused instead of letting it skitter away.

Twenty identical men—and that wasn't the worst of it. They looked like younger versions of the creepy pale guys who had come into the office six months ago, looking for ships. They wanted to know the best place to buy ships in the starbase.

There was no place to buy new ships on the starbase. There were only old and abandoned ships. Fortunately, she had managed to prevent the sale of hers, a year ago. She'd illegally gone into the records and changed her ship's status from delinquent to paid in full, and then she had made that paid-in-full thing repeat every year. (She'd checked it, of course, but it hadn't failed her, and now it didn't matter. Nothing mattered except getting off this damn base.)

Still those old creepy guys had gotten the names of some good dealers on some nearby satellites and moons, and had left—she thought forever—but they had come back with a scary fast ship and lots of determination.

And, it seemed, lots of younger versions of themselves.

(Clones. What if they were clones? What did that mean?)

The drumbeat of their stupid boots had faded. She scurried into the corridor, then heard a high-pitched male scream, and a thud.

Her heart picked up its own rhythm—faster, so fast, in fact, that it felt like her heart was trying to get to the ship before she did.

She slammed herself against the corridor wall, felt it give (cheap-ass base), and caught herself before she fell inward on some unattached panel coupling.

She looked both ways, saw nothing, looked up, didn't see any movement in the cameras—which the base insisted on keeping obvious so that all kinds of criminals would show up here.

If the criminals knew where the monitors were, they felt safe, weirdly enough.

And this base needed criminals. This far outside of the Alliance, the only humans with money were the ones who had stolen it—either illegally or legally through some kind of enterprise that was allowed out here, but not inside the Alliance.

This place catered to humans. It accepted non-human visitors, but no one here wanted them to stay. In the non-Earth atmosphere sections, the cameras weren't obvious.

She thanked whatever deity was this far outside of the Alliance that she hadn't been near the alien wing when the twenty creepy guys arrived and started marching in.

And then her brain offered up some stupid math it had been working on while she was trying to save her own worthless life.

She'd seen more than forty boots stomp past her.

That group of twenty lookalikes had only been the first wave.

Another scream and a thud. Then a woman's voice:

No! No! I'll do whatever you want. I'll—

And the voice just stopped. No thud, no nothing. Just silence.

Takara swallowed hard. That metallic taste made her want to retch, but she didn't. She didn't have time for it. She could puke all she wanted when she got on that ship, and got the hell away from here.

She levered herself off the wall, wondering in that moment how long the gravity would remain on if the environmental system melted. Her nose itched—that damn smell—and she wiped the sleeve of her too-thin blouse over it.

She should have dressed better that morning. Not for work, but for escape. Stupid desk job. It made her feel so important. An administrator at 25. She should have questioned it.

She should have questioned so many things.

Like the creepy older guys who looked like the baked and fried versions of the men in boots, stomping down the corridors, killing people.

She blinked, wondered if her eyes were tearing because of the smell or because of her panic, then voted for the smell. The air in the corridor had a bit of white to it, like smoke or something worse, a leaking environment from the alien section.

She was torn between running and tiptoeing her way through the remaining forty-seven meters. She opted for a kind of jog-walk, that way her heels didn't slap the floor like those boots stomped it.

Another scream, farther away, and the clear sound of begging, although she didn't recognize the language. Human anyway, or something that spoke like a human and screamed like a human.

Why were these matching people stalking the halls, killing everyone they saw? Were they trying to take over the base? If so, why not come to her office? Hers was the first one in the administrative wing, showing her lower-level status—in charge, but not in charge.

In charge enough to see that the base's exterior was compensating for having a hole blown in it. In charge enough to know how powerful an explosion had to be to break through the shield that protected the base against asteroids and out-of-control ships and anything else that bounced off the thick layers of protection.

A bend in the corridor. Her eyes dripped, her nose dripped, and her throat felt like it was burning up.

She couldn't see as clearly as she wanted to—no pure white smoke any more, some nasty brown stuff mixed in, and a bit of black.

She pulled off her blouse and put it over her face like a mask, wished she had her environmental suit, wished she knew where she could steal one right now, and then sprinted toward the docking ring.

If she kept walk-jogging, she'd never get there before the oxygen left the area.

Then something else shook the entire base. Like it had earlier. Another damn explosion. She whimpered, rounded the last corner, saw the docking ring doors—closed.

She cursed (although she wasn't sure if she did it out loud or just in her head) and hoped to that ever-present unknown deity that her access code still worked.

The minute those doors slid open, the matching marching murderers would know she was here. Or rather, that someone was here.

They'd come for her. They'd make her scream.

But she'd be damned if she begged.

She hadn't begged ever, not when her dad beat her within an inch of her life, not when she got accused of stealing from that high-class school her mother had warehoused her in, not when her credit got cut off as she fled to the outer reaches of the Alliance.

She hadn't begged no matter what situation she was in, and she wouldn't now. It was a point of pride. It might be the last point of pride, hell, it might mark her last victory just before she died, but it would be a victory nonetheless, and it would be *hers*.

Takara slammed her hand against the identiscanner, then punched in a code, because otherwise she'd have to use her links, and she wasn't turning them back on, maybe ever, because she didn't want those crazy matching idiots to not only find her, but find her entire life, stored in the personal memory attached to her private access numbers.

The docking ring doors irised open, and actual air hit her. Real oxygen without the stupid smoky stuff, good enough to make her leap through the doors. Then she turned around and closed them.

She scanned the area, saw feet—not in boots—attached to motionless legs, attached to bleeding bodies, attached to people she knew, and she just shut it all off, because if she saw them as friends or co-workers or other human beings, she wouldn't be able to run past them, wouldn't be able to get to her ship, wouldn't get the hell out of here.

She kept her shirt against her face, just in case, but her eyes were clearing. The air here looked like air, but it smelled like a latrine. Death—fast death, recent death. She'd used it for entertainment, watched it, read about it, stepped inside it virtually, but she'd never experienced it. Not really, not like this.

Her ship sat at the far end of this ring, the cheap area, where the ceiling of the base bent downward and would have brushed the top of some bigger ship, something that actually had speed and firepower and *worth*.

Then she mentally corrected herself: her ship had worth. It would get her out of this death trap. She would escape before one of those tall blond booted men found her. She would—

—she flew forward, landed on her belly, her elbow scraping against the metal walkway, air leaving her body. Her shirt went somewhere, her chin banged on the floor, and then the sound—a whoop-whamp, followed by a sustained series of crashes.

Something was collapsing, or maybe one of the explosions was near her, or she had no damn idea, she just knew she had to get out, get out, get out—

She pushed herself to her feet, her knees sore too, her pants torn, her stomach burning, but she didn't look down because the feel of that burn matched the feel of her elbow, so she was probably scraped.

She didn't even grab her shirt; she just ran the last meter to her ship, which had moved even with its mooring clamps—good God, something was shaking this place, something bad, something big.

Her ship was so small, it didn't even have a boarding ramp. The door was pressed against the clamps, or it should have been, but there was a gap between the clamps and the ship and the walkway, and it was probably tearing something in the ship, but she didn't want to think about that so she didn't.

Instead, she slammed her palm against the door four times, the emergency enter code, which wasn't a code at all, but was something she thought (back when she was young and stupid and new to access codes) no one would figure out.

What she hadn't figured out was that no one wanted this cheap-ass ship, so no one tried to break into it. No one wanted to try, no one cared, except her, right now, as the door didn't open and didn't open and didn't open—

—and then it did.

Her brain was slowing down time. She'd heard about this phenomenon, something happened chemically in the human brain, slowed perception, made it easier (quicker?) to make decisions—and there her stupid brain was again, thinking about the wrong things as she tried to survive.

Hell, that had helped her survive as a kid, this checking-out thing in the middle of an emergency, but it wasn't going to help her now.

She scrambled inside her ship, felt it tilt, heard the hull groan. If she didn't do something about those clamps, she wouldn't have a ship.

She somehow remembered to slap the door's closing mechanism before she sprinted to the cockpit. Her bruised knees made her legs wobbly or maybe the ship was tilting even more. The groaning in the hull was certainly increasing.

The cockpit door was open, the place was a mess, as always. She used to sleep in here on long runs, and she always meant to clean up the blankets and pillows and clothes, but never did.

Now she stood in the middle of it, and turned on the navigation board. She instructed the ship to decouple, then turned her links on—not all of them, just the private link that hooked her to the ship—and heard more groaning.

"Goddammit!" she screamed at the ship, slamming her hands on the board. "Decouple, decouple—get rid of the goddamn clamps!"

Inform space traffic control to open the exit through the rings, the ship said in its prissiest voice.

Tears pricked her eyes. Crap. She'd be stuck here because of some goddamn rule that ship couldn't take off if there was no exit. She'd die if there was another explosion.

"There's no space traffic control here," she said. "Space traffic control is dead. We have to get out. Everyone's dead."

Her voice wobbled just like the ship had as she realized what she had said. Everyone. Everyone she had worked with, her friends, her co-workers, the people she drank with, laughed with, everyone—

We cannot leave if the exit isn't open, the ship said slowly and even more prissily, if that were possible.

"Then ram it," she said.

That will destroy us, the ship said, so damn calmly. Like it had no idea they were about to be destroyed anyway.

Takara ran her fingers over the board, looking for—she couldn't remember. This thing was supposed to have weapons, but she'd never used them, didn't know exactly what they were. She'd bought this stupid ship for a song six years ago, and the weapons were only mentioned in passing.

She couldn't find anything, so she gambled.

"Blow a damn hole through the closed exit," she said, not knowing if she could do that, if the ship even allowed that. Weren't there supposed to be failsafes so that no one could blow a hole through something on this base?

That will leave us with only one remaining laser shot, the ship said.

"I don't give a good goddamn!" she screamed. "Fire!"

And it did. Or something happened. Because the ship heated, and rocked and she heard a bang like nothing she'd ever heard before, and the sound of things falling on the ship.

"Get us out of here!" she shouted.

And the ship went upwards, fast, faster than ever.

So fast she could hear the engines screaming—

Which meant she didn't have to.

The thrilling adventure continues with the seventh book
in the Anniversary Day Saga, *Starbase Human*,
available now from your favorite bookseller.

ABOUT THE AUTHOR

USA Today bestselling author Kristine Kathryn Rusch writes in almost every genre. Generally, she uses her real name (Rusch) for most of her writing. Under that name, she publishes bestselling science fiction and fantasy, award-winning mysteries, acclaimed mainstream fiction, controversial nonfiction, and the occasional romance. Her novels have made bestseller lists around the world and her short fiction has appeared in eighteen best of the year collections. She has won more than twenty-five awards for her fiction, including the Hugo, *Le Prix Imaginales,* the *Asimov's* Readers Choice award, and the *Ellery Queen Mystery Magazine* Readers Choice Award.

To keep up with everything she does, go to kriswrites.com and sign up for her newsletter. To track her many pen names and series, see their individual websites (krisnelscott.com, kristinegrayson.com, krisdelake.com, retrievalartist.com, divingintothewreck.com, fictionriver.com). She lives and occasionally sleeps in Oregon.